TROPICAL HEAT

A RINEHART SUSPENSE NOVEL

Also by John Lutz

A RINEHART SUSPENSE NOVEL

TROPICAL HEAT

JOHN LUTZ

HENRY HOLT AND COMPANY

NEW YORK

Copyright © 1986 by John Lutz
All rights reserved, including the right to reproduce
this book or portions thereof in any form.
Published by Henry Holt and Company, Inc.,
521 Fifth Avenue, New York, New York, 10175.
Published simultaneously in Canada.

Library of Congress Cataloging in Publication Data
Lutz, John, 1939–
Tropical heat.
(A Rinehart suspense novel)
I. Title.
PS3562.U854T7   1986   813'.54   85–27129
ISBN: 0-03-006958-0

First Edition

Designed by Katy Riegel
Printed in the United States of America
1 3 5 7 9 10 8 6 4 2

ISBN 0-03-006958-0

For Barbara again

When love's well-timed 'tis not a fault to love;
The strong, the brave, the virtuous, and the wise,
Sink in the soft captivity together.

—Joseph Addison,
Cato

TROPICAL HEAT

A cane was no good for walking on sand. It penetrated to different levels and caused tentativeness. When Carver got to within a hundred feet of the surf, the cane's tip made soft sucking sounds and water appeared in the round holes it left in the sand. A shallow, curved depression shaped like a comma angled forward from each hole, from where Carver levered the cane ahead of him to support his weight for his next step.

He was beyond the sloping narrow finger of land that jutted toward the sea, blocking vision from the north and making his section of beach usually more or less private. Now he could see about a dozen sunbathers lounging along the beach. Carver reached the surf and used the cane for support to lower himself awkwardly to a sitting position. He glanced to his right along the arc of pale sand and array of tanned bodies. There were more people than usual at the beach that day, worshiping a tropical sun that was as fierce and uncompromising as it had been when paid homage as an ancient god. It was odd how the sea's bright edge drew people, Carver mused. It called to them, as it had called to him after his injury.

He sat for a while on the beach, feeling the cold water lap at his bare lower legs, while the late morning sun heated up his face and chest. The sky was clear that day, and the Atlantic was very blue and calm, sporting no whitecaps until it rolled in near the shore and curled forward to break into foam and run gently up onto the beach. A large ship, a tanker, was visible far offshore; nearer in, but still far away, a few white fishing boats bobbed. From off to his right Carver could hear the distant voices of children playing a running game on the beach: a shout, then shrill, uncontrolled laughter. Carver wondered how it would feel to laugh with that kind of abandon. The north beach, to his left, was too rocky for sunbathers or swimmers and was deserted. The breaking sea was noisier from that direction.

He waited for a particularly large swell and timed it right. Before the wave broke onto the beach, Carver tossed the cane back a few feet, leaned to his right, turned over, and used his arms and good leg to propel himself toward the onrushing surf. He grunted and slithered backward on his chest and stomach into the wave, seeking its depths, so that when it withdrew from the shore with its tons of reversed momentum, it would pull him with it toward the sea. The maneuver always reminded Carver of evolution in reverse.

The wave claimed him and carried him into shallow water over a hundred feet from shore. His stiff leg didn't matter so much now; he could stand up and lurch forward into the oncoming swells, using the pressure of his palms against the water to help support his body, which was so much lighter when partially submerged. He continued moving toward the open sea, toward its vast implacability and peace. Sometimes he wondered what it would be like to keep moving in that direction, toward oblivion. But he didn't dwell on the idea. He didn't think of himself as the suicidal type. In fact, he considered himself to be just the opposite; a survivor, that was Carver. Because he could do whatever was necessary. He'd proved it more than a few times. He was proving it now. Every day.

For an instant he thought of Laura. But only for an instant. He diverted his mind from Laura in the same way he did from the vast magnetism of the ocean's horizon.

In deeper water, when he began to swim, the stiff leg didn't matter at all.

It was why he loved the sea.

This was his therapy. Here, he thought, kicking easily from the hips and stroking parallel to the shore, he was as mobile as the next person. And with his increased lung capacity and his long, powerful arms, he was faster and stronger than most.

He stroked harder, reached out farther, rotating his head rhythmically to the left to breathe, in a smooth Australian crawl, and veered east against the swells. Carver had been swimming off the shore there every morning for the past two months; he knew exactly how far out to go before turning back.

When he felt the strain on his thighs and arms, and the dull ache pulsing deep in his chest, he rolled onto his back and floated for several minutes, his eyes closed to the hot, bright sun. It felt good to be tired and winded, exhausted but all the way alive. This was his moment, his fought-for measure of contentment.

"Mr. Carver! . . ."

The distant feminine voice pierced his consciousness like a sharp, thin wire. He rolled over and began treading water.

A woman was standing on the beach, his beach, calling to him. She must have known it was him because of the cane on the sand, and because there was no other swimmer in sight. Despite the heat, she was dressed in dark clothing, what appeared to be a matching skirt and blazer. Poised with her hands on her hips, she was staring out at him in a patient, waiting attitude.

Carver didn't feel like talking to anyone. He rolled onto his back again and continued floating, hoping the woman would take the hint and leave.

She didn't seem to think he'd heard her.

"Mr. Carver! . . ."

3

He opened one eye. She was waving now, with a kind of relentless desperation. She would not go away, maybe ever.

Carver sighed, cursed, and stroked toward shore.

When he got in close enough to walk, he saw her more clearly. She was slender, not very tall, with long dark hair. Her clothes belonged in an office, not on the beach. Dark gray suit, white ruffled blouse, dark high heels. Ms. Efficiency. What could she want here? Was she going to proposition him for sex? Serve him a subpoena? Collect for the March of Dimes? He hoped it was the March of Dimes.

Carver's walk became a crawl. Gravity was doing him dirty again. When a larger breaker roared in, he let it carry him farther toward shore, then he crawled and slithered up onto the beach, feeling embarrassed in front of the woman, resenting her intrusion all the more for it.

She bent down and handed him his cane. He didn't thank her. He sat on the beach, breathing hard, bent slightly at the waist with his good leg straight out in front of him, his other crooked up at the knee. She was good at waiting; now that she'd landed him, she didn't try to talk to him until he'd caught his breath.

"Fred Carver?" she asked.

"Unfortunately," Carver said. He rolled to his side, worked his good knee under him, then levered himself to his feet with the cane. This time the woman didn't move to help him. He liked that. "Bum leg," he explained.

"I know. Lieutenant Desoto told me. I'm sorry about your knee."

"Alfonso Desoto sent you to see me?"

"That's right." She gazed out over the ocean. "Do you swim for therapy?"

"Every morning," Carver said. "It helps fight off atrophy."

"Just in the leg, or in all of you?" She was smiling.

He didn't answer. Didn't smile, didn't frown. Let her wonder. He was wondering.

"Are you finished swimming?" she asked.

"No."

"Then sit back down, please; we can talk here."

Carver lowered himself back into a sitting position. He was getting tired of standing and was glad she'd suggested this. She stooped down to be at eye level with him, settling back on her high heels, her dark skirt stretched tautly across her thighs and rounded hips. He kept his eyes averted from her pelvis and looked closely at her face. Her features were too vividly sculptured to be called "pretty"; "beautiful" fit okay, and yet she really wasn't. There seemed to be an arrogance in the upward tilt of her smooth chin, the directness of her clear grayish eyes. But Carver noticed that she gave the impression of arrogance only at first glance; what there really was about her was an intenseness that had molded her features into a mask.

"My name's Edwina Talbot," she said.

"Why did Lieutenant Desoto send you to see me, Edwina?"

"Because I was pestering him. And because he thinks you need something to do."

"Doesn't he know I'm independently wealthy now?" Carver said. He'd received a fat insurance claim along with his disability pension after being shot in the left knee during a holdup six months earlier, when he was a detective sergeant in the Orlando Police Department. The knee was ruined, locked at a thirty-degree angle for life. Eighty thousand dollars and a pension wasn't much compared to being able to walk without a cane. Not the jackpot some of the damned fools in the department actually congratulated him on. Carver didn't feel lucky.

"Being wealthy isn't the same as having something to do," Edwina said.

"Being wealthy isn't the same as what I am, either."

"Oh?"

"I'm not financially fixed for life, Edwina, unless I wean myself from food."

"Then that's probably another reason Lieutenant Desoto sent me here. He said you were a private investigator now. I want to hire you. I want you to find someone."

Carver decided to be honest with her. Besides, he wasn't sure if he wanted to take on a job just yet. It might be better to hang around there, work on the leg, learn to move as well as possible with what the doctors had left him. "I'm a one-man business," he said. "Larger agencies with more resources are better able to trace missing persons."

"I don't trust larger agencies. Desoto says I can trust you."

"That means something only if you know you can trust Desoto. Who do you want found?"

"His name's Willis Davis."

"A friend? Relative?"

"My lover."

"You've been to the police, obviously," Carver said. "They're good at what they do. Why can't they find Willis Davis?"

"They don't think he's missing; they think Willis is dead."

Carver looked closely at her. It was strange how her angular face seemed so tranquil yet contained such quiet force. "If they think Willis is dead, they must have their reasons."

"If I think he's alive, I must have mine. Want to hear them?"

Carver looked away from her, back out to sea. Desoto was right; he did need something to do. His last case, an industrial espionage matter that had led to the computer operator everyone, even the computers, suspected, had been over a month ago. He'd been loafing since. That was no way to nurture a business, or a sense of accomplishment. His energy had been building rapidly for the past several weeks; he felt frustrated, trapped by his immobility. He'd even occasionally found himself feeling sorry for the new, lame Fred Carver. He didn't like himself very much when that happened.

"I'll listen," he said. "I won't promise to do anything else. Not even to commiserate with you."

She smiled thinly. It was a weary sort of smile, but not at all resigned. It suggested that she had reserves of strength, yet at the same time an odd vulnerability. "Sure," she said, "you can't know what to do until you've listened to what I have to say." There was an edge of sarcasm in her voice, as if she knew he'd already decided to help her and she was humoring him.

She watched him as he planted the cane in the soft sand and pulled himself to his feet. Again she made no move to help. She had him figured out by now.

"I guess I *am* finished swimming for the day," he said. "Come on into the house."

Edwina took off her high-heeled shoes and walked alongside him without speaking, up the beach onto firmer ground. She was still smiling slightly, knowingly. She had cast her line into the sea and he'd taken the hook. Maybe he wasn't a record catch. Or maybe he was.

CHAPTER 2

"Interesting place," she commented, as Carver let her walk ahead of him into his cottage.

"Only one room," he told her, closing the door, "but it's all mine and all I need."

"One large room," Edwina said, looking around appraisingly. "Private. And with a great view." The cottage was mostly glass on the sea side and afforded a wide view of the Atlantic, an airy scene broken only by potted plants dangling on chains from the window frame. When seas were high, the ocean appeared to be above the level of the cottage's flat roof. Sometimes Carver had the feeling that any second he and the beach and the cottage would be engulfed and washed away, torn from the land and lost forever in the sea.

A breakfast counter separated the small kitchen area from the rest of the cottage, and a latticed room divider partitioned off space for a bed and dresser. Beyond the sleeping area were two doors: one to a tiny bathroom, the other to the outside.

"Even though it's on the beach," Carver said, "the land juts out so that the cottage is pretty much concealed from sunbathers or from the road."

Edwina turned her attention from the cottage to Carver. "Why do you live here? Do you want to be concealed?"

Carver wished she'd give up asking probing questions whose answers were none of her business. "I bought the place with part of my insurance settlement so I could be near the ocean. Swimming being recommended therapy for my leg." He limped around the Formica counter into the kitchen area, playing host. "Can I get you something to drink?"

She was still standing just inside the door; there was something mocking in that hipshot stance. "No, thank you," she said. "I want to talk about Willis." She shook sand from her feet, then slipped her shoes back on and walked to the center of the room. It was something to see, that walk.

Carver opened the refrigerator and got out a can of Budweiser. He popped the pull tab and stayed behind the counter while he talked to Edwina. "Willis Davis, wasn't it?"

"*Isn't* it."

He took a sip of cold beer and gazed at her over the rim of the can. "That's right, he's alive. And he's your lover."

She didn't differ with him on that. The ocean rolled and sighed outside, beyond the wide windows and silhouetted dangling plants.

Carver put down the beer can and leaned forward, supporting himself with both hands on the counter. "So tell me about you and Willis."

"Willis is a salesman," she said. "I'm in sales, too. Real estate. We met six months ago at a direct sales convention in Orlando." She paced, not far, just a few elegant steps, then looked straight at Carver. "We met in the hotel lounge, I let him buy me a drink, and we talked for a while. We liked each other. It was late; I'd had too many whiskey sours; I went with him to his room."

Carver nodded. It wasn't called a direct sales convention for nothing. He understood. He knew how it was at conventions. Private investigators held conventions, too, but he'd never been to one.

"I've got a place on the beach, too," Edwina said. "Down the coast in Del Moray. That's where I live and work, in Del Moray. A month after we met, Willis moved in with me. He still worked in Orlando for a while, before he got a job where I was working at the time. He commuted."

"A long commute," Carver said, "but I can understand why he thought it worth his while."

Edwina's features registered no reaction to the compliment. Hers was a face that seemed to have already run the entire range of emotions and was weary of responding. He took another look at her crisp gray business suit. It was tailored and expensive. Del Moray was a wealthy little community with a high percentage of rich retirees. Probably it was a great place to sell real estate.

"Willis enjoyed driving back and forth," she said. "He was happy. I was happy. Neither of us had anyone else. Do you have anyone, Mr. Carver?"

"No," he said, thrown for a moment by the question. Resenting it.

"A month ago," Edwina went on, "Willis began acting strangely, moodily. He hadn't been moody before."

"You hadn't known him very long," Carver pointed out.

"But I knew him very well," Edwina said. "I told you, neither of us has anyone else."

The ocean sighed again, like a huge thing breathing.

Edwina walked to a high-backed wooden chair and sat down, gracefully crossing legs whose curvaceousness even the severe skirt couldn't tame. "One night a week ago, Mr. Carver, Willis made love to me as he never had before. So intensely." One of her hands began absently caressing the top of her thigh. "Even desperately. The next morning, I went to show a piece of property and he stayed behind. He was sitting on the veranda drinking coffee when I drove away." She suddenly realized she was about to rub a hole in her skirt, and the naughty hand joined the nice hand in her lap and they knitted fingers to stay out of mischief.

"When I came back that afternoon, the police were there."

She paused and chewed on her lower lip. Carver waited, wondering if she'd draw blood.

She hadn't. He was disappointed.

"A friend of mine," she continued, "another salesperson, had come by my house to see me on business earlier that afternoon. When she got no answer at the door, she walked around to see if I was outside on the veranda. She was about to leave, when she spotted Willis's sport jacket and shoes on the edge of the drop."

"Drop?" Carver asked.

"Where the Army Corps of Engineers graded the land to rise well above sea level," Edwina said. "They placed rocks about sixty feet below to keep the beach from eroding."

Carver was getting the idea. "Was it your friend who called the police?" he asked.

"Yes. Alice phoned them from my house. The back door was unlocked. Willis had poured another cup of coffee, apparently. It was on the veranda table, cool and full to the brim. There was a glass of grapefruit juice, untouched, and on a plate was a sweet roll with only one bite out of it. And, most important, there wasn't a body on the rocks at the foot of the drop."

"It might have washed away, out to sea. Bodies do that."

"That's what the police say."

"The police know bodies and water."

"I'm reminded of that every time I go to headquarters," Edwina said.

So Willis had decided to commit suicide in the middle of breakfast, Carver thought. What an impulsive guy. He'd suddenly put down his sweet roll and walked to the edge of the drop, then removed his shoes and jacket and dived onto the rocks. Then the sea had pulled his body out to the depths, maybe claiming it for the rest of recorded time. Well, it could have happened that way. The shoes and jacket didn't bother

Carver; suicides often prepared methodically for death, as if in the hereafter they might be graded for neatness.

"Was the jacket folded?" he asked.

Edwina nodded. "It was resting on top of the shoes so it wouldn't get dirty. As if Willis expected to return for it."

"Was anything in the pockets?"

"Willis's wallet, with all his credit cards and over a hundred dollars in it. Also a few other things: a comb, two ticket stubs."

Carver took another sip of beer, noticing that it was getting warm from the heat of his hand on the can. "Miss Talbot . . . Edwina . . . I have to tell you that Willis's behavior isn't inconsistent with suicide."

She raised her eyebrows as if annoyed that Carver had jumped to a conclusion, irritated by a world in general that wouldn't hear her out before passing judgment. "I thought it was suicide myself, until I began to think about how Willis had acted with me that last night we were together. I can't simply close my mind to that."

Carver tried the beer again. It was too warm for his taste. Foamy. Edwina was gazing with unblinking beautiful gray eyes at him.

He matched her stare, trying not to get lost in those eyes. "What do you hypothesize?" he asked. "What really happened?"

"I think Willis is still alive. He knew someone was after him, coming for him; he was afraid. He was taken by whoever came. Or he faked his own death, so he'd be safe, and then ran."

"Ran why?"

"I don't know. Gambling debts, trouble with someone from his past. It could be any of a hundred reasons."

"You must have some specific idea, among that hundred."

"Well, there's something I didn't mention to the police," Edwina said in a measured voice, "because I didn't want to risk getting Willis into any more trouble than he might already be in. There was some money. I saw it the week before he disappeared, in a shoe box in his dresser drawer."

"How much money?"

"I don't know. There were hundred-dollar bills on top, several of them. I don't know what was down deeper in the box. I just got a glimpse of it as he was putting the lid on before he pushed the drawer shut."

"Did you ask Willis about the money?"

"Yes. He said he'd cashed some bonds at the bank. To loan the money to a friend."

"What bank? What friend?"

"He didn't say."

"Do you think the money is connected to his disappearance?"

"No," she said, "but I can't be sure. I do know that the money, shoe box and all, is gone now. Willis is a kind and considerate person, not the sort to get into trouble. But he likes to help people, more than he should. I think he inadvertently got mixed up with the wrong people. He's running from them now, and when—if—they find him, they might . . ." She swallowed hard. Holding back tears? "You have to find him before whoever is after him does."

"Do you know what wrong people might be after him?" Carver asked.

"No, I don't. Honestly."

He didn't know if he believed her. She'd do almost anything to make sure he took the case. He wasn't all that impressed by this money story, didn't know if he believed even that. She might be throwing it at him as added incentive to believe Willis was alive and to find him.

"I only know he isn't dead," she said. "He didn't kill himself. He's still alive somewhere. In danger." Her voice almost broke. "Maybe terrible danger."

"I'm not sure the facts indicate that, Edwina."

"I told you the way Willis made love to me the night before he left, as if he knew it might be the last time, as if he were saying good-bye. I've been told good-bye that way before. I recognize it. I know Willis didn't commit a sudden-impulse suicide. But how do I convince the police?"

How indeed? Carver thought, picturing Lieutenant Desoto's handsome, somber face as the lieutenant listened to a hunch based on passion. It wasn't the sort of evidence to convince a coroner's inquest. It wasn't evidence at all.

"Why are the Orlando police involved?" Carver asked. "You live in Del Moray."

"When Willis moved in with me he kept his apartment in Orlando because he couldn't get out of his year's lease. His official address is still Orlando. I tried to get the police there to list him as a missing person, but they wouldn't."

"Desoto is in Homicide," Carver noted.

"Missing Persons had me talk with him. Willis left no note, nothing. Though Willis is missing, the police see his disappearance as a possible murder officially, only what they really believe is that he committed suicide and the current carried him out to sea. So they're not investigating a murder, and they're not searching for a missing person. They're doing nothing."

"They're officially keeping the case open," Carver said, "and unofficially closing it. Leaving it in limbo in the wrong department—if it *is* the wrong department. If Willis *was* a suicide, they don't have a worry. If it turns out he might have been a murder victim, the department's ass is covered; it's a pending case." For a moment his expression was one of distaste. "Bureaucracy," he said. He poured the rest of his beer down the sink drain, watching it foam and swirl and disappear.

"Your friend Desoto doesn't strike me as a bureaucrat."

"He is, though, in his *bossa nova* way. The Orlando police have a caseload they can barely cope with. It's a fact of life that prevents them from paying proper attention to certain odds-against cases. They call it 'prioritizing.' Maybe it's necessary, but it ignores the human factor. Most cops are human, and

14

prioritizing bothers them. Even Desoto is human. So he sent you to see me so that justice might be served, and to get you off his back."

"That sounds about right. Desoto explained that you'd been injured and were retired from the force. He said you were recuperating here and had gone into business as a private detective. He thought you might want to hear my story. I'm willing to pay whatever you charge to find Willis, Mr. Carver."

"You really should hire a bigger organization."

She was adamant. "Lieutenant Desoto recommended you. He said you could use the business. He also said you were tough, skeptical, had principles, and would surprise me, and you, with your compassion. I'm still waiting for the compassion."

Carver came out from behind the Formica counter and limped across the hardwood floor, supporting himself with his hands on furniture and the wall, then slumped into a chair opposite Edwina's. It was a director's chair, canvas, one he got wet each day after his swim.

"Desoto is a bastard," he said.

Edwina stared at him in that blank, impenetrable way of hers. "I got the impression he was your friend."

"He is. I'm a bastard, too. This knee is locked tight at a slight angle for life, Edwina. I'm finished as a cop, and I don't know any other line of work. Desoto often thinks he knows what's best for me. Right now, he's trying to make sure I succeed in the private-investigation business."

"Maybe he does know what's best for you."

Carver kept silent, remembering times when Desoto *had* known that very thing.

"Lieutenant Desoto says you're a good detective," Edwina said. "He says you think like a criminal."

"I do," Carver said, "but I only think like one. It's Desoto who fixes all his relatives' traffic tickets."

Edwina shifted her weight in her chair, crossing her legs the other way. Her right leg, which had been on the bottom, was pale where its circulation had been impaired by the weight of the left. For some reason the splotchy coloring beneath her light nylon panty hose intrigued Carver. Aroused him. He hadn't thought enough about the opposite sex for a long time. His divorce from Laura had been finalized just three days before he'd been shot. Two deep wounds in one week took it out of a man.

"I'm going to make a guess, Mr. Carver," Edwina said. "It's true that Lieutenant Desoto probably doesn't have the manpower to spare for an investigation into what happened to Willis. Or maybe he couldn't justify such an investigation to his superiors. But he must see a lot of cases like this that he lets drift into official never-never land. I don't think he'd have sent me to see you unless he thought it was worth discovering what happened to Willis, and unless he thought you were the one who could do the discovering."

"You're probably right," Carver admitted.

"Which leaves us only with the question of whether you want to help me. And help yourself instead of vegetating here."

Carver didn't answer. Who was *she*, to talk to him this way?

"That's what Lieutenant Desoto said you were doing out here, vegetating."

"Piss on Lieutenant Desoto. He wouldn't know a vegetable if it jumped up and gave him vitamin D."

"But I suspect he knows you quite well."

"Suspecting seems to be an obsession with you."

"Lately it has been," Edwina said. "I'm looking for someone to share that obsession. Shall we discuss terms?"

Carver stood up, leaned to the side, and got his cane from where he'd left it propped against the wall. He planted it firmly on the wood floor, squeezing its burnished walnut handle hard enough to whiten his knuckles.

"Where are you going?" Edwina asked.

"For another swim. I didn't drip enough water on the floor

from the last time I was interrupted." He tap-tap-tapped to the door with his cane.

"You don't get around so bad," Edwina said, following him outside. The screen door slapped shut behind them and reverberated. "You've got a lean, strong body; be thankful for that."

"I am," Carver said, making for the beach. "You should see me run." A gull wheeled in low and then soared away in an exquisite arc, screaming, as if taunting him with its limitless blue freedom.

"I'm seeing you run now," she said. "Away from this case. But you can find Willis. I know it. I can *feel* it. Lieutenant Desoto knew what he was doing when he sent me here."

"That's your own unreasonable optimism you feel."

"There's nothing wrong with being an optimist," Edwina said. She sounded annoyed.

"Not if you thrive on disappointment." The tip of Carver's cane hit a soft spot and he almost fell. He was walking too fast; he was annoyed, too.

"I was warned you were cynical," Edwina said in disgust. Desoto again.

Near the surf, Carver stopped walking and turned to face her. He didn't want her to see him backcrawl into the water. She got one of her business cards from her purse and handed it to him. It was an expensive thick white card, engraved with QUILL REALTY and her home and office phone numbers. There was a company logo—a red feather—in the upper right corner.

"Don't get it wet," she said. "Consider my offer and phone me."

"Ever think about trying to find Willis yourself?" he asked.

"I know what I'm good at, Mr. Carver. And what I'm not good at."

When she turned and began to walk away, Carver extended his cane and used its crook to catch her elbow, gently pulling her around in the soft sand to face him.

She stared at him, seemingly more amused than angry. She was too tough to be swayed by strong-arm tactics, she was telling him with that look.

"If Willis Davis did commit suicide," Carver said, "he was crazy."

She removed the cane from her arm. "I know. And Willis isn't crazy."

Carver sat down at the edge of the surf and watched her walk away down the beach. Carrying her high-heeled shoes, she strode erectly in her tailored dark business suit among the sunbathers, among all that tanned and glistening female flesh. She was the sexiest thing on the sand. Half a dozen male heads turned in her wake to stare at her as Carver was doing.

He patted his stiff left leg. "Getting well," he muttered to himself. "Getting well. . . ."

After carefully placing Edwina's white business card beneath the cane, far enough up on the beach so it wouldn't get wet, he turned again to the ocean.

It was time to get back in the water.

CHAPTER 3

Carver was awake at five-thirty the next morning, lying in bed in the dimness, turning over in his mind the day six months before when he'd been injured. The kid had taken careful aim and shot him in the knee for the perverse thrill of it. Probably he'd heard about the Irish Republican Army punishing informers by shattering their kneecaps with gunfire, and thought now that he had a cop cornered it might be fun to try this imaginative and permanent imposition of his will. The kid was doing ten to twenty years now in Raiford Prison for armed robbery and assault. Sometimes Carver wished another con would stick a knife in the kid; other times, more and more often now, he didn't much care and had to remind himself that he should lust for vengeance.

He did wish he hadn't dropped his revolver as commanded when the second holdup man had stepped out of the back room of the all-night grocery store.

Carver had been off duty that evening and stopped at the store for a pound of ground beef, when he realized a robbery was going down. Realized it by the studied nonchalance of the only other customer, a young Latino with his right hand in his jacket pocket. Realized it by the rubbery features and scent of fear of the old man behind the counter. The Latino youth had sensed cop, panicked, and begun to run, and Carver drew his revolver, yelled that he was police, and ordered the fleeing suspect to halt. All by the book. And the book worked. The suspect stopped abruptly and raised his hands.

That's when the book failed Carver. A soft voice behind him said, "Drop the piece, Wyatt Earp, and nobody gets their guts shot out." It was the kind of voice Carver had heard a few times before, not scared when it should have been scared, and with a touch of gloating, sadistic humor. Carver let the comforting weight of his revolver drop to the floor. His heart fell with it.

The second gunman had been in the back room. He was a skinny black kid about twenty, with a scraggly *bandito* mustache and a frantically active protruding Adam's apple. When he walked around Carver on his way to the door, gripping a grocery sack full of money in one hand and a cheap oversized revolver in the other, he lowered the aim of the pistol, and blasted away Carver's kneecap. It was as if he'd done that sort of thing almost every day of his life; as natural as zipping up his pants.

Carver was on the floor before he knew what had happened, aware of nothing but a numbness in his leg. And within a few seconds came the pain that was to be Carver's close companion—the blinding, encompassing pain. Pain that absorbed him and shut out the rest of the world. He was unaware that the woman who had been knocked unconscious in the back room had come to and phoned the police, unaware that both youthful holdup men, including the skinny black one with the gun stuck in his belt, had been stopped in the parking lot and arrested. Unaware of anything but the searing everything of the pain, sickening him, sending him in a terrifying plunge down a black well that was bored to the center of the earth.

Then the hospital room. White. Everything white. Clean. Safe.

And the infuriating news about his leg.

For a moment Carver thought he was back in the hospital. Then he realized he was in his own bed at home, squeezing the beaded edges of the mattress so hard that his fingers ached. The sea made soothing whispering sounds outside his open windows, telling him to relax, the pain had ended. Maybe that was why he'd really moved there, for the mothering, comforting sound of the sea.

Carver swiveled to sit on the edge of the mattress, then reached for his cane and stood up. He was dizzy for a few seconds, and sweating heavily, though the morning hadn't begun to heat up. Nude, he limped across the room to the bathroom, hung his cane on the doorknob, and stepped into the shower stall.

The blast of cold water jolted him awake cruelly and lodged his mind firmly in the present. When he was chilled and began to shiver, he turned on the hot tap. He was spending too much time alone since the injury, that was for sure. Planted in the past.

Vegetating.

When he'd finished showering, Carver shaved for the first time in three days. After rinsing the lather from his face, he liked what he saw in the fogged mirror a little better. But only a little. He had never been a handsome man, but now his face had taken on a new, predatory gauntness. He was dark, almost swarthy, except for his sun-bleached eyebrows and pale blue eyes. And he was practically out of hair now, gleamingly bald on top but with thick grayish curls around his ears and growing well down the back of his neck. The line of his nose was long and straight; his mouth was full-lipped and resolute, turned down slightly at one corner by a thin, boyhood scar. Ugly dude. Mean dude. The best you could say about his features was that they were strong.

Carver evened his sideburns and said the hell with it. He didn't want to pose for calendars. He was forty-five and liked fortyish women who had a few nicks and scars themselves.

Stretch marks were kind of sexy; they indicated that the mind had been stretched, too.

He dressed in a blue-and-gray-striped pullover shirt that had some kind of animal embroidered above the pocket, clean navy blue dress slacks, dark socks, and well-worn loafers. The Paris hoodlum look. Then he walked outside to his car.

It was a 1973 Oldsmobile convertible, and Carver had left the top down when it rained. But that was okay; the car had been rusty already and the rain that had gone in the top had run out the bottom. The leather interior was dry and warm and purified by the sun. Carver got in and the Olds started on the first try, as if to confirm that appearances deceived and it could still do its stuff.

He drove down the narrow road to the coast highway, then headed south. The Olds was large, with plenty of room for his stiff leg, and driving was no problem with the automatic transmission.

A mile down the highway was a slow-food restaurant where Carver intended to stop for a big breakfast of hotcakes, sausage, and coffee. He would have a second cup of coffee, and maybe smoke a Swisher Sweet cigar if there was nobody around who looked like they might complain.

Then he'd drive the rest of the way into Del Moray and talk to Edwina Talbot.

Her house was small, like his, only it was worth about three times as much. Carver drove up the winding driveway and parked beneath three tall date palms planted in a perfect triangle marked off by fancy red stones. The house was constructed of brownish brick with a red front door and a low red tile roof. Beyond it Carver could see the blue Atlantic merge with a paler blue sky. When he switched off the engine, the sea muttered incomprehensible secrets to him.

A gate opened in a stone wall that joined the north side of the house, and Edwina walked out. She was wearing a dark blue one-piece bathing suit, Mexican sandals, and was carrying a drink in her right hand. In her left hand was a pair of sunglasses with very dark oversized lenses. Her tanned, slender body was superb but for legs that were slightly bowed. That was the only thing wrong with her legs.

Mustn't grade women like cattle, Carver admonished himself, as he gripped his cane and got out of the car.

"I heard you drive up," Edwina said, walking closer, looking better, worth the blue ribbon. She didn't seem surprised to see him; probably not much surprised her. Her dark hair was pulled back and bobby-pinned, emphasizing angular cheekbones and a graceful jawline. The patient intentness was still in her eyes; they were the eyes of a stalking cat. "Have you decided to search for Willis?"

"Yes."

She smiled; the cat had cornered a mouse. "It's a long drive here from your place. How did you know I'd be home?"

"I didn't. I was prepared to wait for you."

"You could have simply phoned, Mr. Carver. Or did you want to see me again?"

"I wanted to see your house. To see how much you might be worth so I'll know how much to charge you."

Edwina laughed low and melodiously. Carver liked the way the tendons in her throat tightened and moved.

"You're toying with me, Edwina," he said. "Checking to see where you might attach strings to me."

She sobered. The laugh went silent and became a smile. "I'll do whatever I have to in order to get somebody with ability to search for Willis." She dangled the sunglasses, looking down at them. Then she put them on, as if suddenly deciding to effect a disguise. "Come on back by the pool, Mr. Carver. We'll sit in the shade and talk."

She turned and strode through stark shadows back toward the open gate, not waiting for him. Carver limped behind her, watching the switch of her trim hips. He was feeling stronger, getting more competent with the cane.

They sat opposite each other on wrought-iron white chairs at a metal table with an umbrella sprouting like a mutant tropical flower from its center. Edwina set her glass down on a plastic coaster. Carver guessed that the glass contained grapefruit juice. Or maybe it was a Margarita sans salt.

"Would you like something cool to drink?" she asked. "Or coffee?"

Carver declined. He was looking across the small round swimming pool at a brick veranda where another, larger table, with a fringed blue umbrella, was surrounded by four webbed aluminum chairs. Beyond the table was a low, curved brick wall with a long redwood planter on top. There were a lot of colorful flowers in the planter, and something green and viny draped out of one end. On the other side of the low wall the ground sloped gradually to what must have been the drop Edwina had described. They were up high, on a point of land jutting out from the coast. From where they sat, the sea and sky looked incredibly blue and vast.

"Tell me about Willis Davis," Carver said.

Edwina stared at her glass, slowly lifting it just a fraction of an inch off the metal table and putting it back down in its wet ring, as if studying with a scientific eye the amazing adhesion of the water. "Willis is a considerate, gentle man."

"Likewise Bluebeard and Theodore Bundy. Tell me about Willis."

"He's a soft touch who probably got in trouble helping someone. So soft, in fact, that, to tell you the truth, it's difficult for me to imagine him as a salesman. But on the other hand, there's something tremendously persuasive about him. I've seen him use that persuasiveness on a customer. If he believes in a product, he might be able to sell it better than a dozen high-pressure types like me."

"You don't strike me as high-pressure," Carver said. "High-voltage, maybe. It could be you're not as hard as you think."

"You haven't seen me trying to close a real-estate deal." She looked up from her drink. Her eyes were barely visible behind the green-tinted lenses. "I don't mean pushy; that's not what I am. Maybe I'm not exactly high-pressure at that. But I am relentless. That's part of what I saw in Willis—a quiet, calm relentlessness."

"Do you have a photograph of him?"

"No."

"Why not?"

Edwina shrugged. "I didn't know it was required by law. Some people are camera bugs, some aren't. I never took his photograph; I don't even own a camera."

"Don't real-estate salespeople around here photograph the houses they list?"

"No, a professional photographer hired by the company does that."

"So describe Willis."

Edwina drummed her fingertips on the metal table. The sound annoyed Carver. He could feel the subtle vibrations with his own hand, which was resting on his side of the table.

"He's difficult to describe," Edwina said finally. "He's about your height—maybe five-foot-ten. Where you're lean and muscular, Willis is well built but maybe a few pounds overweight. Still, he doesn't have a stomach paunch and isn't soft."

"What color are his hair and eyes?" Carver asked.

"His hair is medium brown. His eyes are what you might call hazel. He's sort of average-complexioned, with handsome, regular features. He has no distinguishing marks that I can think of. Oh—he has a scar on his right shoulder, in front, from an operation he had when he got hurt playing high-school football."

"A shoulder separation?" That was the most common football injury that would leave the kind of scar Edwina had described.

"I don't know."

"What high school?"

"A private school up north. He was the team's quarter-back."

"Where exactly is Willis from?"

"Orlando."

"I mean, before that."

"He never said. He did mention that he'd lived a while in the Midwest."

"Did you get the impression he was a Florida native?"

"Nobody is a Florida native. Willis has a kind of nonregional accent. Which is no accent at all, if you know what I mean."

"Sure. Like one of those talking-suit network TV anchormen: coast-to-coast bland. But what sort of dresser is Willis? Does he favor flashy clothes? Does he wear plaid socks and striped shorts?"

"He's a conservative dresser," Edwina said. "His suits are mostly gray and blue, with vests. He wears white shirts and ties that aren't loud. His jackets don't even have patterns in the material."

"Expensive clothes?"

"Some cost a lot, some didn't. He doesn't wear thousand-dollar suits, but he mentioned once having a tailor."

"You don't have the tailor's name, I suppose."

"No."

"Who are his friends in Orlando?"

"I never met any of them," Edwina said. "It wasn't that long after we met before he moved in with me here. Del Moray is where we spent most of our time together."

"Where did Willis work?"

"At Sun South, just outside of Del Moray. Where I was working when we met. He sold time-share units. Do you know what those are?"

"I'm from Florida," Carver said. Time-share projects were big in Florida. The customer bought the privilege of spending one or more weeks every year in an apartment, usually by the ocean. If he bought one week, he was in effect purchasing one fifty-second ownership of the apartment. Two weeks, one twenty-sixth. And so on. Time shares were a popular way to own at least a piece of valuable beachfront property that might continue to appreciate and be sold at a profit. Might.

"Who was Willis's boss at Sun South?" Carver asked.

"Ernie Franks, the developer who built the project. Willis liked and admired him."

Carver thought it was convenient to have his questions anticipated. Edwina seemed to be ahead of him; he wondered how far ahead. He stood up, bumping his head on the umbrella, and walked around the pool and onto the veranda.

Edwina followed him. As if she thought he might stumble and she should be there to catch him. He didn't like that. She sensed it and fell back.

Carver stepped over another low wall and walked toward the edge of the drop above the sea.

"Be careful, Mr. Carver," Edwina called behind him. She had stayed on the veranda and was staring out at him with what on her stony features passed for alarm.

"Don't worry," Carver tossed back over his shoulder, "I used to be in show business, diving into shallow water from a high platform in the circus."

"Really?"

"No." Carver inched nearer the edge of the outcropping of land and looked down. Diving experience wouldn't help him here anyway; the sea foamed around unevenly piled jagged rocks directly below, and the water didn't appear to be more than a few feet deep. His stomach took the plunge, beckoning Carver to follow. He declined and dizzily moved back from the drop, then turned to face Edwina. "Where were Willis's jacket and shoes found?"

She pointed to a spot on the ground a few feet to Carver's left.

The bare, rocky soil told him nothing. He started back to the veranda. By the time he got there, Edwina was seated in one of the webbed chairs at the table, waiting for him.

27

"Where are the shoes and jacket?" he asked.

"The police kept them."

Carver sat down in one of the other chairs. He saw that his pants were dirty from when he'd struggled over the low walls around the veranda. He brushed at the loose earth and it fell away. "What else can you tell me about Willis?" he asked.

"He loved me."

"You're sure of that?"

"Is it important to you?"

"Yes."

"I'm sure. One other man loved me in my life. It was the same way it was with Willis. I don't want the result to be the same."

Carver stared at her, sensed pain. There was something pertinent she wasn't telling him. "Okay," he said. He stood up, bumping his head on that umbrella as he had on the one by the pool. It felt about the same.

Edwina removed her sunglasses and looked up at him, appraising him with a pawnbroker's squint. She had a way of seeming to see to the center of things.

"You look better than when we met at your place," she said. "Almost as if you don't mind being alive. It's because you have a job now. A challenge."

"I'm not a victim of the work ethic," Carver told her, knowing better. He was like Edwina; he needed an obsession, maybe even one that carried moral obligation, so he could push himself until he was satisfied that he'd done the job: an illusion of forward motion in life. But he had his doubts about whether Willis Davis was worth all of that. "When I find out anything important, I'll let you know," he said. He got a firm grip on his cane and started back around the pool to go to his car.

Edwina walked next to him, her sandals making soft slapping sounds against the bottoms of her feet. Her slow pace was Carver's normal one, with the cane. She didn't open the gate for him, or the car door.

Carver settled in behind the steering wheel, twisted the ignition key, and the Oldsmobile's big V-8 engine growled and rumbled like the dinosaur it was. He felt its powerful vibration in his thighs and buttocks, throughout his body.

"We haven't discussed your fee," Edwina said, standing alongside the car.

"We'll discuss it when I find Willis. If I don't find him, you can cover my expenses and that's all."

"That's fair to the point of being dumb."

"That's me for you," Carver said. He drove away.

CHAPTER 4

Carver took Interstate 95 south, then drove west on the Bee Line Expressway into Orlando. As soon as he got off the highway, he pulled to the curb and raised the Oldsmobile's canvas top; the June Florida sun was high now, beating down on vinyl, flesh, and metal. There would be no sixty-mile-per-hour breeze to cool him now that he had to drive at a slower speed in the city. He switched on the air-conditioner before accelerating back out into traffic.

A van with more windows than a house, and half a dozen Disney World stickers pasted on its rear doors and bumper, honked at Carver for pulling in ahead of it, then whizzed on past the Olds about twenty miles per hour over the speed limit. It seemed that half the cars that passed Carver going north had Disney stickers on their bumpers or trunks. People not letting go of their vacation in Disney-dominated, enchanted central Florida, carrying the good times home with them. Someday it might be comforting to scrape the snow off that bumper and see the sticker.

A small blond kid who might have been male or female stared for a moment out a sticker-papered rear window, just before the van cut across the bow of a truck and took a turnoff toward downtown. Carver followed the van, watching it pull away at high speed. He was on his way downtown, too. He hoped he wouldn't see the van wrapped around a tree on the way.

Carver found Lieutenant Alfonso Desoto in his office on the second floor of police headquarters. The lieutenant didn't get up from behind his cluttered gray metal desk when Carver entered, but he smiled and waved a hand in invitation for Carver to sit down in one of the wooden chairs in front of the desk. A portable radio on the window sill behind Desoto was playing "Guantanamera." In the other window a refrigeration unit purred away, causing a couple of yellow ribbons tied to its grillwork to flutter merrily. The office looked cool but felt too warm.

Carver hooked his cane around the back of one of the chairs and pulled it to him, then sat down. He looked at Desoto without speaking. The lieutenant was as handsome as ever, and would have looked more at home in a bullfighter's suit of lights than in his gray business suit. Desoto was over six feet tall, broad of shoulder and waspish of waist, with flashing white teeth, liquid brown eyes, and a noble Aztec profile. He was only half Mexican, Carver knew, on his father's side. His mother was Italian. Desoto had inherited the best of the gene pool.

He was the first to speak. "You look good, *amigo*. The rich and idle life of the private cop apparently agrees with you."

"Only apparently," Carver said. "I'd rather be back on the job."

Desoto nodded somberly. "I know. But life is change, and we all have to adapt. Sad, but that's the way of things."

"Don't give me that crap."

"Okay."

The music on the radio stopped, and a commercial blared from the tinny speaker, a rehearsed conversation among a group of kids praising the qualities of a popular brand of pudding. Somewhere big business had gotten the idea that cuteness translated into profit. Carver wished they'd hurry up and get some other idea.

"You mind turning that off?" he asked Desoto.

Desoto raised an eyebrow in matinee-idol fashion. He didn't look like the tough cop he was. "You don't like pudding, *amigo?*"

"I don't like cute. It makes me want to spit."

"Ah, you've gotten cynical, bitter." But Desoto's hand reached out and switched off the radio. The room abruptly seemed unnaturally quiet, with only the purring of the air-conditioner and the distant, unintelligible crackle of a dispatcher's voice on the police radio somewhere outside the office, droning relentlessly: Orlando keeping up in crime. "But what about Miss Edwina Talbot?" Desoto asked. "That one is beyond mere cute, wouldn't you say?"

"Is that why you sent her to me, Desoto? To cheer me up?"

"I thought you might need something to make your pecker as stiff as your leg."

"I only need one crutch," Carver said. "You sent me Edwina because the Willis Davis suicide doesn't smell right."

"I didn't tell her that."

"You wouldn't. And you wouldn't tell her that you can't waste money and manpower on a case that probably would end up a fat zero. That the higher-ups on the force wouldn't let you, even if you wanted to take a run at finding Willis Davis or what's left of him. You wouldn't tell her, but she knows."

"Sure, the woman's no fool. I realized that as soon as I stopped looking at her and started listening. And there's something else about her. She isn't nearly as tough as she acts."

"Oh?" It interested Carver that Desoto had come to the same conclusion he had. "Then why does she act tough?"

"You don't understand the female of our species, *amigo.* This one has been hurt, badly."

"Sure. Willis left her." Carver was prodding. He wanted to hear what Desoto had to say about this, his area of expertise.

"No, no, I mean before that. Beyond that. She must have been. That's why she pretends to be so cold."

"So you decided she should be my client," Carver said. "Good psychotherapy for both of us."

"You were going to rust and ruin out there by the ocean, hadn't worked in a month; I heard it from a lot of people. And what other kind of work do you know, huh, *viejo*? You've been a policeman almost all your so-called adult life."

"Even before that," Carver said. "I was a hall monitor in school." He gave a Cagney-like sneer and pretended he was holding a machine gun. He knew Desoto was a late-night TV buff and a Cagney fan.

"You think when things get mean, you can get meaner," Desoto said. "But that doesn't always work in the real world. You can be a cruel man, Carver. Hard. But like Edwina Talbot, you aren't as hard as you think."

"Oh? I know I'm not so hard. Cruel, either. I get mad when I see people jerked around. I've been jerked around too much myself; that's why I use a cane and list like a sinking ship when I walk. When I get mad, I try to do something about what makes me mad. There's nothing very complicated, or wrong, with that kind of behavior."

Desoto leaned back and crossed his arms. "So you get mad when you see people used, and you try to do something about it. You pick and choose. Who the fuck you think you are, *amigo?* Maybe Dirty Harry?"

"No, I'm just a guy who gets mad."

"This is noble?"

"Nope. But if I'm too hard and cynical for some people, that's too bad. I don't apologize."

Desoto leaned further back in his desk chair and looked satisfied. He'd probably meant to get Carver riled; it was sport. Sometimes, for Desoto, getting people mad was like testing their batteries.

He smiled, his dashing devil smile. "So, you're going to help Miss Edwina Talbot?"

Carver nodded. "If Edwina can give herself blindly, so can I. Besides, you're right: It's something to keep me busy."

Desoto widened his smile to wicked. He was the amiable lothario again. "Some busy."

"The people who told you about me were right," Carver admitted. "I was turning to rust because of infrequent activity. It's time to oil up the old machinery and see if the gears still turn."

"They turn," Desoto told him. "They'll always turn. The chase is in your blood."

"Sure, heat-seeking missiles, beagles, and me. Tell me about Willis Davis."

"He's missing," Desoto said, straight-faced. "Other than that we actually don't know much about him. According to Edwina Talbot, he'd been acting strangely before his disappearance, murder, suicide, whatever. And his boss says Davis was a distant kind of guy, a loner."

"Maybe all that was his way of laying the groundwork for a fake suicide."

"Or a real one."

Carver repeated most of what Edwina had told him, and Desoto said that was just about the way the case went.

"Why would somebody interrupt breakfast to commit suicide?" Carver asked.

Desoto waved a hand as if the question were almost irrelevant. "Suicides do these things sometimes, Carver; you know that. They like for their survivors to wonder what really happened to them. Or maybe a person or persons unknown came after Davis, happened to catch him at breakfast, and threw him off the drop. Wanted his bacon or the last danish. Or possibly Davis went insane and was scared over the drop. Maybe he saw people that weren't there."

"Did Davis's jacket and shoes tell you anything?"

Desoto stood up and moved gracefully to a row of filing

cabinets along the wall. He pulled open a drawer, thumbed through it, and withdrew a yellow file folder. It wasn't very thick, Carver noticed.

Seated again at his desk, Desoto opened the folder and scanned its contents. "That information's not here," he said. "You'll have to check with Marillo in the lab."

Carver was surprised. "Not there? How could that be? The man disappeared over a week ago."

"There couldn't be much," Desoto said, unconcerned, "or Marillo would have phoned me."

"What the hell's happened to the department since I left?" Carver asked.

"It's gotten busier," Desoto said. "We've had to prioritize. Such a nice word, eh? Crime is on the upswing, like marriage. The drug business has moved up here in a big way from south Florida. So we've got more men in Narcotics, fewer in Homicide. But Homicide's busier, too. It goes with the drug scene."

"Is that why they labeled the Willis Davis case a homicide?" Carver asked. "So it would get lost with a lot of other unsolvables?"

Desoto shrugged. "You find inconsistencies in Davis's death. Who's to say the man wasn't murdered?"

Carver studied his old friend. The job would never get to Desoto; he'd be the best cop possible under any circumstances, a very good cop indeed, and probably never advance in rank.

Carver folded his hands around each other and the top of his cane, shifted his weight forward in his chair, and stood up. The muscles in his tanned forearms rippled; his arms had gotten stronger since he'd been struggling about with the cane.

"Will you keep me tapped into any developments?" he asked.

"Sure, *amigo*. And you keep me informed. I haven't lost interest in this case. That's really why I sent Edwina Talbot out to see you. We'll help each other, Carver. You're sort of half an answer to my manpower problem; you're still on the job, in a way, only somebody other than the city is paying you. The arrangement could benefit all concerned."

"If I'm the cheapest labor you've got," Carver said, "maybe the department should see to it that some other cops get disabled."

"Ah, if only we had a suggestion box." Desoto laced his fingers on the desk and gazed up at Carver. Glinting gold cufflinks peeked out from beneath his gray jacket sleeves like the wary eyes of concealed animals. "Where are you going now?"

"To the lab," Carver said, "to talk to Marillo."

"Don't tell him I suggested you see him," Desoto said. "I don't want him pestering me unless he finds something startling, like a notebook with Mafia hit men in a pocket."

"What would Mafia hit men be doing in a pocket with a notebook?" Carver asked.

"Marillo is a scientist. Scientists are boring, and I don't want to be bored by one. He's plain vanilla in a white dish, Marillo is."

"He's okay," Carver said. "He smells like formaldehyde but he means well. I like him." He limped to the door and opened it.

"See," Desoto said behind him, "now that you're busy, you've already lost some of your cynicism. Your hard edge. I miss you. You were somebody in the department who could do what needed doing, always, no matter what it was. At the same time, you have ethics and compassion. Almost like a split personality. Officer Jekyll and Mr. Hyde. It's rare, that quality."

"I doubt if you mean any of that," Carver told him, stepping into the hall and slamming the door.

Thinking this was no time to lose his hard edge.

Sam Marillo was at his desk in the lab, in the frosted-glass cubicle that passed for his office. He was a fiftyish, perfectly groomed small man with long, bony features, an erect, fit body, abnormally flawless skin, and short-cropped iron-gray hair pomaded and combed straight back. He looked as if he'd been manufactured rather than born. When he heard Carver's perfunctory, rattling knock on the side of the doorless cubicle, he adjusted his silver-rimmed spectacles and looked up, then smiled when he saw Carver limp in.

He stood up briskly behind his desk, in a way that suggested he'd incorporated exercising into his work regimen, and they shook hands. "How's the leg, Carver?"

"Locked tight as the door to the Narcotics evidence room."

Carver noticed that the desk, as usual, was symmetrically arranged. A marble clock and a calendar were at precise angles, a stack of file folders and the "in" and "out" baskets were situated so their edges were parallel to the edges of the desk. Several sharpened pencils and a ball-point pen had been laid next to each other so that they pointed in precisely the same direction, like compass needles.

Marillo formed a Gothic steeple with his manicured pink hands and gazed thoughtfully up at Carver.

"I need to know about Willis Davis," Carver said. "He's the suicide they're keeping open as a murder case. Or vice versa."

"I know who he was," Marillo said. "It makes no difference to me what they're doing at headquarters with his case. I just tell them what they want to know and don't make waves."

Not even ripples, Carver thought. "What are you going to tell them about Davis?"

"Not much. It's kind of tough without a body. We just have his sport jacket and shoes."

"Did he have athlete's foot?"

Marillo didn't smile. Most humor escaped him. "No, and the wear on the shoes' heels and soles indicated no irregularity in his walk other than a slight tendency to turn his left foot out as he strode. Wait just a second, Carver." Marillo stood up and left the glass cubicle. Carver patiently leaned on his cane and waited. The lab smelled more like Pine-Sol than formalde-hyde.

When Marillo returned he was carrying a results form sheet, an evidence envelope, and a blue sport jacket and a pair of black leather dress shoes encased in clear plastic. After hanging the jacket on a hook attached to one of the cubicle's supports, he placed the envelope on a corner of his desk, then the shoes alongside it with their toes pointed the same way as the pen and pencils. True north without a doubt. Then he sat back down, adjusted his glasses, and scanned the results form. He read aloud in a precise monotone. If voices were flavored, his would indeed have been vanilla.

"The insides of the shoes yielded some black thread, proba-bly from Davis's socks. Also a blade of grass and some lint and blue fibers, all probably picked up from the carpet when he was in stockinged feet before putting on his shoes." He opened the envelope and dumped its contents onto the desk. "Found in the jacket pockets: a comb that contained three strands of straight brown hair; a wallet containing credit cards, identifi-cation, and one hundred thirty dollars; two ticket stubs from the Crown Theater dated May fifth; a wadded Kleenex tissue containing traces of mucus; and a half-used book of paper matches whose cover is lettered 'Earl's Market.' "

"No change or keys?"

"You know men don't usually carry keys or pocket change in their jackets, Carver."

Carver had been chastised. He felt like bowing his head. "Was there anything else?"

"When we vacuumed the coat we got lint, several strands of brown hair that matched those on the comb, two strands of medium-length wavy black hair, and some dirt on the cuff that matched the dirt where the coat was found."

"Are you sure the dirt matches?" Carver asked.

Marillo glared at him. "It contains precisely the same nitro-gen content. And the minerals—"

"I'll take your word it's the same dirt," Carver interrupted.

"The shoes are size ten lace-up dress shoes," Marillo said. "About fifty dollars a pair. The jacket is a Coast Trendsetter, mass-produced but neatly altered as if it's been to a tailor. It was bought fairly recently, maybe a year ago at most."

"Maybe?"

"Sorry," Marillo said. "Finding its origin is your job."

"Used to be my job," Carver corrected. He doubted if finding out where Davis had bought the coat or had had it altered would help much. That hair that wasn't the color of Edwina's could be something or nothing. "Exactly how long were the two strands of wavy black hair you found on the jacket?"

"Five and three-fourths inches and four inches, respectively," Marillo said. "The hairs are fine, broken off."

"Male or female?"

"Could be either. They have a perm solution on them to make them wave, but that doesn't necessarily indicate the sex. Lots of men are getting permanents these days." Marillo's eyes darted to Carver's gleaming pate. "And hair transplants."

Carver ignored the remark; he knew that Marillo's work had imbued him with a protective insensitivity, and the particular, precise lab man actually didn't suspect that he might step on sensibilities while stating facts. It would be interesting if the hairs were female, if Willis Davis wasn't as deeply in love with Edwina Talbot as she thought and was stepping out on her. Might he have left Edwina to be with his other lover? Carver doubted that. A fake suicide was a troublesome and complicated way to break off a relationship. Probably someone with wavy black hair had simply brushed up against Davis, or perhaps hung a jacket on a hook next to his.

"How old would you say Davis's shoes are?" Carver asked, noting the worn condition of the soles and heels through the transparent plastic bag. He used the tip of his cane to poke and shift the bag so he could see the shoes more clearly.

"Judging by the condition of the leather, I'd say at least three years."

"Have they been resoled or heeled?"

"No."

"Would you say a skillful tailor altered the sport jacket?"

"No. But it's still a better job than most department-store tailors do. And more extensive."

"More extensive how?"

"The jacket's a forty-two regular. The sleeves were shortened slightly, and the coat was taken in at the sides—not tucked, the way cheaper tailors might do it, but sewn in tighter all the way down each side seam so the coat wouldn't bell out."

"That pretty well covers everything about the coat," Carver said, impressed.

"Not quite. There was an approximately half-inch-diameter ketchup stain on the left lapel."

"So Davis likes or liked ketchup and is or was an average-sized man with short arms. And a little on the thin side."

"Maybe not thin," Marillo said. "Maybe just particular about the way his clothes fit. I have my own coats altered almost the way his was. And the sleeves aren't all that short. It's possible, too, that he's a meticulous dresser and wants his shirt cuffs to show well below the sleeve."

Carver made a mental note to check with Edwina about Davis's sleeve length. He must have left some shirts at her home along with his other clothes. Carver stepped closer for a better look at the jacket. It told him nothing; it looked as if it might fit him, Carver, without further alterations. It wouldn't hurt to ask Edwina about all of Davis's clothes sizes. Or look himself. A romp through Davis's closet might prove revealing.

"Anything else you want to know?" Marillo asked. It was his way of saying that Carver had learned all the shoes and the coat and its contents could tell him, and Marillo was yearning to return to his true love—work.

"What's your favorite flavor of ice cream?" Carver asked.

The question surprised Marillo. "Vanilla. Why?"

Carver stabbed his cane at the tile floor in disappointment.

"Just curious. Thanks for the help in my quest for Willis Davis."

"*Have* I helped you?"

"Sure. I've narrowed it down to planet Earth." Carver started to leave.

"*French* vanilla," Marillo said behind him. "I like crushed pecans and Kahlúa liqueur over it."

"Ah," Carver said, brightening, "a secret life."

"Huh?"

Carver didn't answer. He left Marillo with this small piece of the day that didn't fit, and walked from the lab.

On his way out of the building, he stopped at a public phone in the hall and used the directory to find the address of Sun South, where, until recently, a man was employed who walked with his left toe pointed out and liked ketchup.

CHAPTER 5

The drive to Sun South took Carver a little less than an hour. He put the top down on the Olds and let the wind dispel the heat of the sun. He was already tanned dark from his therapeutic swims; no need to worry about sunburn. The past few months had toughened him in and out, created a man not only stronger where he had been broken, but stronger everywhere. If he wasn't careful, he might find himself getting fond of adversity.

The Sun South time-sharing complex consisted of over a hundred apartments stacked in half a dozen circular, pale concrete-and-glass towers, stuck in the sand like so many sawed-off tubes. They were nestled together like uncomfortable aliens stranded on the flat beach. As Carver wound the Olds along the highway and got closer, he saw some smaller buildings clustered around the towers' bases: a clubhouse, golf course, and swimming pool, tennis courts, and what appeared to be a restaurant and small shopping mall. Everything for wealthy vacationers gone to a southern respite of sand and sea, and a sun they usually too late learned to avoid. There was plenty of money here, Carver noted; Sun

South had been costly to build and the time shares it sold would be expensive.

Carver parked the Olds next to a dusty Winnebago motor home on the lot that had a visitors sign hung on chains at its entrance. He got out and made his way along a sidewalk toward the tinted-glass panels of the nearest building. The concrete walk gave way to different-colored stepping-stones and strategically led prospective buyers through a small tropical garden. For several steps nothing was visible beyond the low palms except for beach and rolling blue sea. Carver slowed his pace and breathed in deeply, giving himself to the scent and salty weight of the sea air, a heavier scent that overpowered the sweet fragrance of the garden's wildly colored blossoms. The surf pounded regularly like a great immortal heartbeat. The suggestion of eternity was there on the edge of the vast ocean, if not eternity itself.

The sales office was in one of the towers. It was a spacious, circular room carpeted in pale green. There were color photographs and artists' renderings of Sun South units on the even paler green walls, and in the center of the room was a scale model of the time-share project, displayed under glass and complete with plastic model cars, trees, and pedestrians. Carver studied the models, noticed that the pedestrians were all smiling, the cars were all Porsches and Cadillacs.

"Can I help?" a slim, attractive redheaded woman in a brown business suit asked. She was smiling like one of the miniature Sun South residents under the glass, the kind of smile they taught in sales seminars, glossy and bright, with a painted-on kind of sincerity that would dissolve only upon a direct insult or a slap.

Carver looked beyond her to the row of multicolored cubical offices from which she'd emerged, work space created by arranging pastel panels of some kind of rough-textured plastic. "I'd like to see Mr. Franks," he said. "My name is Carver."

Her smile stuck, didn't waver. It was a good one. Her facial muscles had to be tiring. "I'm Chris," the woman said. "I can assist you if you're interested in one of our units. Our one-bedroom Poseidon model is on sale this month, with special financing. There are plenty of prime weeks left."

"I'm not interested in buying a time share," Carver said.

Even that didn't sweep the smile from Chris's freckled friendliness, but it did make her smile a bit crooked. What was this guy with the limp and cane doing here if he wasn't a customer?

Carver gave her back her smile, watched her soften, but just a little. "Tell Mr. Franks I need to talk to him about one of his former employees."

"Which employee is that?" Chris asked, teeth still going at it but eyes not smiling now; but interested eyes nonetheless.

What the hell, Carver thought, and decided to see what reaction he might get from Chris. "Willis Davis."

She didn't seem surprised. She'd expected to hear Davis's name.

"I'll tell Mr. Franks's secretary you're here," she said.

Carver watched her sashay across the pale green carpet, around a bespectacled salesman showing a politely interested white-haired couple some brochures, and through a narrow hall between the pastel, partitioned offices where promises and sales were made, more of the former than the latter. Life was such a game of percentages.

While he waited, Carver walked over to gaze out the wide, curved window that overlooked the sea. To his right was a low, grayish-black building that was supposed to appear as if it had been crudely built of driftwood. But its windows were framed in aluminum, and an air-conditioning unit squatted on its flat roof. SUN SOUTH CAFETERIA, a sign on a landlocked weathered dinghy near its entrance read. Behind and to the left of the cafeteria some of the tennis courts were visible. Carver watched a leggy woman in a pink tennis outfit slap neat base-line returns. Her opponent was out of Carver's sight, beyond the corner of the cafeteria, but whoever was on the other end of the court returned the woman's shots crisply to almost precisely the same location. It occurred to him that she might be playing a machine that launched tennis balls for practice. To Carver's right, two men in a yellow golf cart bounced softly to or from the course. Life at Sun South looked posh and easy for those who could afford to buy a time share or two.

"Mr. Carver?"

He turned from the view outside to see a tall blonde in a navy blue dress smiling at him. Standing well behind her, still smiling but looking a bit uncertain, was Chris. Everyone seemed to smile a lot at Sun South, as if the air were tinged with cheer.

"Mr. Franks will see you," the blonde said.

Carver nodded and followed her toward the hall between the partitions. She walked slowly so he could keep up, which in this case was fortunate, because the spongy green carpeting made walking with a cane a chore.

Franks's office was large and plush, furnished in pale wood and fabric, and decorated in shades of gray. Franks was large and done in shades of gray himself. He was six feet tall, prosperous-looking and fiftyish, and his expensive gray suit couldn't quite hide his stomach paunch. He had flawlessly groomed wavy grayish hair, gray eyes, and a rather unhealthy-looking grayish complexion. This was an aging, handsome man who spurned the sun. He was the only person Carver had seen at Sun South who wasn't smiling.

Franks waited for his secretary to leave before he spoke.

"Sit down, please, Mr. Carver." He did manage a good old Sun South smile as he motioned toward a chair near his desk, then sat down in his gray, executive's chair behind the desk. Behind the chair was a window that bathed the visitor in light but silhouetted and to some degree concealed the features of Franks where he sat facing Carver. A cheap and obvious trick to gain advantage in interviews. Carver resented it; too many of these half-ass, big-money entrepreneurs had their offices arranged this way.

Easy, he cautioned himself, don't be cynical.

But he was cynical. He knew it. Couldn't help himself.

The office was soundproofed, private to the point of defensive isolation; only the soft sigh of cooled air rolling through the ceiling vents, and the ocean view out the window, gave evidence of an outside world.

"You wanted to talk about Willis Davis?" Franks asked. His voice seemed muffled by the silence, yet still managed to convey an amiable but unmistakable authority.

"Actually, I wanted you to talk about him," Carver said. "I'm a private investigator, hired to look into his suicide." He leaned forward and showed Franks his P.I. license.

A flicker of alarm seemed to dance for just an instant over Franks's distinguished gray features. "Hired by whom?"

"I'd have to get my client's permission to reveal that," Carver said. "Professional ethics."

"Oh? You have those?"

Carver nodded.

"One doesn't associate the profession of private detective with ethics," Franks said.

"One is wrong."

Franks raised a manicured hand that looked as if it had never known manual labor. "I didn't mean offense."

"Tell me about Davis," Carver said.

"Willis was quiet for a salesman, but he knew how to close a deal. He could smell blood, sense vulnerability. I liked him."

"Would you peg him as the type to commit suicide?"

Franks looked thoughtful. "No, but I'm not sure there is a specific suicidal type." He leaned back, gazed for a moment at his fingertips resting lightly on the desk. Outside the double-pane window, the ocean rolled soundlessly, as if its power had been tamed. "Are you working with the police?"

"Yes. With Lieutenant Desoto of Orlando."

Franks touched his fingers together, then pressed them with springy persistence back and forth against each other, and digested that semi-accurate information silently.

"Was Willis Davis happy with his job here?" Carver asked.

"Of course. Oh, he'd get restless now and then, talk about moving on, getting financing and starting some development of his own. But his kind talk that way, think that way. I understand that; I came up through sales myself."

Carver just bet he had. So smooth. "How did Davis behave in the weeks before his suicide?"

"I would say normally, for him. He was reserved when he wasn't onto a client. He kept to himself; a private person. Willis Davis seemed to live for his work, knew how to sell and was proud of it. It was like a science to him, Mr. Carver. I have to admit he pulled a few tricks I never heard of."

"Who were his friends among the other employees?" Carver asked.

"Only one other salesperson I'd describe as Willis's friend. Sam Cahill."

"Can I talk to Cahill?"

"He's no longer with the company. He quit and moved on a few months ago. He didn't say where he was going, and I'm afraid I've lost track of him."

"You said earlier that you liked Davis," Carver said.

"Yes, he was a likable man."

"And an honest one?"

Franks's grayish face became flushed. "Of course. That's especially important in this business. In the office where we close deals is a picture of the crucifixion, with an oath of integrity printed on it; I had all my employees sign it, in ink. Sure, sales is like a game, but we're honest here. I mean that. I'm an honest man."

"I didn't mean to imply that you weren't. I have to ask that sort of thing in a possible murder case."

Franks looked startled. He turned away for a moment as if to gather his thoughts. His profile was surprisingly hawkish against the bright window, a glimpse of what he had been before so many years and pounds and three-martini lunches.

When he turned back to face Carver he said, "Whose murder?"

"Willis Davis's."

"But he committed suicide."

"Some people, including the police, think he might have been murdered. Or that he might still be alive."

"Faked his suicide, you mean?" That possibility seemed to interest Franks.

"Maybe," Carver said. "A phony death. A sales job. Maybe he had a reason."

"What kind of reason?"

"Hiding from somebody who was out to harm him, perhaps."

Franks drew a gold ballpoint pen from his shirt pocket, as if he might make a note of something. But he simply rotated the pen a few times between his fingers, then replaced it in the pocket, carefully securing it with its clip. "What do you think?" he asked.

"I'm not sure," Carver said. "I'm trying to find out."

A Lucite button on the desk phone began to blink. Franks lifted the receiver and pressed it to his ear, said, "I'll take care of it," and hung up. Then he stood up.

"Do you have a card, Mr. Carver?"

"Time for a magic trick?"

"Ah, you like to joke." No Sun South smile. "I meant a business card, of course."

Carver gripped the curve of his cane, leaned forward, and straightened up from the chair. He gave Franks one of his cards.

Franks glanced at it, then laid it with a neat little snap on the corner of his desk, as if he were a poker player finishing the deal. The interview was over.

"Thanks for your time, Mr. Franks," Carver told him, meaning it.

"If you find out anything," Franks said, "about Willis Davis, will you let me know?"

"I'm doing that for my client," Carver said.

Franks looked embarrassed, irritated, as if he'd revealed a weakness in himself. "Of course. Afternoon, Mr. Carver."

"Afternoon," Carver said, and limped from the office.

His good leg had stiffened up somewhat as he'd sat talking, but he didn't pay much attention to it as he made his way across the sales-area carpet toward the exit. He was thinking about Franks. Something was bothering the developer, something he hadn't told the police. Carver was sure of it. The uneasy thing that had looked out through the eyes of so many victims Carver had talked with over the years was alive in Franks. Alive and gnawing on him.

Chris was talking to a prospective customer near the sales display, doing her damnedest to sell time shares. She glanced over at Carver and he waved good-bye.

She smiled at him as he left. Not the Sun South smile. A different sort of smile altogether. Time shares. Weren't they what all of us dealt in?

CHAPTER 6

Carver drove inland to a phone booth on Regent Street and called Edwina Talbot at Quill Realty. He was told by a syrup-voiced receptionist that Edwina was out showing property and would be back in about an hour. Carver was disappointed. He needed to talk to her and thought it might as well be over lunch.

After hanging up the phone, he noticed a McDonald's across the street. Even the wealthy residents of Del Moray needed a hamburger fix now and then. He waited for a break in traffic, then deliberately jaywalked and was almost run down by a van laden with teen-agers. He was pleased to find that when really inspired he could move faster with the cane than he'd anticipated.

He ate too many Chicken McNuggets and drank too much diet cola, then walked back to his car. This time he crossed at the corner; he had nothing to prove. On a whim, before getting into the Olds, he stepped into the sun-heated phone booth and tried Edwina again at Quill. He was surprised when he was told she was in.

"Mr. Carver," she said, "have you learned anything about Willis?"

"Not much," Carver said, "but I can pose more questions about him. I think we should meet and talk. And call me Carver without the 'mister' or we won't get along." He'd sounded grouchier than he intended. Too much time spent alone.

"You've grown a protective shell, there by the sea, Carver."

"I'm not by the sea, I'm on Regent Street."

"Maybe we can talk during lunch," she said. "Or have you already had lunch?"

"No, I'm starving."

"Do you know The Happy Lobster?"

"Sure, a fellow crustacean."

"I mean—"

"I know. The circular glassed-in restaurant on the coast highway."

"If that's all right with you, I'll leave now to meet you there."

"Fine," Carver said. "I'll race you."

"You seem to have recovered your zest for life, Carver."

"It comes and goes," Carver said, and hung up. He patted his full stomach, got in the Olds, and tried not to think about lobsters. Even on an empty stomach, he didn't like eating them or watching people eat them; they looked too much like big spiders.

He started the engine and drove toward the coast highway.

"Where does this leave us?" Edwina asked Carver, after he'd described his visit with Ernie Franks at Sun South.

Carver looked out the curved window of The Happy Lobster at the vast blue sea and chewed the olive from his martini. "I'm not sure," he said, swallowing. "The more I try to learn about Willis, the more lost I am. You worked for a while at Sun South; what do you think about Franks?"

"Ernie is a high-priced hustler, but an honest man. And a

mush-hearted one. He found religion somewhere along the line. He prides himself on his fairness and his ability as a big-time developer. Maybe at one time he was the kind of semi–confidence man you find in these kinds of real-estate projects, but he isn't now. Maybe simply because he's reached the age and bank balance where he doesn't have to be. Or maybe he really is born again, like the rest of us yearn to be in one way or another."

"What is his religion?"

"I'm not sure. It's nothing crazy. He doesn't speak in tongues unexpectedly or dress funny on weekends."

"Is he a worrier?"

"No. He's a juggler of things to do and the time to do them in, but he doesn't fret over his decisions either before or after he makes them. He's often preoccupied, energetic and in a hurry, but I wouldn't describe him as a worrier. Usually he's cheerful, full of pep talk."

"He's worried now."

"About what happened to Willis?"

"About something concerning Willis. I don't know what, and Franks isn't talking."

Edwina worked studiously at freeing a strand of meat from one of the lobster tails on her plate. She seemed to be concentrating entirely on the task at hand. Then she gazed out the window, a pained, lost expression on her face.

"You okay?" Carver asked.

She turned back. "Yes. I just miss Willis. I miss him *all* the time. Did you ever feel that way about someone who was gone?"

"Why do you love Willis so much?" he asked her bluntly, without answering her question.

She thought for a moment, a desolate cast to her composed features. "You're asking for a reason for something that doesn't rest on a foundation of reason," she told him. "Love simply *is*, and then it becomes what it will. We don't have much choice in the matter."

"I think we do," he said.

"Sometimes, maybe."

"Is there anything you're not telling me about you and Willis?"

"There's a lot I'm not telling you. Some of it you wouldn't understand; some of it is none of your business." There was no rancor in her tone; she was merely stating facts, keeping the door closed on the intimacy shared by lovers. Not unreasonable.

Yet Carver felt that there might be more to it than that.

She took a bite of lobster meat and watched as he forked another raw oyster from its half shell, dipped it into hot sauce, and popped it into his mouth. Carver had decided he was hungrier than he'd thought, and was on a second plate of oysters. This and two martinis were going to be his second lunch of the day.

"How can you eat something so almost alive?" Edwina asked, wincing in distaste as he let the oyster slide down his throat.

"There is no 'almost alive,' " Carver told her. "There's only alive and dead. There's no difference between these oysters and your lobster and somebody else's steak. We kill, then we eat the dead. But we don't think about it in that light because of mental conditioning. Without all of our carefully developed protective delusions, we'd be in trouble. Me, I never developed the necessary protective layer of delusion about lobsters that have been dropped alive into boiling water."

"Come off it, Carver, the cook isn't a murderer because he boiled my lobster alive. And I'm not a ghoul for eating the carcass. And there's nothing wrong with me because I haven't developed the callousness to eat raw oysters. The damned things can make you sick, anyway. The cook and I don't need any protective delusions."

"You're missing the point," Carver said. "We're the lobsters. It might behoove us to understand the cook."

Edwina stuck the tines of her fork into a bite of lobster meat and held the fork still. She tilted her head to the side and stared at Carver. "What are you trying to tell me with your seafood-soup philosophy?"

Carver took a slow sip of his martini, then rattled the ice in the glass. "Maybe Willis Davis dropped you alive into hot water, used you somehow, and you can't or won't believe it."

She put down her fork and looked out at a distant ship making its way inexorably toward a hazy horizon. Or was the ship really moving? From here it was impossible to tell. "I'm forty-one years old, Carver, and I've been fooled by more than one man. And I've fooled a few; I've been the cook. The thing is, I've played the game both ways and won and lost. It's wised me up. Willis isn't conning me. He loved me. I know enough to know that."

"Maybe it's a new kind of game," Carver said. "Maybe you never met a Willis before."

"I've known a few Willises. I'm not sure if I've ever met another Carver."

"That could be a compliment."

"There goes that protective layer of delusion. What I mean is that your job, your injury, your life, what you were born with—all or some of them have made you tough and cynical."

"I know. I'm working to improve."

"Then accept this: I love Willis, he loves me, something happened to him, I want to know what. I want him back. Simple as that."

Carver grinned at her. "Okay. I'll approach my job under that assumption."

"Good. What next?"

"Dessert?"

"No, I mean in the investigation."

"I want to go home with you."

She dabbed at her lips with her napkin and frowned. He was always surprising her; it wasn't fair.

"I'd like to examine what Willis left behind when he disappeared," Carver said. "Clothing, accessories, whatever."

"He didn't leave much," Edwina said. "It's all in one closet. The only thing of interest was his attaché case, but the police and I have already examined its contents. There's nothing in it other than ordinary papers connected with his job."

"I still might find something pertinent."

"You harbor ego as well as cynicism," Edwina said. "Do you think you're smarter than the police?"

"I'm more interested," Carver said. "They get paid whether they find something or not. Incidentally, did you know Sam Cahill at Sun South?"

"Yes. He was friendly with Willis. We saw him socially a couple of times."

"What did you think of him?"

"Not much one way or the other. He was maybe too much of an operator, but then a lot of salespeople have that fault."

"Do you know where Cahill went after he left Sun South?"

"No. He quit, Ernie Franks said, but there were rumors that he'd actually been fired. I heard he went someplace in southern Florida."

Carver summoned the waitress. As he reached for his wallet, Edwina held up a hand palm-out. "I'll buy," she said. "When you bill me, you'll put it on the expense account anyway."

Only his own lunch, Carver thought, but he kept silent. Edwina was assuming again; now she was thinking of him as the opportunistic private eye who jockeyed for every advantage as a way of life and had a code of ethics slightly higher than Richard Nixon's. Or maybe Carver was the one kidding himself; maybe he fit the stereotype.

After Edwina had smitten the bill with her American Express card, he walked with her from the restaurant.

"I'll meet you at my house," she said, as their soles crunched on the gravel parking lot, "but I'm sure you won't find anything revealing."

"Maybe not, but it's a base that ought to be touched," Carver said, with proper professional arrogance.

She nodded. The warm sunlight on her face lent it a healthy, youthful kind of radiance made beautifully ironic by the faintly crinkled flesh at the corners of her eyes and lips. Her gray eyes caught gold flecks of the sun.

He couldn't help standing for a moment, staring after her, as they parted to walk to where their cars were parked.

The inside of Edwina's house looked as if it had been furnished by a good interior decorator. Everything was in subdued blues and grays, with tasteful accents of red.

"Very nice," Carver said, limping to the center of the living room and making an all-encompassing sweep with his cane, as if he were a visiting potentate bestowing a blessing with his scepter.

"A friend and I designed it," Edwina told him. "You learn a lot about interior decorating while you're showing customers through furnished display houses."

"Is the friend a professional decorator?"

"She used to be. Alice sells real estate now for Quill."

"Is this the Alice who discovered Willis's jacket and shoes at the edge of the drop and phoned the police?"

"Yes. Alice Hargrove." Edwina tossed her purse onto a modern blue chair and walked across the deep carpet, past Carver. "Come on, I'll show you the bedroom."

He limped after her. He felt like using the crook of his cane to trip her by the ankle so he could bolt past her down the short hall.

The bedroom was also done in blues and grays; maybe Alice was a Civil War buff. The furniture was light-grained oak. The bed was king-sized and had a padded blue headboard whose subdued print matched the drapes. It was probably the most restful room Carver had ever been in. One of the windows was open; the sea was whispering not to worry, kick off your shoes and stretch out on the bed, few things are forever.

There was no sign that a man had slept there. No comb or electric razor on the dresser, no tie draped over a doorknob, no worn copies of *Playboy*. A woman's comb-and-brush set lay on the small dresser, which was equipped with a mirror. There was a white push-button phone, and a note pad and pen, next to a reading lamp on a small table by the bed. On a chair in a corner lay an outdated real-estate-listing book. By the chair was a bookshelf containing a single book, a collection of short stories by Stanley Ellin.

Carver looked at the room, then at Edwina. He wondered about Willis Davis's sanity, if Davis had willingly walked away from this.

One end of the room was all closet. Edwina slid open one of four floor-to-ceiling doors. Even the soft rumble of the rollers in their track made a restful sound.

"Almost everything Willis left, I put in here," Edwina said, stepping aside to give Carver a clear view and access to the closet.

Five suits, two blue and three gray, hung neatly on wooden hangers. Next to them on the closet rod hung several white and pale blue dress shirts with button-down collars; also half a dozen striped ties. The shirts' sleeve lengths were 34, not so short; almost Carver's size. On the floor a pair of black wingtip shoes gleamed dully, the kind with thick soles and heels.

Carver leaned against the edge of the open closet door and used both hands to rummage through the pockets of the hanging clothes. They were all empty. He straightened and leaned on his cane. "What about socks and underwear?" he asked Edwina.

She opened the top drawer of a large dresser. Inside were stacks of neatly folded white Jockey shorts and undershirts, along with black socks and two coiled black belts. In the drawer beneath that one were a folded pair of worn jeans and some pullover shirts. Also in that drawer was a flat black-leather attaché case with brass latches.

"The rest of the drawers are empty," Edwina said.

Carver removed the attaché case and sat down on the edge of the bed, surprised by the softness of the mattress; so unlike the board-reinforced hardness of his own mattress. He laid the attaché case on the bed, figured out how the latches worked, and raised the lid.

The contents were pretty much as Edwina had described. Sales brochures, expense-account forms, gas credit receipts, a used book of Disney World tickets, a pocket calculator, a few white business cards. There was a list of price changes for Sun South units, several sheets of plain white typing paper, and a stamped, blank envelope. Apparently Willis had intended to write a letter but hadn't gotten the chance or had changed his mind. A suicide note?

Carver closed the attaché case and stood up.

"Anything illuminating?" Edwina asked. There might have been a mocking edge in her voice. He sensed strongly that she was keeping something from him. Why, really, did she love Willis so fiercely? Why was she holding on so tightly to him?

"Nothing that sheds much light now," Carver told her, "but who's to say when a connection might be made that switches on a bulb? Did Willis wear sport coats very often?"

"No, he usually wore suits. He only owned one sport coat, and the police have it now."

She let the attaché case lie on the bed and abruptly led the way back into the living room, as if she'd suddenly realized Carver was violating a sexual sanctorum and wanted him out. As he followed her along the hall, he noticed the way her long dark hair swung in rhythm to the subtle roll of her hips. Willis Davis, Carver thought, you must be dead.

In the living room she said, "I have a real-estate closing to attend. It's important."

"Good luck," Carver said.

"I'll need it; I'm dealing with lawyers." She led the way to the door, not bothering to look back. It was almost as if she had a leash on Carver. For now, he was content to follow.

"If I learn anything, will I be able to get in touch with you by phone tomorrow?"

"Yes, at the office or here." She seemed pensive, as if she

were talking to Carver and mulling over something else alto-gether at the same time. Had she seen something in the bed-room she didn't want him to notice? Winston Churchill would have liked Edwina. She was a riddle wrapped in a mystery inside a great shape.

She stood in the doorway and watched as Carver got in his car and negotiated the winding driveway to the street. Low branches scratched an unheeded warning on the Olds's canvas top as he made a right turn at the end of the drive.

He didn't notice the rented white compact car that followed the Olds, like a pilot fish trailing a shark, as he hadn't noticed it when it followed him from the restaurant.

CHAPTER 7

Carver drove around Del Moray for a while, looking at the wide streets, neat rows of palm trees, the rambling, expensive houses. As he drove west, away from the ocean, the streets became narrower, with hills and terraced lawns. The houses were still expensive. Only when he neared the western outskirts of town did he find himself in a poorer section, where the streets needed repaving and the houses repainting and the people hope. Most of the faces he saw on these streets were Latino or black, the maids and gardeners of the wealthier residents in the east end of town. There were shabby-looking night spots here, too, and small and obviously struggling businesses. The poor seemed to be a smaller minority in Del Moray than in most other cities. Still, they were there, and were oddly necessary in a way few would admit. Without the poor, there could, of course, be no rich. It was comforting to some people to have clearly defined rungs on the ladder.

Carver stopped at a drugstore and bought a *Del Moray Gazette-Dispatch* and a six-pack of Budweiser. He placed the paper and beer on the front seat of the car and got back in.

Ignoring the taunts of a group of young Latinos lounging on

a corner near a frozen-custard stand, he made a U-turn, then drove back the way he'd come, toward the highway and home.

The next morning Carver swam for half an hour, then showered and cooked up a big breakfast of eggs, toast, and Canadian bacon. He felt good. He could look at his left leg now and not worriedly compare its size or shape with his right. The exercise regimen the therapist recommended would keep atrophy to a minimum if he followed it faithfully, and that was that—all he could do.

Carrying his third cup of coffee and the Del Moray paper from the day before, he limped out to the cottage's small wooden porch and sat in the sun in a webbed aluminum lounge chair. The cup balanced okay on the chair's plastic arm while Carver turned the paper to the classified ads. A glossy bluebottle fly landed on the real-estate section, and Carver watched it wobble down the page to a list of properties for sale by Quill, then take to the air to tend to more important matters.

After a while, Carver took a pen from his pocket, braced the folded newspaper against his thigh, and circled an advertisement for a vacant Del Moray house on Edgewick Avenue listed for an even half a million dollars. If he wasn't going to buy a house, it might as well be an expensive one.

He tossed the rest of his cool coffee over the porch rail, admiring its bright amber arc, then went back inside and phoned Quill Realty.

The conversation worked out fine. He told whoever answered the phone that he was interested in seeing the house on Edgewick, and that someone had recommended an agent named Alice who had experience as an interior decorator. Alice could give him decorating tips while she was showing him the property.

Within half a minute he was talking to Alice, and they made an appointment to meet at the Edgewick property at ten o'clock.

Until it was time to leave for Del Moray, Carver idly watched a taped Atlanta Braves baseball game on television, mostly commercials. Somewhere in this land did flat-bellied cowboys actually drive dogies, then drive Jeeps to saloons with sawdust floors whereon trod barmaids with perfect teeth who served them diet beer? Carver doubted it. But then he hadn't been everywhere.

He was secretly glad the game was a high-scoring dull one; he didn't mind switching off the TV and leaving. He liked pitchers' duels.

Carver remembered Edgewick Avenue from his drive around Del Moray the day before. It was a wide street with a grassy, palm-lined median, still in the desirable part of town, but only by a few blocks. The size and condition of the houses started slipping in this area, and an occasional Latino face could be seen among the residents. But it was still a prestige neighborhood, even if in one of the older sections of the city.

The house with a Quill Realty sign stuck in its yard was a gloomy stone monster that looked as if it might at any moment venture ponderously down from the hill on which it was so forebodingly perched to devour the smaller houses on Edgewick Avenue. It had cupolas that looked like watchtowers, and windows that resembled malevolent eyes. It was probably old when it was built, Carver decided. Also, it had a lot of damned steps.

Carver was breathing hard by the time he'd made it up to the porch, and stood before the house's ten-foot-tall heavy oak doors. When he leaned on his cane and extended a hand to ring the doorbell, one of the doors opened smoothly and an attractive thirtyish woman with blond hair framing a roundly pretty, tiny-featured face smiled out at him. He had the strange feeling that she was the maid and would usher him into the den to await the master. Would she curtsy, call him "sire," and step aside?

"Mr. Carver?" she said crisply, and held out a hand. When he nodded, she said, "I'm Alice Hargrove." She spoke with the slightest suggestion of a lisp, had dark crescents beneath her eyes, as if she hadn't slept the night before, and her too-fine short hair had been rudely mussed by the wind. Her smile made everything else about her seem unimportant; it was a light that warmed.

Carver shook the slender cool hand gently, so as not to break fine bones, and stepped into the house. Alice's blue eyes flicked to his cane, registered no change of expression. He knew she was thinking about all the steps leading up to the house and how she might talk him into ignoring them if he turned out to be a serious prospect. You had to be wily to survive in sales.

The house was bare and needed a lot of interior work. The walls were faded and paint was peeling from the ornate wood-work. A kidney-shaped water stain marred the high ceiling. There was a large stone fireplace in the room they were in, flanked by bookcases beneath fancy stained-glass windows that muted the sun and did wonderful Technicolor tricks with the light.

"As you can see," Alice said, "the place needs work but has tremendous potential." Her voice bounced around in the emptiness.

Carver tapped the hardwood floor with his cane. The clatter might have been heard for miles. "I plan on putting some heavy manufacturing equipment in this room," he said. "We build locomotive engines. Do you think the floor will support the weight?"

For only a second she was confused. "Mr. Carver, I don't think the zoning on this property . . ." She stopped talking. An expression of fear, then admirable determination and cunning subtly transformed her round, sweet features. She tried not to move her eyes toward the door; he was between her and it, and that might mean everything. Here was the real-estate lady's nightmare. "You're not actually interested in buying this property, are you, Mr. Carver? Or is Carver your real name?"

"Relax, Alice," Carver said reassuringly. "I'm not interested in anything you'd object to. Anyway, you could outrun me if I tried anything."

She exhaled slowly and seemed slightly more at ease, looking dubious, waiting.

"My time is pressing and this is the surest way I could get to talk to you," Carver explained. "My name really is Fred Carver. I'm a detective."

"Police?"

"No, private." Carver got out his wallet and showed her his investigator's license.

Still dubious. He hoped she wasn't the type who carried Mace.

"I'm working for a friend of yours," he said. "Edwina Talbot. I think you might be able to help me help her. You can tell her about this conversation when we're finished."

"We could have met in a more conventional way, Mr. Carver. I'd say that the reason we didn't was that you didn't want me to know beforehand that the conversation was going to be about Edwina." Perceptive lady. "Were you afraid she and I might agree on some sort of lie?"

"No," Carver said. "It's true that I didn't want you and Edwina to talk before I met you, but only because what she told you might color what you'd tell me."

"Is it so important to you that I don't have any preconceived notions?"

"It is. I'm probing for nuances as well as hard information."

"I thought detectives dealt only in facts."

"We do, but first we have to catch the slippery things. That's why I need your help."

Alice breathed in and out noisily, got a filter-tipped cigarette from her purse, and began to pace. Beneath one of the stained-glass windows, she turned. The softened light made her twenty again. "You're trying to find poor Willis." She flicked a dainty silver lighter and touched the bluish tip of its flame to her cigarette in a lingering way that suggested the cigarette might enjoy it.

"Do you think he's findable?"

"No, I don't." She dropped the lighter back in her purse. "What specifically do you want to talk about?"

"I want to know more about Willis Davis."

"Such as?"

"Such as why is he Willis? Why doesn't anybody ever call him Willie?"

Alice smiled—not as bright as her saleswoman smile but definitely more genuine. "A Willie is more casual than a Willis. A Willie might wear a shirt even though it has a stain on it, or he might miss a belt loop. A Willis wears laundered, starched shirts and has a matching belt to go with each pair of pants and never misses a loop. Believe me, Willis was a Willis. He was a fastidious dresser, fastidious about everything he did."

"How many times did you see him?" Carver asked, remembering the ketchup stain on the sport jacket. "And for how long?"

"Oh, a dozen times, I guess. Social get-togethers. Or he'd be there when I went to Edwina's house to see her. Willis was an okay guy; I liked him. And you could tell he cared a lot about Edwina."

"Did Edwina care a lot about him?"

Alice looked closely at Carver, gauging him. "Edwina cared everything about him. She's had a tough time with the men in her life, with her former husband. She's been knocked around some. Abused physically and emotionally. It changed her, gave her a hard veneer. You might say she never met a man before Willis who could match her strengths, or maybe understand her weaknesses."

"Do you mean a man she could look up to?" Carver always thought of Wilt Chamberlain when he used that expression.

"No, I mean a man who wouldn't need her to be dependent,

one she could look upon as her equal. The Edwina I know doesn't do much looking up to anyone."

Carver thought about his broken marriage to Laura. That hadn't been exactly a fifty-fifty proposition. He'd demanded too much of her, made some classic male mistakes. And now she was living in St. Louis with their son and daughter, and he missed them, all of them at times. He'd needed to let Laura be Laura, but he hadn't.

"Despite his kind and quiet manner, there must have been something steely-strong in Willis Davis," Alice was saying, "because even though they'd only known each other four months before he disappeared, Edwina loved him with complete commitment. She told me that; she used those words."

Carver wasn't surprised. And he remembered that Edwina had told him that she and Willis met six months before. A mistake? An approximation? A lie? "What kind of words did Willis use?" he asked. "Did he seem educated? Did he use a lot of profanity? Did he say *throwed* and *ain't*?"

"He seemed well educated, now that you mention it. And I don't think I ever heard him curse. He seemed basically a good man, decent. That was how he struck people, as decent."

"What sort of things did he talk about?" Carver asked.

"He talked about everything—but somehow without really saying anything. Yet he was interesting, even fascinating. He was great at cocktail parties."

"How did he treat Edwina?"

"He was kind to her, attentive. Always the gentleman."

"Don't you find it unusual that a savvy woman like Edwina would fall so hard and so thoroughly for a man after knowing him only a matter of months?"

"Not at all," Alice said. "It's like that sometimes with some women, no matter how knowledgeable they are in other matters."

"Did you ever get the impression that Willis was using Edwina?"

"Not in the sense you mean, not deceptively. She helped to

get him his job at Sun South. Edwina's the one who talked Ernie Franks into hiring Willis, but I wouldn't call that using her."

"I guess not," Carver said. "And I suppose he could have left her afterward."

"Actually, not right away," Alice said thoughtfully. "From what I know of Ernie Franks, he might have thought badly of Willis if he didn't stay with Edwina after getting the job at Sun South. Franks has the reputation of an honest, no-nonsense developer, a nice guy but no patsy. And that's how he impressed me when I did some of the decorating for display units at Sun South. He even made me sign some kind of oath of integrity printed on a picture of the crucifixion."

"Did you meet Sam Cahill when you were at Sun South?"

"Briefly. The fast-shuffle type. Full of glib talk and easy promises to get a client's name on a contract. And he had big ideas. Wanted to get financing and start some kind of development of his own in central Florida."

"With Willis Davis as a partner?"

"They talked about it. The usual slow-salesday gab to pass the time. I'm sure nothing ever came of it. I think they knew nothing would when they were tossing out their grand ideas."

"You're the one who phoned the police about Willis's disappearance," Carver said.

"Yes." She told him about going to see Edwina, getting no answer at the front door, then walking around to the veranda and seeing the jacket and shoes at the edge of the drop.

"What went through your mind at the time?" Carver asked.

"There was something about the way he'd neatly folded the jacket and laid it on top of the shoes. Something final. As soon as I saw them near the drop's edge, I thought he'd jumped."

"Do you still think so?"

"Yes. I'm sorry about it—for Edwina, for Willis—but that's what I think, that he's dead."

Carver was running out of questions. Sometimes that was

when he asked his best ones. "Is there anything in particular about Willis that sticks in your memory?"

Alice considered that one, drawing again on the long filter-tipped cigarette and frowning. "No," she said at last, slowly, "there's nothing." She raised her head slightly. "It was kind of touching, the way Edwina talked about him at times. She often referred to him as a gentle man. Not *gentleman*, but the two words separated."

"Considering her past treatment," Carver said, "that's not surprising." He shifted his weight and moved his cane a few inches to the right; he'd been standing too long in one spot and was getting uncomfortable. His good leg was falling asleep. "Are you going to tell Edwina about this conversation?"

Alice stared at him through a haze of exhaled smoke, a pleasant, moon-faced woman who would always seem young at first glance. "No," she said. "I want to help her get over Willis. I think the way to do that is to keep quiet and help you."

"I get the feeling Edwina isn't playing exactly straight with me. Is there anything about her that I don't know but should?"

"You'd have to ask her about that."

"Does she confide a great deal in you?"

Alice watched a wisp of cigarette smoke curl in the muted light, then said, "There's a part of Edwina she keeps private. I respect that and have never pried, and I don't intend to start now."

"All right." Carver braced himself with the cane and moved toward the door.

Alice was standing rigidly with her arms folded, watching him. He paused at the door, turned, and looked around the cavernous bare room.

"Half a million dollars seems a little high," he said. "Do you suppose they'd dicker?"

Alice smiled. It was a lot like the smiles he'd seen at Sun South.

After leaving Alice Hargrove he drove down Palm Street toward the ocean. The morning was heating up. There were a few clouds in the west, blowing in from the gulf, making soft and empty threats of rain. Ahead of Carver, the sky was a flawless blue backdrop for the gulls to soar against. The scent of the sea wafted into the Olds with the increasing humidity.

When Carver saw a phone booth, he stopped, called his home, and listened to the messages on his answering machine. There were only two. The first was a recorded sales pitch promising a free book of tickets to Disney World with an appointment for an estimate on home remodeling; a recorder talking to a recorder. It reminded Carver of the old question about whether a sound was made if a tree fell in the woods when there was no one around to hear it. The second message was Ernie Franks suggesting that he and Carver talk again about Willis Davis. He claimed to have some important information for Carver.

Carver used the back of his hand to wipe perspiration from his forehead. Then he called Franks's office, made an appointment to see him, and drove in the direction of Sun South.

Above the coast highway, the gulls seemed to soar and circle deliberately in front of the Olds, vying for Carver's attention with unintelligible screams he could barely hear over the sounds of the motor and the wind.

Screams like shrill warnings.

CHAPTER 8

Carver walked alongside Ernie Franks down some concrete steps leading to a man-made, landscaped plateau below the level of the Sun South towers but above the level of the beach. They strolled slowly along a walkway above the beach, through brilliant sunlight and stark shadow. Beyond the protective metal railing bordering the walk, Carver could see half a dozen sunbathers lounging on the pale sand. The heads of a few adventuresome swimmers bobbed out beyond where the waves began to rise for their rush and break onto the beach. Farther out, a small boat with a canvas-topped flying bridge lazily trolled for deep-sea fish. The strip of ground where Carver and Franks walked was grassy and dotted with small palm trees whose trunks had been painted white halfway up. At random between the palms, lush and colorful tropical flowers, like bright exotic birds perched on stems, swayed in the warm ocean breeze.

Sunk in the side of the hill was a sign, the words *Sun South* lettered with seashells that had been artistically and elaborately set in concrete. As he walked past the sign, Franks absently extended his hand and let his fingertips brush the shell-letters. In so large and powerful a man, the gesture seemed oddly gentle and pathetically possessive.

"I talked to Lieutenant Desoto about you," he said. "And I did some checking into your background."

Carver said nothing, watched the white surf rage beneath them on the beach.

"You were a good cop. And you're an honest private cop now. Bad luck about the injury."

"It's the sort of thing that happens to good cops," Carver said, not without a touch of bitterness. Edwina would arch an eyebrow at him if she were there. Cynical Carver. Pessimist. Maybe she was right. It took a while to get over a bullet. Catching one wasn't like catching a cold.

He watched a teen-age boy hop up from where he'd been stretched out on a towel and run to dive with splashing abandon into the surf. Carver thought about how he had to enter the water. How he had to crawl.

Then he thought about how he might be dead now, how the kid at the grocery store might have aimed higher with the junk revolver. The jasmine scent of the flowers became sharper, sweeter.

Franks stopped walking, leaned on the iron rail, and gazed out over the beach and ocean, his domain on the edge of the world. Disney didn't have a monopoly on magic kingdoms in Florida; they were dotted up and down the coasts. "There's something I didn't tell the police when they asked me about Willis," he said. "I've decided to confide in you."

"Why me?"

"Practicality. My sources tell me you can be trusted, and you're already into this thing, already searching for Willis."

"Then you don't think he's dead either?"

"I'm not sure," Franks said, "but my bet would be on him being alive. Your earlier visit helped me to decide that. I think he knew it was time to get out, so he faked his suicide and went into hiding."

"Time to get out of what?" Carver asked.

Franks straightened up from the railing. Still looking seaward, he lit a cigar, shielding the flame of his gold lighter expertly with a pale, cupped hand. He exhaled heavily; the breeze shredded the smoke and whisked it away. There was pain on his seamed, congenial salesman features. The gray, suave guy was suffering; this wasn't going to be easy for him. "For each Sun South unit there are, of course, only a maximum of fifty-two potential buyers, one for each week of the year. I discovered that Willis was selling some of the units more than fifty-two times, writing contracts to different customers for time shares for the same prime weeks. He'd collect their down payment or earnest money, in some cases a large percentage of the time-share price, and deposit the money in a secret Sun South bank account that operated on his signature."

"What was supposed to happen when two or more 'owners' showed up at the same time to claim their week in the same unit?"

"Willis planned to have disappeared by then. He made sure the weeks he sold were for next winter, or for units still under construction that wouldn't be completed until then, so he had months to work his scheme before he had to get out."

"How did you discover what he was doing?"

"Two days after he disappeared, someone at the bank where he had the account contacted me on routine business, keeping up personal contact so Sun South would continue to use the bank. He thought we were happy with their service, and he was surprised when we'd drawn out so much money without explanation. He was even more surprised when I told him we didn't have an account at his bank. Then *I* was surprised when he told me Sun South had carried an account there for the past four months, and had drawn out over a hundred thousand dollars the previous week." Franks smiled helplessly around the cigar, puffed some more smoke, then withdrew the cigar from his mouth and flicked gray ash for the wind to take. "He told me the account's balance was two hundred dollars."

Franks tried to laugh; it caught like a barb in his throat. "Just enough to keep the account open and not attract too much suspicion."

Carver walked away from the railing, to a small concrete bench in the shade of a palm tree, but he didn't sit down. He looked from the shade out into the sun, where Franks was standing just a few feet away as if he sought the heat to help purge him of what had been done to him.

"He was an even better salesman than I thought," Franks muttered. He bowed his head for a moment, saddened by his capacity to trust. A virtue in his faith, a weakness in the world of commerce.

"So Willis is gone, along with a hundred thousand dollars," Carver said. That answered and also raised some questions.

"One hundred twelve thousand dollars exactly," Franks said. "I have a copy of the signed withdrawal slip. It carries Willis's signature, along with a phony signature of a make-believe Sun South treasurer."

Carver asked the most obvious of the recently raised questions. "Why didn't you tell the police?"

Franks shook his head, as if the police had never been one of his alternatives. "I decided there was a better way," he said. "Time-share projects already don't have the best reputation in Florida; public knowledge of what Willis did would put me out of business. It would be especially bad because I'm a member of the Florida Real Estate Commission; there wouldn't be anything left of my reputation after the news media finished with me. I'm an honest man, Carver, but that wouldn't make any difference to the wolves who are just waiting to attack another crooked land developer."

"It's not easy being honest these days," Carver said.

"Or inexpensive," Franks added. "I got the names of the customers Willis had bilked, contacted them personally, and returned their money or gave them deals on other time-share units. It's about all I've been doing these last two weeks. That and worrying."

"If you've satisfied the victims," Carver said, "why are you so concerned about negative publicity?"

"I'm not sure I found all the victims. Maybe there are more whose money was placed somewhere other than in the bogus bank account. They could rear up and bite me any time. Ruin me." Franks had lost interest in his cigar. He let it go out by itself and held the butt, unwilling to drop it and desecrate the pure landscaped world he'd created. "Willis—if he's still alive—is the only one who can set my mind at ease as to whether there are more victims. I want to hire you to find him, and to recover what's left of my hundred thousand dollars. You can tell Willis I won't prosecute if he returns the money and a complete list of the buyers he bilked."

"I already have a client who wants Willis," Carver said.

"Edwina Talbot, no doubt."

"Did you ask her about Willis and the missing money?"

"No. I definitely don't want anyone else to know about it. Anyway, I trust Edwina and don't think she was involved, despite her relationship with Willis. And her hiring you convinced me she doesn't know his whereabouts."

Carver hadn't actually said Edwina had hired him, but he didn't bother to point this out to Franks.

"You can inform your client about me," Franks said. "I don't care. Or let's just say I'm hiring you to recover the money. The duplication of effort should make things easier for you. And I'll pay you half of whatever money you recover. It's a dead loss otherwise."

It didn't take Carver long to work basic mathematics and make up his mind.

"I want to make it clear to you that I already have a principal client when it comes to locating Willis Davis," he said. "Your offer to find Davis, and the recovery of the money, are secondary to my first client's interests. It has to be that way."

Franks smiled. "Your ethics could prove costly."

"Yours already have proved costly."

There went the smile. "Maybe I can give you a starting point," he said. "Sam Cahill."

"Do you think he was in on the racket with Willis?"

"No, Sam would never be involved in anything of that magnitude. But he and Willis were friends, and I never trusted Cahill completely. I had to fire him when I found out he'd been supplying cocaine to some of the other employees. But it was small, recreational amounts; I don't think Sam was actually dealing. It was just something I had to stop or the law might have."

"You told me you didn't know where Cahill had gone when he left Sun South."

"After you told me Willis might be alive, I found out. Through the real-estate commission. Sam kept up his Florida broker's license and is selling backwater property in and around a little town called Solarville, on the edge of the Everglades. At least he was a week ago. If he's moved on, you should be able to locate him."

"Do you think Willis Davis might be in the same area?"

"I doubt it. Davis is too smart to stay in Florida. But Cahill might know where he is."

"He might," Carver agreed. He felt a subtle heightening of his senses, a racing of his blood. A cop's hunch, a hunter's instinct, the sort of thing a department-bound policeman often had to ignore, but that a private cop couldn't. Carver wanted badly to find Sam Cahill.

Franks somehow gauged Carver's piqued interest, took a deep breath and let it out slowly, as if in relief. "Then we have a deal, Mr. Carver." He switched the dead cigar to his left hand and held out his right. The acrid scent of tobacco rose with the hand. Along with the perfumed scent of the flowers, it got to Carver's stomach, made him a little nauseated.

Carver pumped Franks's hand a few times, sensing that the handshake was as binding as a written contract. But also knowing that Franks's money would be in his possession first, for him to deduct his percentage before turning it over to

Franks. Cynical Carver again, jaded by his job. He found himself wondering if *Franks's* signature was on that crucifixion oath.

Carver didn't feel quite right about this new aspect of the case, and he wasn't sure why. He'd have to be a fool, or someone who couldn't figure percentages, to turn down Franks's offer. As Desoto often pointed out, Carver hardly had the financial means to discriminately choose his clients and remain in the private-investigation business. This was an occupation, not a series of causes. And Desoto was right about Carver not knowing any other line of work. Not wanting any other. But Carver, even as a cop, had relied too much on hunches, on the subtle stirrings at the back of his mind. And there was a silent and persistent something back there now that kept telling him he was getting deeper into where he didn't belong, and he might have no way to climb back out.

He realized he had lived with that feeling since he'd met Edwina.

As he followed Franks back up the zigzagging flights of concrete steps to Sun South's main grounds, he resolved not to be so unceasingly suspicious. It was unrealistic. Unhealthy.

Half a mile out to sea, the man on the canvas-shaded flying bridge lowered his binoculars and shouted an order in Spanish. A shirtless man on the deck reeled in the trolling lines, and the boat turned away from the beach.

It chugged and pitched into the waves, then gained speed and headed south along the coastline.

CHAPTER 9

The yellow ribbons tied to the air-conditioner in Desoto's office in Orlando police headquarters were strained horizontal in the cold air rushing from the vent, fluttering madly, as if they longed to escape and soar from the room. The office was hot despite the tireless effort of the window unit, but Desoto, as usual, appeared cool. He flashed his white grin at Carver and motioned elegantly with an arm toward the chair before the metal desk. He had his radio on as usual, too, tuned to a Spanish-speaking station that played *mariachi* music. The volume was just loud enough to be irritating. Before Carver could request it, Desoto reached back and switched off the radio.

"You're here to tell me you found Willis Davis," he said to Carver.

Carver sat down and shook his head.

"You're going to marry Edwina Talbot?"

"I'm here to report a crime," Carver said. "It's my obligation to let the police know when I've learned that a crime has been committed."

"Ah," Desoto said, still grinning, "we are official today, eh?"

"I didn't say that," Carver told him.

Desoto straightened his tie, adjusted his cuffs, as if he thought Edwina might walk into the office next. If Willis Davis was still missing, and Carver didn't want to bed the wench, she was fair game. Or maybe Carver had Desoto wrong.

Nope. He had him right.

"If you're not interested in the lonely Edwina, *amigo*, send her in my direction."

"She came in your direction of her own accord," Carver said. "You deflected her to me."

Desoto nodded sadly. "My lament. I thought I was doing you a favor, but apparently it's one you won't accept." He leaned forward in his desk chair; the breeze from the air-conditioner ruffled the black hair above his right ear ever so slightly. "What about this crime you're here to report?"

Carver told him about his conversation with Ernie Franks at Sun South, about Willis Davis and the missing hundred thousand dollars plus change.

Desoto leaned far back in his chair and thought about it. "Interesting," he said. "But the perpetrator is officially dead, and it seems that Mr. Franks has settled with all the victims, so there are no complainants. No charges have been brought. I see no justification for the police to pursue the matter."

Carver had been sure Desoto would come to that conclusion. There wasn't much else he could do, except cause a lot of trouble that would produce little result. Desoto wouldn't do that; he knew there was a kind of Newton's third law to trouble, a direct and opposite reaction. It seemed that however much trouble you launched, at least that much came back at you.

"So, you've discharged your professional duty of informing the police of a crime," Desoto said. "Now what? Are you going to Solarville to locate this Sam Cahill?"

"It's the logical next step."

Desoto shifted position and deftly used his fingertips to

smooth his hair where the breeze had mussed it. "I know a little about Solarville, Carver. It's on the edge of the swamp. Narcotics-smuggling country."

"Isn't it too far inland to receive drug shipments?" Carver asked.

"Some shipments find their way through the Everglades by airboat. Others are dropped by plane and picked up by boat. Some of the stuff is actually grown in the swamp, harvested, and cut right there in town for sale for street use. Solarville is one of those places that mostly look the other way when it comes to drug activity because it provides a lot of the town's income, supports some of the leading families."

"What about the local law?" Carver asked.

"It's better than you'd think. As honest as possible, in a town like that, but at the same time practical. If you understand my meaning."

Carver understood. The law in Solarville was doing the best it could while avoiding political quicksand. It was that way everywhere, but in some places more than others. "What kinds of drugs pass through there?"

"All kinds. Marijuana, cocaine, heroin. The people there would sell ground-up alligator tails if they could get away with it."

"It's illegal to poach alligators," Carver said.

"Ah, that would be the attraction." Desoto chewed for a moment on the inside of his cheek. "What does the delectable Miss Talbot think of the fact that her Willis is a thief? And of you switching the emphasis of your investigation to Solarville and Franks's money?"

"She doesn't know yet. And the emphasis remains the same—Willis Davis. Cahill might lead me to him."

Desoto shot his handsome grin at Carver again, below dark eyes that calculated. He knew Carver. "There's something else," he said.

"Yes," Carver admitted.

"I'm listening, *amigo*. Your friendly police ear."

"Here's how I see it. Willis connected with Edwina Talbot so he could use her to get the job at Sun South. And he worked it into a sweet scam, one that could still be running. Franks found out about the operation only because someone from the bank handling the phony account contacted him. The reason was that Willis had virtually closed the account. If he hadn't, nothing would have come to light. He could still be at Sun South pulling in big money."

"Then why isn't he?" Desoto asked.

"He had enough money."

"People like Willis Davis never have enough money."

"Exactly. So why would he walk away from getting richer?"

"That's my question," Desoto said.

"It's possible he wanted to move on and use what he had to make even more money. It could be that Willis was conning clients at Sun South for seed money for an even bigger kill. He needed a certain amount to swing a deal, and once he reached the magic number he was ready to step up to bigger things."

"A drug buy," Desoto said thoughtfully. "Yes, once he had enough to make the buy, he could cut the stuff and make a great deal more money than at Sun South. A hundred thousand on the front end of a drug operation can easily turn into half a million dollars. What you suggest is possible."

"Cahill was fired from Sun South for supplying some of the other employees with coke," Carver said. "He's no stranger to the drug scene, at least on a lower level. It's possible that he's Willis's liaison man or partner. Which would explain why Cahill headed for Solarville when he left Sun South."

"All so neat," Desoto said. "Too neat, *amigo*. You know that."

Carver knew. Maybe it was all structured so logically because it was solely the product of his mind and not reality.

"But if what you say is true," Desoto said, "it follows that Willis Davis might be found around Sam Cahill and Solarville."

"And it follows that I should go there to look for him," Carver said.

"And for the money, *amigo*."

"I hadn't forgotten."

"And Willis Davis—he never really loved Edwina Talbot?"

"It looks that way," Carver said.

Desoto shook his head slowly. "The lady's a treasure no one will claim."

"Maybe Willis looked at her as currency to be spent," Carver said, "and he already used her to buy what he wanted."

"So it seems. I feel sorry for her, when you explain to her about her Willis."

"Don't waste your sympathy, Desoto; she won't believe it even after I go through the steps with her."

"Dedication," Desoto said, with a hint of admiration. It was the quality he most valued in women; his ego demanded it.

"Or blind stupidity."

"No, not stupidity. Not in that one."

"Do you get the feeling there's a lot we don't know about Edwina?" Carver asked.

"Of course. It adds to her mystique."

"What if it's the money she's after, and not Willis? What if Willis ran out on her and she concocted this whole thing?"

"No," Desoto said, "if she was in on the scam with him, she would never have come to the police when he left her."

Carver agreed. And despite the uneasy feeling he had about Edwina, he didn't think she was lying about Willis. Of course, there was no way to be sure. Of anything.

Carver bore down on the cane and stood, feeling his perspiration-soaked shirt come unstuck from the chair. The cool breeze from the air-conditioner was steady on his face. "You're right," he said. "It's a mistake to take her too lightly. It might be the biggest mistake Willis Davis ever made."

"If he's still alive," Desoto said, clinging to the official view, making his job and Carver's easier. "If he wasn't murdered or didn't really commit suicide."

"Any personal opinions?" Carver asked.

Desoto said, smiling, "On one hand it seems that he's dead, on the other that he's alive."

"I'm getting tired of both hands," Carver said, and limped from the office. Police work and politics. Some bedfellows.

As the door swung shut behind him, he heard *mariachi* music.

A part of him hoped he was right about Edwina not believing him when he told her about Willis and the illegal Sun South money. Willis was gone; it was Carver who would have to witness her initial disbelief and hollow denial. Her desperate loyalty to a delusion. He found the thought of that surprisingly hard to bear.

He didn't want to hurt her.

CHAPTER 10

"There's another side to all of this," Edwina said. She took a quick sip of her whiskey sour, probably not tasting it.

"You mean Willis's side?" Carver asked.

"Of course. Someone must have forged his signature on that withdrawal slip. I'm sure Willis didn't steal that money."

They were sitting at a table in the bar of The Happy Lobster. Carver had suggested lunch, but Edwina declined. That was okay with Carver; like Edwina, he wasn't hungry.

"I'd be interested in hearing Willis's side of what happened," Carver said. "And so would Ernie Franks."

There was a piano at the other end of the lounge. A middle-aged blond woman sat down and started to play a slow, lilting melody that Carver had never heard. It was the sort of song that used to be played as the refrain in B-movie *Casablanca* imitations.

He rested his fingertips on Edwina's hand, finding her flesh startlingly cool. "You can't go on believing after your reason to believe is gone," he said. "It only makes it hard on you; it changes nothing." He realized he sounded like Bogie talking to Ingrid Bergman.

She finished her drink hastily and stood up. Moisture glittered in her eyes as she turned and walked toward the door. Carver noticed her shoulders quaking and knew she was leaving so he wouldn't see her cry.

He put down a ten-dollar bill to cover the drinks and tip and followed Edwina. The woman at the piano began to sing now, something about love smoothing all of life's rough spots. There wasn't much conviction in the lyrics or in her voice. Or maybe that was just Carver's interpretation.

He kept Edwina in sight, but he stayed well behind her, stood at a distance in the sun-washed parking lot while she leaned with one hand on her car and composed herself. Her stunted shadow lay huddled at her feet.

After a while he walked toward her, prepared to shout her name if she started to get into the car.

She heard his soles crunching on the gravel, the gritty drag of his cane, and turned. No moisture in her eyes now; she had a grip on herself, but a tenuous one. For a moment her lower lip trembled, then she bit it and seemed to relax her body, muscle by muscle, standing with exaggerated looseness and watching him.

He stopped a few feet in front of her, looking at her. The pain in her eyes stared back, then retreated to a far, dark place in her mind. Just then Carver hated all the Willis Davises of the world. Hated them hard and cursed the fact that there were so many of them. And so many of their victims.

Carver and Edwina stood silently for almost a full minute. He felt perspiration trickle down his neck and realized he was uncomfortably warm. He could feel the heat from the parking-lot gravel radiate upward through his soles. Edwina wasn't perspiring. She was cool-looking and pale. Her gray eyes were flat now, like shades drawn to conceal her thoughts.

"When are you leaving for Solarville?" she asked.

"This afternoon. It won't take long to get there. Maybe not even an hour."

"It doesn't take long to get anywhere in Florida," she said. "You get on an interstate or a pay turnpike, drive for an hour or so, and you're where you want to be. Or think you are."

"It's better to face reality and learn to live with it than to run from the facts," he said, still being cruel to be kind. He wondered if that had ever really worked.

"That's a predictable philosophy," she said calmly. "Much less complicated than your lobster analogy, but bullshit nonetheless."

Carver had no answer for that. She might be right. He used his palm to wipe sweat from his face, dragging his hand painfully downward from forehead to chin. He checked his palm to see if his face was there.

"I'll join you in Solarville tomorrow," Edwina said, which didn't surprise Carver. "When we find Willis, we'll get to the truth about the money." She smoothed the material of her gray tailored suit. "I have a business appointment today."

A business appointment. There it was. Carver saw into her then, saw the way the past few years must have been for her. She was using her work as a shield, probably had been since the end of the jinxed marriage Alice Hargrove had mentioned. It had been effective; Carver knew from experience how work could blunt the pain. Business, keeping ceaselessly busy, could fill the void, absorb the wild energy of volatile depression.

"You shouldn't go to Solarville," Carver told Edwina. "That's why you hired me, to sniff around and get my nose dirty."

"Phone me at home tonight," she said. "Let me know where you're staying and what you've learned. I'll decide whether I'll join you, when that will be."

Carver shrugged and nodded. Those were the rules. She was the boss, he was the bird dog. He could overlook her tough act. Everybody who was tough had an act, some better than others.

When she turned to open her car door, he gripped her upper arm, then held it gently.

She looked up at him. She began to cry again and tried to whirl her body away from him. He tightened his grip on her arm, pulled her to him. He would look at her tears, make her blend with reality. It was impossible to be a romantic in today's world; didn't she know that?

For a moment she clung to him; he could feel the heat of her body, vibrating against him. He wanted to comfort her, reassure her. With lies, if necessary. Especially with lies. He raised a hand and caressed her hair where the sun touched it; he felt her grasping fingers feel their way down his back, nails sharp and urgent through his shirt.

Then she pulled away, stood up straight, and briskly smoothed her suit again. Her business suit.

Her gray eyes were cool. This hadn't happened, they said. That woman hadn't really been Edwina Talbot. Two strangers in another dimension had momentarily felt something that bore no relevance to here and now.

He stepped back, silently agreeing with the eyes, which didn't quite meet his. The hell with this. He was afraid. He didn't want this any more than Edwina did. Too soon. Too soon after Laura. He remembered the legalese and pain.

"I'll be waiting for your call," she said crisply, and ducked into her car, swiveling gracefully on the seat before pulling the door closed. The pale turn of her ankle below the gray of her skirt was breathtaking.

The Mercedes' tires spun and caught hold. Gravel pounded against the insides of the fenders; a few small stones flew free and bounced off Carver's shoes.

Edwina didn't look back at him as she wheeled the car to the driveway, then out onto the highway.

Carver leaned on his cane in the sultry heat and watched her drive away, pondering the mystery of her. He wondered if part of her appeal might be that hidden chamber of her life, and the fact that she might be manipulating him. He was always one for puzzles.

He felt like following her, but he didn't. Instead he went home and packed.

CHAPTER 11

It was early evening when Carver reached Solarville. The flat terrain and endless orange groves of central Florida, geometrically sectioned by flat, dusty roads, had given way to lusher, more tropical country as he neared the northern edge of the Everglades. He exited from the main highway when he saw the sign signaling the turnoff for Solarville and several other small towns. After following a tree-lined side road for ten miles, he turned south on another road and found himself on Solarville's main street, Loop Avenue.

The town was larger than Carver had imagined; a sign proclaimed that the population was over four thousand. Most of the buildings on Loop Avenue were clapboard, the rest were brick. The heat and humidity had done its work. Almost every painted surface was discolored or peeling. There was the usual string of businesses found in towns that size: a barbershop, two service stations, a small movie theater, several restaurants, a hardware store, variety store, Laundromats, a medium-sized supermarket. Solarville was big enough to boast a McDonald's halfway down Loop. The golden arches seemed about to sag in the heat.

Carver had the top up on the Olds. He drove through town slowly, ignoring the pedestrians who glanced at him as he sized up Solarville through the bug-splattered windshield. He'd passed a citrus processing plant a few miles before reaching town; he supposed that was where many of the residents worked.

Not far from McDonald's was the city hall, a small stone building with an elaborate, weathered dome on it, an architect's scaled-down dream that had probably been built with federal money during the thirties. Directly next to city hall was police headquarters, not nearly so grand: a low, white-shingled building with a sand-and-gravel lot next to it. There was a dusty blue patrol car parked on the lot, and not far from it a pickup truck with oversized tires, and a winch mounted on the front bumper. The word *traffic* was lettered on the truck's door, and on the front near the winch in smaller letters was painted *Ditch Bitch*. Considering the swampy terrain off the roads, Carver figured the Ditch Bitch had hauled many an errant motorist's mistake from the muck.

At the end of town, where Loop fulfilled its promise and began its curve back to the alternate highway, the swamp began and some of the buildings were elevated on stilts. The neighborhood was shabbier there, where people existed closer to brackish water, hordes of mosquitoes, and maybe even an occasional alligator that wandered over to see how the vertical creatures lived.

Carver turned the Olds away from the gloom of the swamp and drove back the way he'd come, to a sign with an arrow that pointed down a side road to the Tumble Inn Motel.

The Tumble Inn was a tan brick two-story structure less than a mile outside of town, built in a U as if to embrace its small rectangular swimming pool. A pimply-faced kid who introduced himself as Curt blinked bulbous blue eyes at Carver as if it were a first for anyone to be checking into the place, then accepted Carver's Visa card, had him sign a registration form, and gave him a tagged key and directions to room 17, the end room on the north leg of the building. "Near the ice machine," Curt told him conspiratorially, as if ice were the gold of the region and he'd done him a special favor.

It wasn't a bad room. Clean. And not so musty once Carver figured out the controls on the air-conditioner and got it humming. The place was decorated in shades of beige, with motel-modern furniture that had been stamped out at some factory where they must make all cheap motel furniture.

Carver pulled the beige drapes closed, tossed his suitcase up on the beige bedspread and opened it, then rummaged around until he found a clean shirt. He didn't know how long he'd be staying, so he didn't unpack; everything he'd brought would resist wrinkles and the press of humidity through the miracle of polyester.

He entered the tiny, tiled bathroom, rinsed his face with cold water that carried the faint, rotten-egg smell of sulfur, then changed shirts and left the room to drive back into Solarville.

Carver drove past police headquarters. He'd decided it might not be wise to contact the local law yet; he didn't want anyone tipping Sam Cahill to the fact that someone was in town watching him. He stopped at a self-service Shell station, filled the thirsty Olds's tank, then went into the office to pay a greasy little guy with jug ears who was standing behind a greasy counter.

"Where can I find a local real-estate office?" he asked the jug-eared man, whose uniform name tag identified him as Wilt. Carver peered closely at the sewn-on tag. Yep, Wilt—not Walt. "I'm interested in looking at some property around here."

"There's several places here in town sell real estate," Wilt said. He punched the keys of a jangly old cash register until the drawer popped open, deposited Carver's twenty-dollar bill, and handed Carver back his change, two slippery quarters.

"Which is the closest?"

"Bain Realty, just down the street," Wilt said, scratching an oily, protruding ear. "But they'd be closed now. Then down a few blocks the other way is World Real Estate. They're mostly commercial stuff, though. Or is that the kinda property you're lookin' for?"

"Is that a fairly new phone directory?" Carver asked, ignoring the question and pointing to a pay phone and its slender directory dangling beneath it by a chain.

"Just a few months old," Wilt said. He rubbed a greasy forefinger on the right side of his nose, leaving a dark smudge to match the one near his left nostril. He did like oil. Liked it a lot.

Carver thanked him and stepped over to the phone. Sam Cahill would have to put up some sort of respectable front to satisfy the law here. Carver leafed through grease-marked pages, and there was Cahill listed as a broker along with half a dozen other real-estate agencies. Cahill's home and office address was on Pond Road. Carver asked greasy Wilt where that was.

"Not far outside of town. Forks off to the west, where Loop starts to curve." He pointed vaguely to the south end of town.

Just then a raggedy-haired fat woman pushed through the door and asked to buy a can of Valvoline. She'd come to the right place.

Carver gave Wilt a casual half salute and limped back outside to his car. He got a Kleenex from the glove compartment, wiped the grease from his fingers, and drove toward Pond Road.

It took him less than five minutes to turn the Olds onto Pond. The homes there were well kept up, separated from each other by trees and high swamp brush. They were low ranch-style houses that had the same basic character, probably built within months of each other. Medium-priced houses, but nice ones considering they were in a backwater town like Solarville. Cahill's address was one of the models with a two-car garage. A four-wheel-drive Jeep was parked in the driveway, the ideal vehicle for showing customers the kind of property Cahill was selling in that area. The garage's overhead door was open. Inside was a low-slung red Corvette with a chrome luggage rack on its trunk. The car was polished to a high gloss, gleaming like a ruby set in the dimness.

Carver parked down the road, off to the side, where he could watch the house but where his car wouldn't be noticeable.

As darkness fell, no lights came on in the house. Apparently Sam Cahill had a third vehicle that he'd driven away in, or he was away with someone else who had driven.

There was little point in staying parked there. Carver wondered it he should talk to some of the neighbors, ask them if Cahill stayed alone at his home and office, or if they'd seen another man, one fitting Willis Davis's description.

He decided that wouldn't be wise. It probably would net him nothing, and might alert Cahill to his presence in Solarville. And it wasn't likely that Willis Davis would make himself so easy to find, even if he was in the Solarville area.

Carver drove back into town and had supper at the motel restaurant. One of the side dishes he ate was unidentifiable, but it was tasty. Something from the swamp? He decided not to ask the waitress.

In the booth across from him sat a man and woman in pinstripe business suits that might have been fashioned by the same tailor. The man had the side dish Carver had eaten, but he'd pushed his plate away after a few exploratory bites. The woman, a cool, scrubbed-looking blonde with unblinking green eyes, had played it safe and ordered a roast-beef sandwich. The two of them looked out of place sitting in the vinyl booth in a second-rate motel in a backwater town. The expensive cut and fabric of their conservative clothes, the woman's subdued but quality jewelry, and their refined but alert behavior suggested that they were high-level executives on a slumming expedition. Maybe corporate lovers getting away to a place where no one they knew would spot them. They didn't seem the sort to have business other than of a very private nature in Solarville. Lawyers in love? Corporate copulation? Unlikely, but possible.

Carver shook off that kind of baseless musing, futile speculation. Dirty occupation, dirty mind. He was beginning to think too much like the kind of private detective that kicked open motel doors and snapped photographs. These two were probably nothing more than wealthy tourists driving around the state with time and money to waste. Their type wasn't unusual in almost any corner of Florida.

When he got up to pay his bill and leave, the woman glanced at her watch. Carver noticed that it was an expensive-looking Mickey Mouse watch, with what appeared to be diamonds set in each of Mickey's hands. He walked past the man and woman toward the cashier, wondering what it would be like to have enough money to live and to buy so frivolously.

Outside he smoked one of his infrequent after-meal cigars, then he drove into town and had a few beers at a local tavern that featured a stuffed alligator suspended by wires above the bar. He said nothing, listened to the conversation around him, and learned nothing. This kind of sleuthing worked mostly on TV and in novels. Or in Desoto's old movies.

At nine o'clock he got up and left. He was older now but no wiser. The alligator had been a nothing. If the beer and the air-conditioning hadn't been frosty cold, the evening would have been a complete waste.

He walked around town for a while, then bought a *Solarville Bugle* from a newspaper vending machine and drove back to the Tumble Inn.

When he got to his room, he phoned Edwina and let her know where he was staying. She told him she'd join him in Solarville sometime the next day. He tried to talk her out of coming, but she was in no mood to be talked out of or into anything.

When Edwina had gotten off the line, Carver called Desoto and asked him to check with Records on Sam Cahill.

"Have you found Cahill?" Desoto asked.

"Sure, it was easy. He's listed in the phone directory."

"Under *A* for 'accomplice'?"

Carver didn't reply. He wasn't in the frame of mind for snappy repartee. If Desoto wanted to play Abbott, let him find somebody else to be Costello.

"Did you talk to Cahill?"

"Not yet," Carver said. "I'm going to hang back and watch him for a while. Why?"

"A description would help with Records. Cahill might be an alias."

"I haven't even seen him yet," Carver said.

"Well, he's a he," Desoto said. "That narrows it down to a little less than half the population, *amigo*. Should be no problem. Do you want me to call you back on this tonight?"

"Sure." Carver told Desoto where he was staying and gave him the phone number.

"The Tumble Inn Motel, eh? Is Edwina Talbot with you?"

"No."

"Oh." Desoto sounded disappointed.

"She's arriving tomorrow."

"Ah!"

After thanking Desoto and hanging up the phone, Carver took off his shoes, stretched out on the bed, and started to read the *Bugle*. A banker named Jackson was marrying a girl from Miami and the newlyweds were going to live there after a honeymoon in Hawaii. The liquor store on Loop had been robbed of several hundred dollars the day before. A skinny but pretty teen-ager who looked embarrassed in her bathing-suit photograph had been nominated by the hardware store for that year's Gator Queen. When Carver got to the page-two article about an argument among the winners at a church bingo game, he fell asleep.

Two hours later, the jangle of the phone awakened him.

That and something else. He sat up in bed, breathed in dizzily, and sank back down. He opened his eyes in the darkness and they stung; he couldn't keep them open. Couldn't see anyway. Tears rolled down his cheeks and he clenched his eyes shut as tightly as he could. Instinctively, he continued to grope for the ringing telephone.

Wait a second. Darkness? What about the bingo argument and the Gator Queen? He'd fallen asleep reading the paper—with the lamp on!

He breathed in, coughed violently, tried again to open his eyes but couldn't. What the hell? His right arm flailed wildly, and he heard the clatter of his cane as he knocked it from where it was leaning against the table by the bed.

With a cold pang of fear, he suddenly understood.

The fear deepened, rushed him straight down in a roller-coaster plunge. It took him a few seconds to fully accept what was happening.

The room was full of smoke.

CHAPTER 12

C arver rolled off the bed and dropped to the floor, pressing his cheek to the rough carpet and sucking for breathable air, praying for it. He pulled more smoke into his lungs, gagged, and coughed.

For a moment he lay still, willing himself to control the terror that threatened to panic him, trying to blot out the vision of a man he'd discovered in a burned car when he was still in the police department. He hadn't recognized the thing on the front seat as a man at first. He'd—

Carver actually snarled at himself, jolting his mind from surrender and certain death. He groped for the bed, the legs of the nightstand, to get his bearings, and began to crawl toward the door, dragging his stiff leg. Every few feet he'd press his face to the carpet and draw a cautious, shallow breath, enough air to allow himself another foot or so of progress.

Finally his rigid fingertips bumped into the smooth hard surface of the door. He scrambled against it, raising his body, found the doorknob and turned it.

The door was locked.

Carver grasped the knob tightly, squeezing frantically to

keep his sweaty fingers from slipping off the slick metal, and pulled his body higher.

He found the sliding bolt lock, fumbled with it, feeling a shock of pain as he bent back a fingernail and instinctively jerked his hand away.

Grasping the lock again, more carefully, he gradually forced the bolt sideways, until it jammed. He shoved hard against it. He lost his footing then, supporting his entire weight for a second by painfully squeezing the hard metal lock between his thumb and forefinger. Then his grip was torn loose.

He wasn't sure if the bolt had slid free. But when he fell backward, the door swung open.

Immediately the air down low was breathable, as dark smoke rolled from the room. Carver heard voices, the wailing yodel of a fire truck or police car. The siren got closer, louder, deafening, then growled to reluctant silence like a record running down. He dragged himself forward, over the hard-edged threshold, out onto the concrete in front of the open door. Then he wriggled off to the side, away from the black pall of smoke.

Multicolored lights were suddenly dancing around him. People were shouting. Soles scraped on concrete. Another siren sent up a wail in the distance. Hands grabbed him roughly beneath the arms and pulled him away. His stockinged feet bounced painfully over the rough concrete and he struggled awkwardly to stand and walk on his own, forgetting for a moment that he had only one good leg.

"Easy, fella," a very calm voice said. He was allowed to slump down against a wall. Something soft and confining, a mask, was placed over Carver's mouth and nose. For a moment he panicked and tried to shake it from his face. "Breathe in, buddy, not too hard," the calm voice instructed, making it all routine.

Carver obeyed and instantly knew he was breathing in oxygen. He'd experienced the heady sensation before, during a police training session. He held the mask to his face himself, sucking in more of the clean, smokeless nectar.

He fought off dizziness, then sat for about ten minutes taking in oxygen, his head thrown back. There was the very stuff of life, usually taken for granted.

At last he experimentally removed the mask, drew a breath, and found that his respiratory system had returned more or less to normal.

He began to take an interest beyond his survival. Two yellow fire engines were parked at angles in front of the motel. From one ran a jumble of hoses. Several uniformed firemen were busy at the motel-room door and window, feeding water into the room. One of the hoses ran around to the back of the building. A police car was parked next to the swimming pool, and a skinny redheaded man was in discussion with a tan-uniformed patrolman. There was an ambulance parked next to the police car. The roof lights on both vehicles were flashing red and blue, playing off the still water in the pool with a kaleidoscope effect.

Carver used the wall to brace against and drew himself to his feet. A hand gently touched his arm; a fireman had been standing nearby to make sure he didn't fall. The man had a round, concerned face, a wild shock of graying hair. The one who'd supplied the oxygen?

"Do you need medical attention?" a voice asked. The cop had walked over to stand next to Carver. A young medical attendant from the ambulance was with him.

Carver glanced at the ambulance and shook his head no. "I think I'm okay," he said. "A phone call woke me up just in time to get out."

"Thank God for that!" the redheaded man who'd been talking with the uniformed cop said. He introduced himself as Jack Daninger, the owner of the Tumble Inn, and assured Carver that the motel sincerely regretted this and would do everything possible to ensure Carver's comfort. Daninger was solicitous enough to be embarrassing. He wouldn't go away until Carver flatly told him that he wasn't going to sue the motel. Carver thought, not for the first time, that lawyers had screwed up the country.

An unmarked white Plymouth sedan rocked to a stop behind the patrol car. From the Plymouth emerged a short, paunchy man in a rumpled brown suit. Despite his lack of physical stature and his near-obesity, there was a suggestion of carefully contained power in the way he looked over the scene and walked toward Carver and the uniformed patrolman. He'd been in places like this before, his glance and his walk said; he knew the steps to this dance.

"What happened here?" he asked.

"Fire, sir," the patrolman said, offering the short explanation.

The paunchy man glared at him.

"Don't know yet where or how it started," the patrolman said, trying to recover status in the eyes of a superior. *The* superior. No doubt about the pecking order here.

"Find out."

When the patrolman had hurried away, the man said, "I'm Harvey Armont, police chief here in Solarville." He shook hands with Carver. He had beefy, rounded cheeks, with an oddly sharp nose that didn't appear to belong on such a face. His dark eyes were searching, uncompromising cop's eyes; his permanently arched black eyebrows gave him a worldly expression. "It looks as if the fire was pretty much confined to your room," he said.

Carver twisted his body, his palm still flat on the wall, and looked. Armont was right; Carver's seemed to be the only room affected. There was no more smoke, only the scorched, acrid scent that hung over every water-soaked fire scene. He realized he hadn't seen flames.

"You here on business, Mr. Carver?" Armont asked. His voice was amiable but insistent, demanding a reply. That voice would probe, soothe, cajole, trick, seep like water through any cracks in the truth.

Carver knew he might as well give Armont what he was going to get anyway. "Yes, I'm a private detective." He dug his wallet out of his wrinkled pants and showed the chief his license and some identification.

Armont looked over at the open door and soaked carpet of Carver's room. "That's interesting, considering the nature of the fire."

"What nature?" Carver asked. "It might have been spontaneous combustion, or faulty wiring in a light switch."

"There's really no such thing as spontaneous combustion," the chief said.

Another police car pulled into the lot and parked near the driveway, a gray Ford, from a nearby town, its driver drawn by radio traffic to the fire. The driver nodded to Chief Armont, one curious professional to another, but didn't get out of the car.

The uniformed cop had returned, eager to make amends and get back on the road to promotion. "The conflagration started in a trash can behind the building," he said. "The wooden eaves over the can caught fire, and part of the second-floor railing. The air-conditioner to this one room sucked in most of the smoke. It looks like somebody might have tossed a lighted cigarette into the can. Or maybe, hot night like this, it was spontaneous combustion."

Armont looked at Carver without changing expression. The tone of his voice was the same, too. "In this kind of situation, the motel will fix you up with another room, Mr. Carver. Come morning, you drop by my office and we'll talk."

Carver nodded, catching sight of Armont's wristwatch. Eleven-thirty. He realized that most of the illumination there was from the lightbars of emergency vehicles, fooling him into thinking it was early morning. He'd only been asleep for two hours when the phone had rung. Desoto, almost certainly, waking him and saving his life.

"One thing," Carver said. "My cane is in there." He nodded toward the disaster of a motel room.

The chief looked down at Carver's legs, realizing perhaps for the first time that Carver was lame. Then he shot a commander's sharp glance at the patrolman, and said, "Rogers."

Rogers bustled into the room, lifting his black regulation

shoes high on the spongy carpet. Carver could hear the slosh of the officer's footfalls.

A minute later he returned, handed Carver the cane, and smiled. He waited around for a moment expectantly, like a dog that had recovered a stick for its owner and anticipated a biscuit in reward.

Carver thanked him; it was the best he could do. He got the impression that with a little incentive, maybe two biscuits, Rogers would charge alone into a Mafia stronghold.

"You lock your door now, Mr. Carver," Armont said, as Carver turned and limped toward redheaded Daninger, who was standing before an open door to a room at the other end of the motel and maintaining his sickly, don't-sue-me grin.

"Is there anything you want from your room before morning?" Daninger asked. "Anything at all?"

Carver told him no. His wallet, with all his money in it, and his keys, were in his pants pockets. One of the few advantages of falling asleep with your clothes on. He was missing only his shoes, and knew they'd be soaked and unwearable.

"Curt will launder all your clothes and get them to you in the morning," Daninger said through his uncertain, pleading grin. "And of course anything you've lost will be replaced."

Carver found himself feeling sorry for Daninger, small-town businessman staring into the loaded barrels of years of expensive litigation. It was enough to make any entrepreneur jittery. "You've done everything possible, Mr. Daninger," he said. "Thanks."

Daninger was at least somewhat relieved. Carver accepted the key to his new room, went inside, and locked the door carefully.

He lay awake for a long time, listening to the emergency vehicles racing their engines and departing one by one. The fire-truck drivers blasted air horns and clanged bells, as if they were merging with traffic on a crowded four-lane highway.

Finally Carver dozed off.

He slept two hours out of the next eight, popping awake now and then, imagining he smelled smoke.

CHAPTER 13

In the morning, Curt showed up as promised. The friendly, pimply teen-ager grinned at Carver and sauntered past him to the closet. Slung over his shoulder were all of Carver's cleaned clothes draped on hangers.

"Got most of the smoke smell outa these," he said. He ducked back outside and returned with a suitcase about the same size as the one Carver had lost to smoke and water the night before. Best of all, he was carrying a new pair of black dress shoes similar to the ones Carver had lost in the fire. The design was much the same, only these were wingtips, thin-soled and flexible; not the thick, clompy kind Willis Davis wore. The shoes were 10½s, Carver's size.

"You're pretty lucky," Curt said, standing by the open door.

"Yeah, I made out okay; this is a new pair of shoes."

"I mean about still being alive," Curt said. He wasn't one for subtlety.

Carver tested the zipper on the suitcase, running it back and forth. Smooth.

"This town is rumored to be a haven for drug runners," he said, glancing at Curt. "Any of that true?"

"Naw. There's always talk about the Malone brothers. Sean and Gary. But believe me, they blow a little grass now and then and that's it. Some drugs at the high school, too, even with a few of the teachers. Some hard stuff, but not much. Like it is everywhere. Big deal, huh? Folks just need somebody to talk about."

"That's the truth," Carver agreed, thinking they wouldn't be likely to talk to Curt if they didn't want their words spread around like flu at an orgy.

He attempted to give Curt a tip, but Curt would have none of that. Not from a poor cripple the motel had almost smoked like a ham.

"Daninger said to tell you there'll be no charge for the room as long as you wanna stay," he said.

"Thank him for me," Carver said. "Tell him I'll send home for the family and the rest of my things."

Curt's acne-marred face split into a mottled grin. Nothing bled; a testimonial for Clearasil. "Really?"

"No," Carver said. "I'll be here a few more days at most."

Still grinning, Curt hitched up his faded Levi's and ambled slowly out to return to the office. Walking at normal speed seemed alien to the boy's nature.

His clothes might be fresh, but Carver still smelled faintly like charred hickory. He went into the bathroom and took a long shower in lukewarm water, lathering up twice.

He stayed in the shower until he no longer smelled like a forest fire. Then he toweled dry, dressed in some of his freshly laundered clothes, and tried out his new shoes.

The shoes fit well. Someone had even pressed his clothes, and Daninger had managed to have Carver's blue sport jacket dry-cleaned. No expense or effort had been spared in the attempt to sidestep litigation.

Carver felt okay after the night before, only a little tired. But he knew about fire; another ten minutes in that small room that was filling up with smoke and he would never have awakened, except perhaps for a few terrified, airless last seconds before eternity.

He smoothed the thick, damp gray hair above his ears, palmed water from his bald crown, and was about to leave the room when the phone rang.

Carver thought it would be Daninger, checking on his well-being, wondering if the clothes were to his satisfaction. But it was Desoto. The Cahill report.

"I phoned you last night," Desoto said. "You didn't answer."

"You saved my life last night," Carver said.

"Hey, don't blame me. I wasn't near you."

Carver explained what happened.

"This fire I saved you from," Desoto said, "was it an accident?"

"Maybe. It could have been spontaneous combustion. What about Sam Cahill?"

"He was in trouble over in Fort Lauderdale nine years ago. Assault with a deadly weapon, suspended sentence. A domestic quarrel over a woman when her husband showed up unexpectedly. The treacherous paths of love. Cahill tried to bean the guy with a lamp. Relatively minor stuff. There's nothing else on him in Florida."

"Nothing? No drugs?"

"Not on the record." Desoto paused. "You know what the Chinese say, *amigo*?" he asked, mixing cultures without a qualm. "When someone saves your life, you're responsible for them, share the blame or credit in whatever they do from then on."

"You've got it backward," Carver said. "*You* share the blame for whatever *I* do."

"If that's the way it is," Desoto said, "I'm going to hang up and stay away from the phone, in case there's another fire there."

"Thanks for the call last night," Carver said, "and for the rundown on Cahill."

"Part of what makes my job a joy," Desoto said. "It's possible that you might be onto something too big for you to handle, *amigo*. Something nobody else has noticed."

"I don't know yet what I've got hold of," Carver said honestly.

"You're out there alone, Carver. The first to suspect something. Not healthy, my friend. The early worm gets devoured by the bird. Maybe you should get out of there, count your bullets, and look forward to another day, eh?"

"Not yet. The fire might really have been an accident."

"You seen the local law yet?"

"No, I'll get around to that this morning."

"You worry me."

"That Chinese thing."

Desoto snorted. "I got to go, Carver. Crime calls. A busy day shaping up. Folks killing each other at a brisk pace." Latin music came faintly over the phone; Desoto had turned on his radio, building rhythm and momentum to carry him through the day.

"Thanks again," Carver said. "Really."

Desoto hung up without answering. No sentimentalist he.

Carver left to talk to Chief Armont, as promised, locking the door carefully behind him, catching a whiff of charred wood from the direction of his old room.

The morning was hot. And the air was filled with clouds of some kind of tiny insect that had ventured out of the swamp to mate or die or act out some other mysterious rite of nature. The bugs were good at being pests. They flitted abruptly this way and that and had no respect for humans. Carver brushed the irritating insects away as he limped toward his car.

The man watching him from behind the trees at the end of the parking lot didn't seem to mind the insects at all. Until he was sixteen, he'd endured worse inconveniences every day of his life, indoors and out. Inconveniences that to others had seemed an inexorable grinding that had finally worn them down, destroyed them.

That kind of background gave a man certain hard-won advantages, if he followed the right course and played his own game. A man like that could do things some people would faint just thinking about, because they'd always had a choice; it had never been necessary for them to learn what they could really do on sheer nerve, what they might even come to enjoy.

He grinned, tasted and then spat out one of the unpredictable tiny bugs, and started walking through the moss-draped woods toward town.

CHAPTER 14

S olarville's police headquarters had once been somebody's home. The ordinary problems of life had been shared there, solved or not solved, and probably children had romped and brooded to maturity within its shelter. Now the inside of the low white house had been purged of hominess and rearranged into a booking area and offices. Carver figured Chief Armont's office was in what had once been the master bedroom. There was what appeared to be a closet door on one wall, on another a window that looked out on a sloping stretch of ground ending at a tall chain-link fence bordering the backyard of the house in the next block.

Behind the fence a large black and tan Doberman pinscher paced like a caged dark spirit, as if contemplating escape for malicious purposes, or daring anyone to come into the yard. Carver wondered why someone whose house backed up to police headquarters thought they needed a watchdog.

"That's King," Armont said, noticing Carver looking out the window at the dog. "He looks tough but he's a marshmallow." He stared speculatively at Carver. "How about you? Are you really a marshmallow?"

"Do I look tough?"

"Yeah. Even with the cane."

"You look tough, too. Even without the cane."

The chief paced around the room for a while, not so unlike a chunky counterpart of the unimaginatively named King. His tie was loosened, and his short-sleeved white shirt had crescents of dampness beneath the arms. He wasn't compatible with the climate of his town. His thick arms were layered with muscle. As he paced, his stomach paunch preceded him aggressively like the confident prow of a ship. He looked like a square-fisted, solid cop, all right, and Carver suspected that his center was as hard as his exterior.

"That fire last night," Armont said, "it wasn't necessarily accidental. You said you were here on business. Anybody in town have a motive to try to barbecue you?"

"I doubt it. I just arrived yesterday."

Armont stopped his restless roaming, then sat on the edge of his desk and crossed his arms, propping them on the shelf of his stomach. "Why are you here, Mr. Carver?"

Carver told him, mentioning the possible connection between Sam Cahill and Willis Davis, but not between Cahill and drugs. Maybe Cahill wasn't involved in drug trafficking. Or maybe he was and Chief Armont knew it. Right now, it was a box better left unopened.

"No sign of this Davis around here," Armont said. "Any stranger draws at least some attention in a town like Solarville. Nobody fitting Davis's description, vague and average as it is, has set down around here." He spoke as if he knew everything that went on in and around Solarville. He probably did.

"What can you tell me about Sam Cahill?" Carver asked.

Armont shrugged; the powerful muscles in his arms danced. Carver thought it was a shame he didn't have one of those tattoos of a hula girl on his forearm, so the girl could wriggle when the muscle did. "He's been here about six months. Deals in real estate out of a home and office he rents out on Pond Road. Drives a fancy red car. Got himself some money."

"It there enough real estate dealt around here to make it worth his while?" Carver asked.

"There might be. And he talks now and again about building a subdivision outside the north edge of town. He could be serious; ground's flat out there, and fairly dry." The arms resting on the stomach paunch unfolded. Armont gripped the desk edge with thick, gnarled fingers. Carver had seen fingers like that on an old major-league catcher. "You musta checked on Cahill," the chief said. "He got any priors?"

Carver knew Armont could easily run his own check on Cahill; this was a test of cooperation. Carver cooperated. "A nine-year-old assault conviction," he said. "Never served time. It was a domestic fracas; a husband came home at the wrong time and caused a problem. Cahill tried to solve the problem with a lamp. Used it as a club. The traditional blunt instrument."

"Humph. He's been quiet enough here. Maybe he's grown out of his temper." Armont's flat yet curious eyes flicked up and down Carver, considering him. "You can find Cahill most mornings about this time at The Flame restaurant down on South Loop. He's probably having breakfast there as usual, trying to suck up again to Verna Blaney, one of the waitresses."

"Was Cahill involved with this waitress?"

"For a while he seemed to be; then whatever was going on cooled off, at least with Verna. It's the sort of thing folks around here would notice and probably make too much of. Myself, I wouldn't be surprised if there was nothing between Verna and Cahill but acquaintanceship. Verna's dad, Ned Blaney, ran airboat rides for tourists through the swamp south of town before he died of a heart attack nine months ago. People wondered what would happen to Verna. She got the job at The Flame, and she's still living out on her hundred or so godforsaken acres in the ramshackle swamp cabin she and her dad shared before he died. She's a good woman, maybe went a little touchy and withdrawn after Ned died, then she seemed to right herself." Armont recrossed his arms; he was done talking, finished with his own gesture of cooperation.

Carver thanked him for the information and started toward the door.

"You were a cop once, weren't you?" Armont asked, in a way that made it clear he knew the answer.

Carver turned, leaning on the cane. "That's right. In Orlando."

"It shows," Armont said. His tone suggested he was complimenting Carver, in his own begrudging manner. He sat down heavily behind his desk and got busy in a rough way with paperwork that apparently had him frustrated. "You'll keep me informed," he said.

Carver said that he would.

Armont didn't look up from the disorganized spread of papers on his desk. He drew a plastic ballpoint pen from his shirt pocket, and with powerful darting motions of his big right hand, he began gouging signatures into some of the papers. A man who attacked his work.

Carver continued out of the office. He nodded to the uniformed patrolman at one of the desks, and to the elderly woman at the switchboard, when they looked over at him as he limped past. They nodded back. The woman smiled in grandmotherly fashion, as if she'd like to pat Carver on the head, give him some cookies, and fix his leg. She looked as if she might actually be able to do that.

Carver levered himself into the sun-heated Olds, wincing as his bare hand pressed too long against the baked vinyl upholstery. The car's top was up, but the sun had invaded through the windshield and rolled-down side windows.

He drove from the police-department lot, then down Loop Avenue to The Flame restaurant. After making a U-turn, he parked the Olds behind Sam Cahill's gleaming red Corvette and smiled. Time for breakfast. Bacon, eggs, and information.

The Flame was a white clapboard building close to the curb on Loop Avenue. It had a long, green-tinted window that featured a fancy decal of a dancing flame above the restaurant's name in red letters. Through the window Carver could see several tables and booths, and a long serving counter with stools. There appeared to be about a dozen customers inside, most of them at the tables or booths.

One of those electrified insect traps that attract and then zap bugs on contact was hung above The Flame's entrance. War was hell, even war on insects. Carver stepped gingerly through the previous night's bounty of crisp casualties and went inside.

He sat at a table near the counter, not far from one of the big ceiling fans that were rotating their broad blades too slowly to stir any air. A huge antique jukebox was playing a country-western tune, a sincere lament that had to do with cowboys and trucks and desperately unhappy rich women. The place was old, slightly worn at the edges, but it looked prosperous in a small way and clean, except for the insects. Carver felt better about ordering breakfast there.

Two men in jeans and work shirts sat at the counter, sipping coffee. A man and a young blond boy with a mouthful of braces were in one of the tape-patched booths, and an older couple sat at a table near the back. Some teen-agers giggled not far from them. No one in there looked as if he might be Sam Cahill.

A squarish, gray-haired woman bustled out of the kitchen, carrying a tray with platters of eggs and toast on it. She took the tray to the table where the man and boy sat. While the boy went at the eggs, the man smiled and thanked her, called her Emma. Which meant the dark-haired woman behind the counter was probably Verna Blaney.

Carver studied the counter waitress while she drew a refill of coffee from a tall stainless-steel urn. She was older than he'd expected, in her mid-thirties. Slender yet somehow sturdy. He suspected she was built with deceptive lushness beneath her ill-fitting white waitress uniform, the sort of peasant-stock voluptuousness that used to play hell with princes. Her hair was thick, pinned up and back, and would probably fall to shoulder length when she let it down. She turned to set the cups on the counter and Carver got the full impact of her broad-featured face. Her eyes were brown and set far apart, beneath unplucked brows that almost met above a broad, perfectly aligned nose. She had vaguely Slavic, prominent cheekbones, and her wide lips were full, slightly inverted to reveal even, very white teeth. She was feminine, not close to beautiful, but there was a coarse sensuality about her. The air around her seemed to hum with vibrations aimed at the male libido.

She turned in the other direction then, and Carver saw the wide, ugly scar that disfigured the right side of her face. Raised and red, it ran from her misshapen ear, down her cheek, and curved beneath her jaw.

Her eyes met Carver's, didn't look away. A direct stare, almost daring him to react to the scar. She was probably a woman direct in everything, one who had come to accept her disfigurement and alternate futures not lived.

"Yes, sir?" Emma said. She was standing alongside Carver's table.

She waited while he glanced over the menu, then she licked a pencil point and jotted in her note pad as he ordered the Gator Special and coffee. He could swear she gave him a crocodile smile.

As Emma walked away, a man came out of the rest room and strode toward the counter, absently checking to make sure his fly was zipped. "Leavin', Sam?" Emma asked.

"Not yet, sexy," the man said. He sat down on a stool close to the far end of the counter. Without being asked, Verna poured a cup of coffee with cream and carried it down to him. Sam Cahill. Had to be.

He didn't look much like Carver had imagined. He was tall and rangy, in his mid-forties but still lean, in good shape. A cigarette-ad cowboy in jeans and a plaid shirt with the sleeves rolled up. Not the sort who'd sell Sun South units. Did he have an act for each set of customers? Was he the polished smooth-talker for wealthy Sun South buyers, then rough-hewn and one of the boys for the swamptown property he was selling now?

Verna stayed near the end of the counter, leaning on it, and they talked. Carver couldn't understand what they were saying, but they didn't seem particularly intimate. There were no lingering looks, no magnetic gestures that prompted and prolonged contact. But Carver noticed that she did keep left and front face toward Cahill, concealing the scar.

After about five minutes, Verna wiped down the counter around Cahill's coffee cup and walked away, finding things to keep her busy behind the counter. Things she'd just as soon be doing as talking to Cahill. Whatever fire there had been between them, if indeed there had been one, seemed to have burned itself out.

Even before Emma brought Carver's Gator Special, Cahill got up and strolled out of the restaurant. A still-busy Verna saw him leaving, from the corner of her eye, and waved, managing to keep her scar toward the wall. He nodded an easy good-bye to her, his western boots thunking out a slow rhythm on the floor.

It would have attracted attention to walk out of the restaurant after Cahill without having eaten breakfast. Carver stayed where he was; he knew what Cahill looked like now and could find him easily enough. He wondered about the woman who might have been Cahill's lover.

Carver ate his eggs, bacon, and toast, drank his orange juice and coffee. It was the kind of salty, greasy breakfast he liked more than was good for him. If he hung around Solarville, he'd return to The Flame for the food if nothing else.

Verna doubled as the cashier. Carver stood up from the table and picked up his check, which somehow had gotten wet at one corner in the way of restaurant checks, and limped over to where the register sat on the counter. The restaurant floor was waxed linoleum, tricky to walk on with the cane.

When she sensed him standing there, Verna turned from the grill she was scraping with an oversized iron spatula and wiped her hands on a towel. She looked at the check. Close to him now on the other side of the counter, she gave off a soapy but vaguely musky scent that cut through the restaurant's smells of fried grease and perked coffee, like a perspiring athlete not long after her shower.

"Can I still get an airboat ride outside of town?" Carver asked.

"Not anymore," she said. "Three seventy-six with tax."

"I rode an airboat here about a year ago," Carver went on. "I remember you from then."

She raised her head and gave him a neutral, distant look. "My dad used to take tourists out on those rides. He's dead now."

"I'm sorry," Carver said, and laid a five-dollar bill on the counter. "An accident?"

"Heart attack." The neutral expression remained.

"Hearts cause a lot of grief. Sometimes I think it would be better if people had been designed without them."

Verna said nothing as she counted out his change. Then she told him, "Thanks, come again" in the voice of an automaton, and she laboriously resumed scraping the grill. Her efforts made a sound he could feel in the edges of his teeth.

Carver left a tip for Emma and went outside to his car.

He'd driven halfway back to the motel, along the tree-lined narrow road, when the Olds's front end dipped and it tried to veer to the right, down an embankment and into the swamp.

Carver yanked the steering wheel left and the car crossed the road and almost plunged down the other embankment. It had developed a yen for an accident. It bounced, skidded, fishtailed, a vehicle with a mind of its own, bent on suicide.

He wrestled the slick steering wheel, feeling it slip in his sweaty grasp.

Finally he braked the big car to a stop, half off the right shoulder of the road, and switched off the ignition.

After sitting still for a few minutes, calming down, he got out and stared at the flat right front tire. There was no clue as to what had made it suddenly lose air. He probed the misshapen tire with the tip of his cane, as if checking for signs of life. The faint scent of heated rubber wafted up to him.

Though it was still late morning, the sun and dampness were of the intensity that sapped the energy from a man changing a tire on a dusty road. Or from one thinking about changing a tire. Carver already felt half melted and unenthusiastic. But there was very little traffic on the road, so the odds of being able to flag down a car, so he could ask the driver to send back a mechanic to change the tire, were long.

The clouds of insects that had invaded the motel were there, too. Carver brushed away one of the insistent little bugs as it buzzed around his mouth and tried to flit up a nostril. Then he sighed and walked around to open the trunk and see if the spare still held air; he hadn't checked it in months.

He was about to insert the key in the trunk lock when a car rounded the bend, slowed, and pulled onto the shoulder a hundred feet beyond the Olds. It was a plain white Ford Escort, the kind used frequently for rental cars in the area. When it stopped, its cloud of dust caught up with it, and the driver waited until the haze settled before opening the door.

A young Latino got out of the Escort. He was wearing a red short-sleeved shirt and dark blue, grease-stained pants. Maybe he was a mechanic. He gave a movie-*bandito* smile beneath a drooping, ragged mustache as he approached Carver. His teeth were bad. His dusty feet were clad in leather sandals that flopped wildly as he walked, yet he moved very gracefully.

"Trouble, hey?" he said. He looked both ways on the deserted road.

"Flat tire," Carver said. "I think the spare has air in it."

The man nodded, still smiling. Pancho Villa with charm. His dark eyes took in the cane and Carver's stiff left knee. He reached beneath his shirt and drew out a long folding knife, the sort used to cut produce. Metal clicked on metal as, with a deft twist of his wrist, he flipped the knife open. The blade caught the sun.

He was no stranger to knives. This one nestled like a deadly pet in his right hand.

Holding the gleaming blade straight up and far out in front of him at eye level, as if it were a mystical object magically drawing him forward, leading him where it wanted him to go, he began to move in on Carver.

CHAPTER 15

C arver said nothing as the man came toward him. He waited for a demand for his wallet but got only silence. The man kept advancing, not smiling now, in a slight crouch and holding the knife expertly with the experienced knife fighter's peculiar deadly daintiness. He was suddenly all grim business. He wanted to finish what he'd started; another car might come along at any time. What he'd started wasn't robbery, but murder. He wanted to lose the long blade in Carver.

Behind the man, far away above the swamp, a large bird was slowly circling, looking for prey. For some reason it drew Carver's eye, a figure in the scene in which he was trapped, but so distant, out of danger.

The man's advance became slower, more cautious; he was almost within killing range. Life and death here. It made sense to be careful, even with a cripple.

Years ago on the force Carver had learned from a veteran cop how to use a nightstick not as a club but as a lethal jabbing instrument. A cane should be even more effective than a nightstick. Or so Carver tried to convince himself through his fear, waiting for the young Latino to pounce for the kill.

A cripple deserved some respect, but not much, said the expression on the man's intent face. There wouldn't be much sport to this, so he might as well go right for the heart. It was survival time. Carver decided it was nice to be underestimated.

The man bent low at the waist, holding the knife well out in front of him. His arms were skinny but muscle-corded; his body was wiry and he moved neatly and economically on the balls of his feet. He had a matador's meticulous balance and calm instinct for death.

Carver backed a step and made a deliberately feeble attempt to knock the knife away with the cane. The man drew back his arm easily, swelled with confidence, and stepped in fast for the kill.

Surprise. This time the cane snapped up off the ground, flinging dust with it. Its tip found the soft space just beneath the startled man's sternum. Carver ignored the knife and eternity and drove the point of the cane hard into the man's chest; he heard the loud *whoosh* of air explode from shocked lungs, saw spittle arc in the sunlight.

The man staggered back a few steps, almost fell. Surprise and rage contorted his face, along with the sickly expression of someone struggling to regain his breath.

He came at Carver again, more hunched over now rather than bent in a knife fighter's classic stance. Carver crossed him up and struck with the cane instead of jabbing, laying the hard walnut across the side of the man's face and quickly withdrawing the cane before it could be grabbed. That made the man pause, and Carver whipped with the cane and knocked the knife from his hand, maybe breaking the Latino's wrist.

But the man gave no sign of pain. His hissing breath broke for a moment, then regained its relentless rhythm, was perhaps louder.

The Latino was game. He picked up the knife with his left hand and came again. Carver jabbed at him, missed. The man twirled like a dancer and rushed him. Carver let himself fall to the left, dropping to the ground to avoid the slashing knife blade, and as the man flashed by him he hooked a bare ankle with the crook of his cane, held on tight against the sudden yank of checked body weight. The slippery walnut cane sprang alive and tried to fly from his perspiring fingers, then suddenly lost its life-force and became once more inanimate.

There was no scream. No sound other than the scuff of a sandal in the dirt. Abruptly, the man with the knife was gone.

At first Carver didn't understand what had happened. Then he used his arms to scoot to the road shoulder and the edge of the embankment. He looked down.

The man lay sprawled on his back in black shallow water at the base of the embankment. Somewhere during his roll down the slope, he'd taken his own knife high in the stomach. Probably, as he'd continued to roll, the blade had slashed around inside him, caught the heart. His hand was curled around the knife as if he'd tried to remove it before he'd died. The red shirt and blue pants were twisted on him, making his limp body seem thin and childlike, harmless. As Carver watched, something long and green—a snake? lizard? the man's soul?—slithered quickly away into the lush foliage, fleeting as an illusion.

Carver gripped the cane and stood up. He was trembling so violently that he had to lean against the sun-heated metal of the Olds to keep from falling back down. The fetid, rotting scent of the swamp almost overcame him, sending waves of bitter nausea through him. He swallowed, hearing phlegm crack in his dry throat. *The man had tried to kill him.* For what? For his money? his wristwatch and ring? for pleasure?

Beneath the Florida tropical sun, Carver was sweating beads of ice. He'd never killed anyone, not as a cop or as a private detective. Hadn't come close to it. That kind of thing done with light consequence was for books, television, and movies. Having killed the Latino was going to take some hard getting used to.

A steady, pulsing sound helped to calm him, as if his wildly hammering heart were adjusting its pace to it. He realized then what he heard. The white Escort's engine was still idling; he could see the car's whiplike antenna vibrating.

Now what?

Carver had heard about small-town southern police. They were tough, bureaucratic, and suspicious. The man he'd killed might have been a local, popular, never known to get in trouble. One of those with a dark side known only to himself and briefly to his victims. How could Carver explain this to Armont? Or should he try to explain?

Why not? he asked himself. He hadn't done anything wrong, God damn it! The man had tried to kill *him*. He, Carver, had nothing to hide or fear! He reminded himself of some of the rape victims he'd seen, the wronged and ravaged, uncomprehendingly wondering at their guilt.

It was all emotion, had nothing to do with logic.

But he could change the tire, get in the Olds, drive away, and his part in the man's death probably would remain unknown. The prospect was tempting, but Carver couldn't bring himself to run from the awesome finality of having killed a man. That would make it worse for him somehow, even if he was never suspected.

Carver realized that his hands were shaking. He felt cold. He glanced to the side of the road where the man had gone over the embankment and his mind flashed on the lifeless face, the unseeing but infinitely wise flat eyes staring up at him.

Carver reminded himself that he'd been a cop in a city with problems. He was supposed to be used to that kind of thing. But how many cops, of the public or private variety, ever actually killed someone?

He again felt the desire to change the tire, climb into the Olds, and get out of there. But he resisted it. He began to feel better. The trembling had passed; his hands were steady now.

Ten minutes later, a pickup truck loaded with jagged sections of broken concrete came laboring around the bend. Carver flagged it down, stood in the dust and told the shirtless kid behind the steering wheel there had been an accident and that a man was dead, and asked him to drive into Solarville and send the police.

Then he spat grit from his mouth, sat down on the hard ground in what little shade the Olds provided, and hoped he'd done the right thing.

High and far away, the large bird was still circling above the swamp, its arced wings fixed to the wind.

CHAPTER 16

C arver was free to leave Solarville police headquarters late that afternoon. Armont had waited for the coroner's preliminary report and lab findings before speaking with him. The chief didn't like somebody coming into his quiet if corrupt little town and causing problems. Not that he seriously thought Carver had murdered the Latino, but problems of the sort that were raised could lead to problems of another sort. And Armont didn't need more problems of any sort.

"We snooped around and found the dead man's clothes and identification in a locker at the bus station," he'd said to Carver, when Carver had sat down before Armont's desk. Armont remained standing behind the desk, absently rubbing his protruding stomach with his left hand, as if he suspected he might give birth to something he had grave doubts about. "His name was Silverio Lujan. He was a Marielito."

Carver knew about Marielitos. In 1980 Castro emptied the prisons and mental institutions of Cuba and sent the inmates, along with legitimate refugees, in the boat lift from Mariel harbor in Cuba to Florida. Only a small percentage of the Mariel refugees were Marielito Banditos, as the press called them for a while. But their numbers were in the thousands.

Some of them never were set free on American soil. And many of them had been returned to Cuba by agreement with Castro in 1985. But thousands remained in the United States, and they were criminals of such fierce nature that even the hardest homegrown criminals feared them in or out of prison. It hadn't taken long for the Marielitos to become deeply involved in drugs, prostitution, and murder.

Murder.

"Why would a Marielito try to kill me?" Carver asked.

Armont stopped massaging his stomach paunch and let both hands drop to his sides, as if suddenly they had become unbearably heavy. "Maybe somebody hired him. He did an expert job of driving a honed piece of steel into your tire, so it would go flat suddenly in a short distance when the metal worked its way loose. Nifty. Or maybe he wanted to rob you."

"He never asked for money," Carver said.

Armont sneered. "Hah! Why should he ask? You might deny him the pleasure of slicing your guts out. You don't know these Marielitos, Carver. Not the ones that stayed in southern Florida, anyway."

Carver thought that some of the Marielitos he'd dealt with in Orlando weren't the sort you'd want your maiden aunt to date, but he said nothing.

"This Lujan might have just felt like killing somebody today," Armont said. He wanted to believe that, Carver knew. That would be the simplest explanation for him.

And maybe it was the most likely explanation. Carver hadn't been in town long enough for Lujan to take a bus in, rent a car, and try to do a contract murder. Unless Lujan had been following him before he'd come to Solarville.

"What bus did he arrive on?" Carver asked.

"No bus," Armont said. "He drove. He rented the car five days ago in Miami under another name with forged identification. It looks like he didn't expect to be in town long enough to have to get a motel room, so he set up housekeeping in a bus-station locker."

"Do you know when he got into town?"

Armont shook his head. "There's no way to pin down the time. Even come close. But I know what you're thinking. I had my men ask around; nobody remembers seeing him earlier, either in town or around the Tumble Inn before the fire."

"What about priors?"

"Lujan's got a record of playing with knives in Miami. But the police there don't have anything on him before 1981. And there's no way to know his background in Cuba. He cut up a few people seriously in Miami, though; seems he was one of those guys fascinated by sharp steel."

"Which is why he might have tried to kill me just for sport."

"Exactly. He's killed for sport before, even though he managed to avoid prosecution." Armont suddenly dropped into his desk chair and sighed, as if some silent signal had allowed him finally to take his weight off his feet. "You probably know that some Marielitos have tattoos on the webbing between the thumb and forefinger. Lujan's tattoo was of an arrow and the word *madre*. That's 'mother' in Spanish, but to a Marielito that tattoo signified that Lujan's specialty was murder. His mother probably wouldn't claim him. He was fond of killing."

Carver had gathered that, on the road outside of town. "Any drug arrests on Lujan's record?" he asked.

Armont arched an eyebrow at him. "Sure. Cocaine possession. I'd be surprised if there hadn't been any narcotics charges against a hard-ass guy like Lujan. Against any Marielito." Armont shifted to the side in his chair and frowned. "Funny you should mention drugs. There's a DEA agent named Alex Burr who's coming into town tomorrow to talk with you. I'm supposed to tell you to be available."

Carver had seen the Orlando police work in conjunction with the Drug Enforcement Administration. It was a federal organization formed for the express and vital purpose of winning the government's declared war on illicit drugs and the people who sold them. And the DEA had slowed the flow of narcotics coming into the U.S. by ship or plane, though the width and density of that flow was such that it could be temporarily lessened but not stemmed. Carver didn't like the idea of talking to a government agent. They had a knack for stuffing things into cubbyholes where they didn't fit.

"What's the DEA got to do with this?"

Armont shrugged his muscle-bunched shoulders. "Federal. You know how they are. They got ways of finding out things almost before they happen. Sometimes they even *make* them happen. And the DEA is all over Florida these days, what with the government's war on drug trafficking. Florida is where it's happening, all that coastline, the little inlets and islands where boats can go without being seen, where drugs can be transferred. Most of the drug game is played south of here and along the coasts, but to the DEA Florida is a war zone. All of Florida."

Carver took a chance. "I've heard narcotics crops are grown in this part of the state."

Armont grinned at him. Carver didn't like the grin. "I've heard that too, Carver."

"The Malone brothers have been mentioned in that context."

The grin stayed. "You'll have to ask them about that. I already have asked; it'll get you nowhere."

"Maybe the rumors are only that."

"Tongues do wag of their own accord," Armont said.

Carver thought now seemed a good time to go, if he was still free. He stood up. "Will you let me know if you learn anything more about Lujan?"

"Sure," Armont said. "And you let me know what you learn." He seemed to dismiss Carver from his mind and bowed his head to size up the paperwork that had accumulated on his desk while he'd been delving into attempted murder. Carver remembered how the chief had wielded his pen viciously on the last visit. Judging by the sour expression on his wide face, Armont didn't care for paper. Crinkly, irritating stuff. He gave the impression that any second he might wad it all up in one big ball and toss it aside.

Carver set his cane, leaned on it, and headed for the door. It would be good to get out into the free, hot air.

"Make sure you stick around for this Burr character," Armont said behind him.

After leaving police headquarters, Carver walked down the street to Wilt's Shell Station, where his car had been towed. Wilt was there, full of grease and gab. He tried without luck to sell Carver a new set of radial whitewalls. Carver put the cost of the tow and tire repair on his Visa card, then drove from the station.

On the way to the Tumble Inn, he began thinking about the expression on Lujan's face when he'd come with the knife and the gleaming dullness of death in his eyes staring up from the swamp. Sudden death always carried with it surprise and a hint of prophecy. When Carver drove past the point on the road where it had all happened, his hands began to tremble on the steering wheel. It took a few minutes for them to be still.

He parked the Olds by his room, then walked back across the parking lot to cut through the lobby to the motel restaurant. He needed something to eat, and a couple of cold beers.

The swamp seemed to loom around him, dank and threatening, full of life, full of death. None of it subject to reason. There were eyes watching from the black shade beneath the moss-draped trees. And eyes not watching. Eyes like Lujan's.

When Carver entered the Tumble Inn lobby, he saw Edwina sitting on the stiff vinyl chair near the desk. She was wearing a white blouse and a pastel yellow skirt and had her long, nyloned legs crossed. The air-conditioning in the humid lobby was fighting a losing battle, but Edwina looked cool as a glacier queen on her throne. She sensed him near her and looked up from the tattered *Newsweek* she'd been reading. The magazine had a photograph of a marijuana plant on its slick cover.

She said, "I hope you've kept busy."

CHAPTER 17

After Edwina had checked in at the Tumble Inn, Carver took her to dinner at The Flame. They sat in a booth near the back, where they could see the regular customers, and the few tourists who'd been driving through and stopped to eat. The place was crowded; Carver noticed that most of the regulars—easy to spot by their casual clothes and familiarity with the waitresses—were having the Seminole Sizzler steak special.

There was a boisterous conversation among half a dozen men at the counter over the relative merits of different types of shotguns. It interested Carver because two of the men had been referred to as Sean and Gary. The Malone brothers. They were short, muscular men with similar strong, handsome faces. Sean was the heavier of the two, in his mid-thirties, about five years older than Gary, who told everybody to hell with shotguns, he was a good enough shot to use a rifle; shotguns were for blind men and pussies. Both Malone brothers had amused blue eyes, and noses that seemed to have been broken several times and never set. Sean dribbled his beer when he drank, and he laughed a lot with an annoying, nasal giggle; Gary's remark about blind men and pussies ranked high on his list of things funny.

"Is this the best place in town to eat?" Edwina asked.

"It is for us." Carver sipped his water, which was cold but tasted as if it had been pumped straight from the swamp. "This is where Sam Cahill has some of his meals. Besides, you might be surprised by the food and service here."

"I thought you were watching Cahill on the sly, to see if Willis contacted him," Edwina said. She sniffed her water, turned up her nose. City girl.

"I was," Carver said. "But there's no point in that now. He knows I'm in town, why I'm here." Carver told Edwina everything that had happened since he'd arrived in Solarville. She leaned forward over the table, her expression serious, when he got to the fire that had almost asphyxiated him, then the murder attempt and the death of Silverio Lujan. He found it disturbingly gratifying to see the concern in her eyes.

"But maybe none of this has anything to do with Willis," she said. She wouldn't let go. Willis didn't deserve her.

"Maybe not," Carver said, "but it would be quite a stretch of coincidence if it didn't. Cops, present or former, don't believe in coincidence. Except for Chief Armont. He believes hard. It's a prerequisite for his job."

"Sam Cahill will recognize me if he comes in here," Edwina said. "We worked together for almost a year at Sun South."

"It doesn't matter. It might be interesting to see his reaction when he notices you."

A waitress Carver hadn't seen before approached the table and asked if they were ready to order. Edwina asked for a tuna salad sandwich. Carver played it safe and ordered the steak special. The waitress, a very tall woman with dark hair and elongated, horsey features, tucked her order pad into her belt and walked off. Carver didn't see Emma, but Verna Blaney was working behind the counter, passing orders back to the kitchen. When the tall waitress handed her their order slip, Verna glanced over at Carver and Edwina blankly, then looked away. The scar on the side of her face and neck flushed fiery red.

"Maybe Sam Cahill is just what he appears to be here," Edwina said. "He might be selling real estate, trying to line up financing for the subdivision the police chief mentioned." A thought startled her. "You're not suggesting that Willis is going to back him with the supposedly stolen money, are you?"

"No," Carver said. "A hundred thousand dollars might help procure financing, provide collateral for the first installments. But I don't think Cahill intends to build anything in or around Solarville."

"Why not?"

"Cynical me, I guess. And I don't see people lined up to live in the swamp." He took another sip of water. "I'll take my cynicism further. We can't be sure anything going on in Solarville involves Willis. We stepped into something nasty and dangerous, but it could be unrelated to what we're after. However, since they're so friendly, if it involves Cahill, it might very well involve Willis. Or it might only involve those two muscle-headed types at the counter. The Malone brothers. They're reputed to be active in drug smuggling."

"They don't act like they have enough sense to know which end of a joint to light," Edwina said.

Carver had to acknowledge that point. It had been bothering him, too.

"Maybe they're working for somebody."

"Not for Sam Cahill," Edwina said. "It's not his style to get involved with that sort."

"Is it Willis's style?"

She appeared uneasy. "I don't think so. But I'm getting surprised a lot about Willis, aren't I?"

Carver looked across the table at the agony in her eyes. He wanted to reach across and squeeze her hand, wanted to hold her, reassure her. Wanted to kick Willis Davis where it hurt for doing this to her.

Emotion, he warned himself. Don't let it get in the way of

your life, your judgment. Remember your children you seldom see, Anne and Fred Jr. Remember Laura, how it felt when she left. Not again. Not yet, anyway.

"Sorry to keep you all waitin'," a voice said. The tall waitress with their supper. She set dishes and glasses about on the table quickly and expertly, then loped away.

The tuna salad sandwich looked okay. At least some small thing was going right for Edwina. Carver took a bite of his pan-fried steak. He understood why the special was popular at The Flame, and why he'd never be a gourmet like a P.I. he'd met in Boston.

The Malone brothers finished drinking beer and arguing about guns and swaggered out. The place was much quieter in their absence, and the food tasted better.

"The waitress behind the counter," Carver said, "the one with the scar on her face. She and Cahill had a thing going, I'm told. Or at least they had a strong friendship."

Edwina lowered her sandwich onto her plate and turned slightly to study Verna. "I'd bet on friendship," she said. "This isn't a criticism of the girl, but it isn't like Sam Cahill to be with a woman disfigured that way. He prides himself on perfection. The kind of guy who suddenly runs outside to buff a smudge from his car. He sees his women as having to pass inspection, like all the rest of his possessions. They're reflections of himself, or how he sees himself."

"Maybe," Carver said, "but who knows about love?"

"Who knows?" Edwina repeated. She swallowed, not tuna salad.

"Cahill seems to be putting on the outdoorsman act here," Carver said.

Edwina shrugged. "Sales technique, probably. Cahill will do whatever he has to in order to swing a deal. He enjoys that part of the business, fancies himself a manipulator of people."

Carver took another bite of steak, wondering how Edwina could see Cahill so clearly, but not see Willis.

"How's your sandwich?" he asked.

"Like the rest of Solarville. Tolerable."

Carver kept quiet and chewed.

Sam Cahill didn't come into The Flame that evening. After supper, Carver and Edwina drove back to the Tumble Inn in the Olds with the top down. The heat of the night was moderated by the breeze that whipped around the windshield and rushed back to splay Edwina's dark hair across her cheeks and forehead. In the constant flow of wind she looked oddly like a beautiful woman underwater, drowned and alone. When Carver slowed the Olds to take a curve in the road, the breeze lessened and the close scent of the swamp crept in for a few seconds, until he built up speed again. The secret of life: keep moving.

"We might as well leave here tomorrow," he said, glancing over at Edwina. "If Willis was here when I arrived, he isn't anymore."

"Why not tonight?" she asked, as if she were afraid.

"A DEA agent named Burr wants to talk to me about Lujan."

"Drugs," Edwina said. "They think everything in Florida is drugs."

"If you want to return to Del Moray tonight, you could get your rental car back and drive," Carver said. She had left her Mercedes in the shop in Del Moray for service. He was afraid of the same thing she was; he wanted to make it clear to her that it made no difference to him if she drove back to Del Moray alone, tonight, without him.

She seemed to consider the idea. Then she said, "No, that would be stupid. We're both going in the same direction, and my room is already paid for."

As Carver turned the Olds onto the Tumble Inn's parking lot, a black Lincoln coming out braked to make room for him, then turned left on the highway, traveling away from Solarville. The Lincoln's windows were tinted, but not so darkly that Carver didn't notice that the driver was the three-piece-suit type he'd seen earlier in the Tumble Inn restaurant, and his passenger, sitting as far away from him as possible on the front seat, was the executive-tailored blonde woman who'd been with him. Off to new diversions, Carver thought, wondering how it would be to have that kind of money, that kind of leisure. Lately he'd found himself envying other people too often.

He parked the Olds halfway between his room and Edwina's.

Neither of them moved to get out of the car right away.

"Do you want some coffee?" Carver asked. "Or a drink in the hotel lounge?"

"No, it's late. I'm tired." The car's engine ticked, cooling.

For the first time Carver realized it was almost ten o'clock. They'd had a late supper, sat longer than he'd planned in The Flame. Against the dark sky, a huge full moon was plastered like a decoration at a dance, low on the haze above the swamp. Night insects were screaming as if they were dismayed about the world in general.

"What time are we leaving tomorrow?" Edwina asked.

"I don't know. I'll call you after I talk with Burr."

She worked the chrome handle, started to push open the door to get out of the car. Carver's hand was on her shoulder before he knew it had moved, feeling the sharpness of bone and the warmth of flesh beneath the crisp white material of her blouse. There was something desperate in the action. She twisted on the seat and looked at him, confused and a little angry in the moonlight.

"Not a good idea," she said. "Wrong." But her own hand rose and her fingertips brushed the side of Carver's face, so lightly he might have imagined it.

She got out of the car and he watched her walk to her door. She unlocked it and went inside without looking back.

Carver put up the canvas top on the Olds, then went to the Tumble Inn lounge and sat nursing one beer for almost an hour, listening to an unbroken string of sad love songs wafting from unseen speakers. It was almost as if the bastards who'd set up the music knew.

Not a good idea. Wrong.

131

He didn't feel like sleeping. But he didn't feel like sitting there and drinking and feeling mawkish any longer either, so he left the lounge and walked back across the parking lot to his room, listening to the solemn sound of his soles crunching on gravel, the growling drag of his cane.

It took as much willpower as he'd mustered in years not to stop and knock on Edwina's door.

But she was waiting for him in front of his door. So much for willpower.

He touched her shoulder and she came to him, clung to him. He bowed his head, sought her eager mouth, found it with his own. Her grip on him tightened, and her body writhed tight against his.

Somehow he managed to fit his key into the lock.

CHAPTER 18

The next morning, Carver studied Edwina over the rim of his coffee cup. She kept her eyes averted from him, her gaze downcast. She wasn't wearing makeup; her face was fresh-scrubbed and her eyes were puffy. Her dark hair gave off a faint, clean perfumed scent and was drawn back from her forehead, parted and combed oh so neatly. She was wearing a denim skirt and a tailored blue pinstripe blouse, no jewelry. She might have been a nun in street clothes.

But Carver remembered her fierce and desperate softness of the night before. He'd been awkward at first, with his lame leg, having to support and lever himself carefully with his good knee and his arms. But within a few minutes Edwina had made him forget all about the leg, about everything but her. Her intensity had amazed and delighted him, taken him away. His own intensity had shocked him. She was like a hand grenade tossed into his mind.

But now it was Willis Davis again. He could see that. Or was it something more than Willis?

How had she viewed the night before? As a lapse, a temporary surrender to desire? An unfortunate, never-to-be-repeated interlude?

Carver knew that now he had every reason to find Willis Davis, to lay Willis to rest alive or dead in the mental landscape of Carver's relationship with Edwina. Otherwise Willis would continue to haunt them, to sour what could be between them. Willis was one of the world's spoilers, all right. Carver disliked him more than anyone he'd never met.

"I'd use your toothbrush," Carver said.

Edwina stared at him. "What?"

"That's the test of true intimacy, if you'd use your partner's toothbrush."

She didn't smile. "That's disgusting. And you've already brushed this morning. Finish your coffee."

They sat for a while without speaking in the cool motel restaurant. It was as if the night before had been cut from the calendar. Carver stared out the window at the cloudless sky, the morning heating up in the glare of slanted sunlight. At the edge of the swamp beyond the parking lot, Spanish moss and vines seemed to drip from the trees as if the branches were melting in the sun. Carver looked at his watch. Nine-thirty. Alex Burr had phoned half an hour ago. Carver was to meet him in town at eleven. He had time to kill; he knew how he wanted to kill it.

"Do you want to take a walk?" he asked Edwina.

"No, I'll stay here for a while."

The implication was clear: Carver could take a walk. Alone. Down love's rough road. With a pang of jealousy, he remembered how, the night before, she had called him Willis without realizing it.

He thought he'd better not push Edwina any further. When the waitress wandered by, he waved her down and had her refill both coffee cups. Edwina didn't look up, absently added cream and sugar to her coffee, and stirred. She seemed listless, somewhat confused beneath her brittleness.

"What are you going to tell Burr?" she asked.

"Whatever he wants to know. He'll probably have the answers to everything he's going to question me about anyway, or he wouldn't ask. It's the way the feds work."

"That doesn't make sense."

"Think of your tax form."

Daninger walked past the restaurant entrance from the lobby, looked in, and smiled tentatively at Carver. Everything was all right now, the smile said. Wasn't it? Carver hoped Daninger didn't come into the restaurant for added reassurance that the legal profession wasn't going to pounce on him.

Outside the window, along the line of ground-floor rooms, Carver saw Curt, wearing jeans and a gray T-shirt lettered *Slow Is Better*, sauntering along carrying a gas-powered weed trimmer. Carver wished people would run out of things to say on T-shirts.

"Do you think I should be there when you talk to Burr?" Edwina asked.

"No. I might be able to learn something from his questions. And he might not ask the same questions if he knows the extent of your relationship with Willis. DEA agents have the suspicious minds of witch burners who've been to college."

"You mean he might think I know where Willis is."

"He might. On the other hand, he might take the official view that Willis is dead. It's Silverio Lujan who drew DEA attention. He was a Marielito who died an unnatural death. To the government, that means narcotics."

"I know Willis wouldn't be mixed up in drugs."

"You might be right."

The weed trimmer kicked into life behind the motel and began to chortle and buzz, like a gigantic insect in the swamp making determined passes at its prey. The wavering sound made the heat outside seem thicker, palpable as clear, still water.

Edwina stood up without having touched her fresh cup of coffee.

"Where are you going?" Carver asked. There were things he

wanted to say to her, even though she wouldn't listen. He preferred having her around in case she changed her mind.

"To my room. To pack, to rest, to think."

He watched her walk from the restaurant. He didn't ask her what she was going to think about. He knew. Willis.

Carver thought about Laura. But not for long, and with lessened pain. She was definitely alive and had made it abundantly clear that she no longer wanted or needed him. Not like Willis and Edwina. Emotional ties had been cut, the loose ends knotted. That was the critical difference. Finality.

He sipped his coffee and watched the shadows and sunlight sharpen in contrast on the parking lot.

Alex Burr had borrowed Armont's office to talk with Carver, but he acted as if it were his office. He was a trim and athletic-looking blond man who wore a black eye patch. The patch might have made him a romantic figure ten years ago, but his lean features had become a bit jowly with his forty-odd years, and there was a pouch beneath his visible unblinking blue eye. His hair was straight and professionally styled, worn longish to hide the straps from the eye patch. He'd removed his coat but hadn't loosened his small, neat tie knot. His pants had sharp creases and his white dress shirt was spotless and starched and would do any laundry-detergent commercial proud. He hadn't rolled up his sleeves; that would be giving in to mere heat. He reminded Carver of a middle-aged German duelist lost in time.

But Burr didn't say *Achtung!* or flip his gloves in Carver's face. Instead he stood up behind Armont's desk, smiled, extended a hand, and assured Carver he wouldn't take up much of his time. Carver figured he had probably said that to people who were serving twenty years.

They shook hands, and Burr waited while Carver sat down and rested his cane against the desk.

Then Burr sat down slowly, with an odd familiarity, in

Armont's chair and said, "Do you have any idea why Lujan would try to kill you?"

"No," Carver said. "I was hoping you might."

"Had you had any contact with him before yesterday?"

"Not that I know of."

Burr began to rotate back and forth slightly in Armont's swivel chair, as if it were something he did habitually every day. "We checked on you with the Orlando police. You come out clean, at least on the surface. Lujan doesn't look clean by any standards. He was involved in smuggling schemes and drug dealing in the Miami area since the early eighties. The company he ran with is rough, but no rougher than Lujan. He liked to cut people. He killed before with a knife, we're sure, though we could never nail him. The gang he was with used him to even scores. Nobody knows how many times. He wasn't a big fish, but he was the kind that swam in a big pond and would lead you to larger fish. We've been keeping track of him."

"Then maybe you know what brought him to Solarville," Carver said.

"No, we don't," Burr admitted. His single blue eye blinked in annoyance. There was a sharp intensity about it from its task of doing double duty. "But if we knew what brought *you* here, maybe we could guess about Lujan."

"Was he mixed up in something current around Miami?" Carver asked.

Burr smiled; it made him look positively dashing. "Guys like Lujan are always mixed up in something current. He was a Marielito."

"I thought we'd sent the worst of them back to Cuba last year," Carver said.

"Not the worst and the smartest. They slipped through the net early and set up shop. They're organized. They're into drugs, prostitution, gambling, extortion; the gamut of crime, anything illegal and profitable. But especially drugs. And they're bad people, Carver. Bad beyond belief. Narcotics has always been a rough business, but now it's rougher."

"Do you know who Lujan worked for in south Florida?"

"He worked for whoever wanted somebody killed."

Carver thought about that. This knife for hire. It reduced the odds on Lujan's attack on him being a coincidence, unrelated to his mission in Solarville, almost to nil.

Burr leaned forward and rested his elbows on the desk. "Now, about what brought you to Solarville and led to a dead Marielito. . . ."

Carver told him about everything, including the missing hundred thousand dollars. He had no choice. Burr was federal and not to be crossed. Too many of these guys suffered from the Eliot Ness syndrome.

None of it quite tied in with Lujan. When he had finished talking, Carver sat and watched Burr consider it all. The blue eye caught the light from the window and looked perplexed.

"Lujan might have come here to meet the Malone brothers," Carver suggested. "Snowbirds of a feather. . . ."

"We know about the Malones," Burr said. "Lujan was small-time, but even he wouldn't get involved with a couple of backwater bunglers like the Malones."

"Big oaks from little yokels grow," Carver said.

Burr frowned at him. Apparently he wasn't one for puns or maxims. But that was to be expected: The DEA didn't joke much. "It might be a good idea if you left Solarville," he said. The line about the oaks must have done it.

"I'm planning to, as soon as we're finished with this conversation. There isn't much I can do here now."

"Except maybe finally get burned or stabbed to death."

"Had Lujan ever been a firebug?"

Burr shook his head. "Never. That bothers me." Like Carver, he couldn't quite see the Tumble Inn fire as an accident, even though there was nothing to rule out that possibility.

Each man knew what the other was thinking. "Not Lujan," Burr said. "He liked knives, not flames. What fire does for a pyromaniac, knives did for Lujan."

Carver nodded. He understood. If the motel fire had been deliberate, probably someone other than Silverio Lujan had set it. This was a world of specialists.

"Where are you going when you leave Solarville?" Burr asked.

"Del Moray."

Burr leaned over the desk and gave Carver a white business card with several phone numbers engraved on it in official-looking small black print. "We want to know what you know, when you know it. Understand?"

"Sure," Carver said. He knew there was no need to tell Burr how to get in touch with him. He angled the cane straight down, set the tip, and levered himself to his feet. "Anything else?"

"Not for now."

Carver knew Burr was watching him limp from the office, wondering how a cripple like Carver could have killed a hard-ass Marielito. Wondering a lot of things. Some of them the same things Carver was wondering.

CHAPTER 19

On the road back to the motel, Carver didn't notice the flashing red and blue lights in his rearview mirror. There was too much glare from the sun.

The sudden wail of a siren, abruptly cut off as if a hand had been clamped over a screaming mouth, startled him.

He checked the Olds's rearview mirror and saw a police car inches off his back bumper, its lightbar flashers rotating on its roof but simply not up to overpowering the intense tropical sunlight. Only when the cars passed through dappled shade were the flashing lights even noticeable.

Carver braked the Olds and swerved to the side of the road, feeling the car's right front wheel go off the gravel and sink slightly into marshy ground beyond the shoulder.

The police car had pulled in behind the Olds, as if it had been towed there by a string between the two vehicles. Carver sat quietly and watched it in the mirror.

Chief Armont got out of the car, hitched up his belt, and walked up to lean on the passenger-side door of the Olds. The Olds's canvas top was up; Armont crouched to peer in at Carver.

"Am I going to get a ticket," Carver asked, "or is this just a warning?"

Armont's beefy face was flushed, perspiring. It hadn't taken him long after getting out of the air-conditioned cruiser to break into a sweat. "Neither," he said. "I just want to talk to you. I knew you were leaving, so I figured I could catch you here driving back from your conversation with the DEA."

"I could have hung around your office and waited for you," Carver said. "If it's still your office and not Burr's."

Armont chuckled. "Assertive bastard, ain't he?" He settled down more comfortably with his elbows on the car door, where the window rolled down into it; that would leave nasty grooves in his arms, Carver thought.

"The fact is," Armont said, "I got some information about twenty minutes ago that might interest you. That's why I decided to try to catch up with you here, before you were on the road back north. It concerns our departed friend Silverio Lujan."

"Why don't you get in the car and sit down?" Carver suggested.

Armont shook his head; perspiration dripped from his chin. "Just as soon stand out here." He folded his gnarled hands. "A few days ago the University of Florida called my office. They were worried about a naturalist from their faculty, a Professor Raymond Mackenzie. Mackenzie left last week to spend some time here in the Everglades, cataloging wildlife, or whatever naturalists do. He was supposed to phone a female student of his who he lives with, but he never called. She alerted the university, kept bugging them to inquire and stir up some kind of action. I drove out and found his campsite two days ago. His four-wheel-drive Jeep was parked next to his little camper trailer, but he wasn't there. There were signs that he'd left suddenly some time ago. A rotting, half-eaten meal; the butane cookstove switched on, and out of fuel. Mackenzie hasn't turned up since at his campsite, or been seen by anyone around here."

Carver waited patiently for Armont to get to the point.

"I remembered something from Mackenzie's campsite," Armont said. "Footprints in the soft ground around there. So I drove out this morning and made casts of some of the prints. They match the sandals Silverio Lujan was wearing when he tried to kill you and got dead himself."

Carver sat with his hands on the steering wheel, remembering Lujan coming at him with the knife.

Armont said, "They're the kind of sandals whose soles are made from tire carcasses. The treadmarks are identical."

"They sell a lot of those," Carver said. "How do you know these were Lujan's that made the campsite prints? Were they both B. F. Goodrich, or what?"

"Goodyear, actually. The one with the blimp. But they also have individual distinguishing marks on them. Lujan's sandals made those prints. Whatever happened to Mackenzie, Lujan was out there at some point—during, before, or after. What I want to know from you, Carver, is had you ever had any contact with Mackenzie?"

"I never heard of him until a few minutes ago," Carver said. "From you. Are you telling me you think Lujan killed him?"

"I'm not sure what to think right now," Armont said. "There's quicksand in that part of the swamp south of town. Sinkholes that go down deeper than imagination. A man could have an accident there, disappear for good. Even a trained naturalist like Mackenzie."

"Still," Carver said, "those sandal prints. It's possible Lujan knifed him, maybe in a robbery, maybe for twisted sport, and there's no connection between that and his attempt on my life."

"Yeah," Armont said, "it's possible." He didn't seem to believe it. "Could be we'll never know, with Lujan dead." More perspiration dripped from his chin.

"Thanks for the information," Carver said. He reached over and shook Armont's hand.

Armont stood up straight, so that only his ample stomach was visible out the window. He slapped the canvas top of the car to get Carver's attention. "You take care now," he said, loud enough for Carver to hear.

Carver watched him walk back to the cruiser and get in.

Armont started the car immediately. Its tires kicked up mud and rock as it swerved back onto the road and accelerated past the parked Olds.

The chief tapped the horn and waved to Carver, an oddly wistful good-bye.

Carver sat for a while longer, thinking about what Armont had told him. Something had happened to the naturalist Mackenzie out there in the swamp. Considering Lujan's history with knives, it wasn't at all unlikely that Mackenzie and Carver were simply meant to be fellow victims, by chance and nothing more. Or Lujan might have visited the campsite but had nothing to do with Mackenzie's disappearance.

Coincidence again? Hah!

Carver started the Olds and gunned the engine to free the right front wheel from the pull of the swamp.

It was almost noon when Carver and Edwina drove out of Solarville in the Olds and headed toward the main highway, then north. Not toward Del Moray but toward Orlando. Edwina wanted to get some of her things from Willis's apartment, she'd said. Carver thought she probably wanted to visit the apartment to get a renewed sense of Willis, to make the ghost more real.

They stopped for a light lunch at a truck stop that served free orange and grapefruit juice in paper cups, then continued through the grove country with the Olds's top raised to block the brooding tropical sun. Carver sat disconsolately behind the steering wheel, thinking about the night before and listening to flying insects smack against the windshield and meet sudden, unexpected oblivion.

In the rented Pontiac that followed the Olds were three men, well dressed in expensive if slightly flamboyant fashion, seated calmly in the air-conditioned oasis of the car's spacious blue interior. They were large men, and each had about him the perfect stillness of the truly dangerous, the calmness of the carnivore conserving energy for the kill. Two of the men had been on the boat off the shore near Sun South when Carver was talking to Franks.

The three had spent most of their lives in Cuba. Hard lives, not without violence. They were Marielitos.

The driver, a bulky man with a receding hairline above a peasant's sunbrowned face of blunt angles and planes, was Jorge Lujan. Silverio's brother.

He liked knives *and* fire.

CHAPTER 20

About an hour after lunch they were close to Orlando. The smiling, sunny presence of Disney World began to make itself felt, radiating far beyond the Magic Kingdom. Signs began to give mileage and directions to the land of Mickey and Pluto and the Monorail. Carver stopped and filled the Olds's tank at Gas World. A roadside shop with a display of clocks made from waxed slabs of cypress billed itself as Souvenir World. A produce stand not much larger than a phone booth was Citrus World. In the station wagon in front of the Olds, anywhere from four to six children (they were moving around inside the car too fast to count) all wore oversized mouse ears that kept getting knocked crooked on their small heads. The man and woman in the front seat took turns twisting awkwardly and shouting at the kids. Frantic World.

Willis Davis's apartment was on Escalera Street, in an Orlando neighborhood of newer brick apartment buildings interspersed with older stucco two-story structures with terra-cotta roofs, wrought-iron balconies, and unkempt gardens. Most of the stucco was cracked, missing in spots, its pastel colors faded from the sun. The brick buildings were clean-lined and functional and looked as if they might have been built two hours ago. It was a fascinating juxtaposition of old and new. Willis's apartment was in one of the new brick buildings, on the third floor, front.

He had virtually moved out of the place, long ago. A very fine layer of dust covered everything, evenly settled, like dust on waxed fruit in a bowl. It seemed not so much to make things dirty as to remove their luster, make them something less than real.

The furniture was fairly new, traditional and nondescript. A couple of outdated magazines lay on a round coffee table; a bookshelf near the window held a stereo tape deck and two speakers, and some more magazines, *Time* and *Real Estate Weekly*, stacked in a jumble down below. The wall hangings looked like dime-store prints, and most of them listed sharply in the same direction, as if the building had been tilted slightly by a curious giant, then straightened.

Edwina switched on a lamp to make the place brighter. It didn't help much; the fine dust seemed to absorb the illumination. She looked around, breathed in deeply, then walked toward a hall leading to the bedroom, which Carver could see from where he stood.

Carver found the thermostat and turned it to Cool, then he followed her. Air rushing from a ceiling vent in the hall brushed the back of his neck. "When's the last time the police looked around in here?" he asked.

"Unless they used the landlord's passkey, they were only here the day after Willis disappeared."

Carver thought that was about right. The apartment of a probable suicide wouldn't be subject to as much attention as that of a suspect in a crime. The Orlando police had probably given the place a quick but thorough once-over, searching for a note or anything that had suggested self-destruction.

While Edwina was rummaging through mostly empty dresser drawers, Carver walked around and did some nosing about of his own. Obviously Willis hadn't lived in the apartment for months, and had visited it only occasionally while he was living with Edwina in Del Moray. The medicine cabinet held nothing but a rusty Gillette razor and a dehydrated stick of deodorant. The soap in the tile dish by the bathtub was also dry and cracked. One of the tub's faucets was dripping loudly and steadily; the sort of thing that would get on Carver's nerves if he let it. He bent down and turned the faucet handle tight, but the water still dripped at the same rate.

Carver went into the kitchen, where he could still barely hear the steady *tap! tap! tap!* of water hitting the tub. The refrigerator held two cans of Budweiser and what had once been a tomato. The cupboards contained a sparse assortment of half boxes of cereal and crackers, a few cans of Campbell's soup.

In the bedroom, Edwina was still going through drawers. She'd found a necklace and a pair of black spike-heeled shoes. "We spent some time here before Willis moved in with me," she explained. She checked a bottom drawer and pulled out a wrinkled, man's tie. Holding it high to examine it, she quite consciously caressed it before laying it back in the drawer. Something of Willis.

"Did you expect to find some sign that he'd been here?" Carver asked.

"I don't know. Possibly I did. It would at least tell me that he has some choice in his movements, that he's reasonably well, and whatever danger he might be in has left him still alive."

"If he's in danger."

Edwina shot him a brief glare. She began to speak and then stopped, her lips trembling. She'd been about to defend Willis but seemed to realize that her carefully managed composure might crack under the pressure of emotion.

Carver limped over to the closet and slid open the door. A gray suit with wide lapels was draped over a hanger, out of style. Willis hadn't figured it worth taking with him to Edwina's. The shelf above the hanger bar was empty. Carver went through the suit pockets. They were empty, too.

He walked over to the window, his cane leaving quarter-sized depressions in the plush, rose-colored carpet. For a while he stared down at Escalera Street, thinking. If Willis had anything in his possession he hadn't wanted Edwina to find, he might have left it there in the apartment, well hidden. And if he hadn't been able to predict the precise time when he had to fake his suicide and disappear, whatever might be hidden could still be there. It was possible he'd returned to get it—if there was an "it." But he might not have needed to return for it. The kind of hiding place Carver had in mind was one that wouldn't be uncovered by less than a major police search, perhaps not even by new tenants.

"I'm going to look around," he told Edwina.

"Isn't that what you've been doing?"

"I mean more thoroughly."

"For what?"

"I don't know. Probably there isn't anything to be found. But there are places to hide things, and I might as well check them."

"Another one of those bases that need to be touched?" Edwina asked.

"Maybe home plate," Carver said. "The winning run. Who can tell about Willis?"

He thought she'd reply that she could, but she knew better. She silently checked the drawer in the nightstand.

Carver started with the bedroom. He removed light bulbs to see if anything was hidden in the sockets. Using a dime for a screwdriver, he checked the cavities behind the switchplates. Then he went over the mattress and springs, tested the corners of the carpet to make sure it hadn't been peeled back and replaced, made sure the hanger rod in the closet wasn't hollow.

He found nothing in the bedroom and moved on to the bathroom. By this time Edwina had finished retrieving her things and was sitting patiently on the living-room sofa. All she had found were the shoes and necklace, which were beside her on the cushion. When Carver glanced in at her, she crossed her legs and looked unhappy. He wondered how she'd look in the black spiked heels and necklace, nothing else.

Back to business, he told himself.

Or maybe without the necklace.

The bathroom took only about ten minutes, and yielded nothing of interest other than an unusually large palmetto bug that scurried into the woodwork. Carver moved on to the kitchen. He would do the living room last. Room after room, by the book.

In the kitchen, he had luck. When he removed the access panel to the plumbing, at the back of the cabinet beneath the sink, he discovered a coffee can attached to the water pipes with electricians' tape so it wouldn't fall between the walls.

He removed the can and pried the lid from it.

Inside were a snub-nosed .38 Colt revolver, a clear plastic packet of white powder, and several credit cards, library cards, driver's licenses, and Social Security cards. There was also a folded piece of gray paper.

Carver set the gun aside, opened the packet, and looked closely at the fine white powder. He wet his finger, touched it to the stuff, and tasted a few particles. Cocaine. He resealed the packet and examined the cards. The Social Security cards looked forged and probably were. Maybe Willis had used them to obtain the rest of the phony identification.

When he sorted through the cards, Carver found that they were made out to two names: Arnold Givers and David Verrac. Carver guessed that Givers and Verrac were names pulled from Willis's imagination, or from old gravestones so Willis could contact local government agencies and obtain genuine birth certificates to start the chain of false I.D.s. Building a new identity link by link was easy if you knew how.

Carver unfolded the gray paper. It was a detailed map of Solarville, with an area of swamp south of town neatly circled in red pencil. He refolded the map and put it with the gun.

149

"What's all that stuff?" Edwina asked. She had approached quiet y behind Carver and was staring over his shoulder where he sat on the floor in front of the sink.

"That's a gun," he said, pointing to the revolver.

"I mean the rest of it."

"Ever hear of Arnold Givers or David Verrac?" he asked.

"No."

He gathered everything in his right hand, beneath his right arm, and stood up with difficulty using the cane. Edwina didn't move to help him. He spread out the gun, the cocaine, the map, and the phony identification on the butcher-block counter and watched her step close and peer at the revealing display.

"What does it all mean?" she asked finally.

"It suggests that Willis was up to something you didn't know about. That Solarville was in his thoughts. That he tooted or dealt in coke. And that he used several identities for whatever he did in life. He might be living somewhere now under an assumed name, if he isn't dead. When you get involved with dope, guns, and false identities, usually you're also involved with people whose flip sides are dangerous."

Edwina walked back to the sofa and sat down; Carver watched her through the kitchen doorway.

He returned the can with its contents to where he'd found it, screwed the painted plywood access panel back on, and went into the living room to join her. His good leg was aching from all the straightening and stooping, and the awkward position he'd had to hold under the sink. He was perspiring; the air-conditioning he'd switched on when they'd entered the apartment hadn't caught up with the heat.

"Willis didn't do dope," Edwina said, staring up at him.

"Not in front of you, maybe," Carver said. "Or maybe he didn't do drugs at all but had something in common with people who did." He wondered if the packet in the coffee can might be a sample in a major narcotics deal. A hundred thousand dollars would buy a lot of cocaine or pure heroin near the source. It was all beginning to point that way. Willis Davis dealing in all kinds of dreams, romantic and otherwise.

"Maybe the coke belongs to somebody else," Edwina said.

"Maybe," Carver said, rolling with her optimism.

She stood up, started to pace, then turned to him and said, "God damn it, Carver."

"I'm sorry," he said. "But you should have thought about where whatever I learned might take you. Take us."

Edwina looked away from him. He suspected she was crying. The Willis Davis she knew was dissolving in front of her. Fading like someone who'd never quite existed for her from the beginning. He was too good, and then too bad, to be true. But she couldn't turn loose her idea of him. Drugs? Guns? Fake I.D.? Hidden in his apartment? Not her Willis. Like hell not!

"There has to be a logical explanation," she said, turning again to face him, trying not to think about the actual logical explanation. Her eyes were moist, her mouth soft and unsteady. She bit her lower lip and swallowed. Pressure, pressure. Carver could almost see her shell cracking.

"It might be an explanation you won't like," he said, pushing it. He felt mean now. Let her get a clear look at reality. Shake her past, shake Willis, forever.

Then she was pressed against him, sobbing. He hadn't expected that. He could feel the wet heat of her tears through his shirt.

He stood still and held her close for a long time. Her back and shoulders eventually stopped quaking, then began moving steadily with her regular breathing. She was in control again, but barely, hanging on in a tumult of emotion that might snatch her away again any second.

Carver ran his hand down her back, aware of the firmness of one of her breasts pressing against his side. Firm yet soft. She raised her reddened face, said, "Carver—"

He kissed her. She hesitated, then leaned hard into him. Maybe he was Willis just then, maybe not. He moved his mouth, his tongue, over her tear-streaked face. She clung to him, staring up blankly at him, something deep turning in her eyes.

Carver moved as gracefully as he could with the cane, leading her toward the bedroom. He was breathing rapidly, faintly grinning. Willis's bedroom, Willis's bed, Willis's woman. Carver anticipated the next half hour with perverse pleasure. This is what happens when you play dead, Willis. You wrongheaded asshole. You lose. Big. At least for a while.

But he knew that really he was about to lie down with Edwina and Willis. A threesome. Carver knew that should matter to him more than it did. The hell with it. He didn't care. And right now Edwina didn't seem to care. Maybe this would help to ease the bastard from their lives.

The cane was a hindrance. By the time they reached the bedroom door, she was ahead of him.

CHAPTER 21

It rained hard at three o'clock, but not for long. The sun was out again immediately afterward, making up for lost time, reheating the concrete so that shimmering waves of vapor rose and formed a low, multicolored haze, like a rainbow that had fallen and lost form but hadn't dissolved.

It was much hotter outside than in Desoto's office; the window had fogged up like a medicine-cabinet mirror after somebody's steaming bath. It made Carver feel confined, as if there were no outside world. Nothing except the low and crackling metallic voice of the dispatcher on the radio in the squad room, the clacking of a teletype or printer, the inexorable official stirrings of the law. This was Police World, with nothing beyond.

Desoto leaned back behind his desk, held up a paper clip he'd bent, and stared at it with a kind of wonder, as if it were a piece of surrealistic sculpture. "Have you gotten on better than friendly terms with Miss Edwina Talbot?" he asked.

"You have a dirty mind," Carver told him, shifting in his chair.

"You bet. It's fun. I think of myself as an erotic romantic."

"You think of yourself," Carver said.

Desoto seemed glad that he'd irritated Carver. He smiled. He speculated. "Do you sleep with that cane?" he asked.

Carver glared at him, told himself to calm down. This was Desoto, who had always been like this and wouldn't change until his glands did. If they ever did. Carver suspected he was looking at a dirty old man in the making. Desoto would serve out his time on the force, retire, get collared for lascivious conduct in the park.

"Why do you think this Silverio Lujan tried to knife you?" Desoto asked. No more men-of-the-world talk; time for business. The DEA had been in touch with Desoto.

"Who knows?" Carver said. "He was a Marielito, and a tough one. A guy like that, maybe he just felt mean. Maybe he hadn't stabbed anybody for a while." He told Desoto about the missing naturalist and the matching sandal prints.

"It's possible that Lujan knifed Mackenzie and hid the body in the swamp," Desoto said.

"Some insight," Carver told him. "Have you got anything more on Lujan?"

Desoto shrugged and shook his head. "He only goes back to 1980, after the boat lift. There's no way to get a line on him for when he was in Cuba. He and his two brothers came over here together on the same boat."

"Brothers?"

"Jorge and Alejandro," Desoto said. He pronounced the names with a Spanish flare, made them sound beautiful, not the names of thugs. "Alejandro was killed in gang warfare in Miami."

"What about Jorge?"

"Who can say?" Desoto adjusted his white cuffs. "Marielitos don't notify the post office when they change address. The last anyone seems to have heard of Jorge was when he was arrested for torching a tavern in Daytona. Doused the place with gasoline and set fire to it, customers and all. He'd been in a scrap, got outfought because he was outnumbered, then left and came back fifteen minutes later with a can of gas and a match, mad at everybody. What a sore loser. Fortunately there was a back door to the place, so everyone got out. A few people were burned, one of them seriously. Jorge was tried for the crime, but witnesses declined to testify and there wasn't enough evidence to convict."

"Fire, huh?" Carver said, feeling the ice of fear trickle down his spine. He thought about the night he almost choked to death in his room at the Tumble Inn, the searing pain in his near-bursting lungs, the panic that had threatened to engulf him and deliver him to mindless, agonizing death.

"Fire and knives and guns and piano wire. Anything that kills," Desoto said. "It all fits Jorge Lujan's style. He's probably heard his equally humanitarian brother Silverio is dead by now." Desoto's dark eyes took on a sad seriousness. "*Venganza*," he said. Vengeance.

"You think Jorge might be after me for killing Silverio?" Carver asked. He didn't like to think about being stalked, especially by someone with a compelling reason to kill. A reason that ran in the blood.

"Maybe," Desoto said. "Hot Latin temperament and all that. But not to worry, *amigo*, the DEA will protect you."

"You've met Burr?" Carver asked.

Desoto smiled, white teeth flashing. "Sure, he's the one who filled me in on the notorious Lujan brothers. They have brief but nasty backgrounds in the U.S., Carver. Burr thinks Silverio Lujan was part of a drug scam in Solarville. But then Burr thinks everybody everywhere is part of a drug scam."

"Lujan ran with known dealers and users," Carver said. "According to Burr, that's all part of being a Marielito. But Silverio Lujan and Solarville don't necessarily add up to drugs."

"Marielitos go where there's money," Desoto said, "and there is no more money anywhere in Florida than in drugs. Not illicit money, anyway. So a Lujan in Solarville means money for the Marielitos, a drug deal. It means that to Burr, anyway."

"Burr might be right," Carver said. He told Desoto about the coffee can with the gun, map, false I.D., and packet of cocaine, hidden behind the access panel beneath the sink in Willis Davis's apartment.

"We went over that apartment the day after Davis disappeared," Desoto said. "My men usually check plumbing access panels."

"Not this time," Carver said. "Not for a plain old uninteresting suicide."

"Have you told Burr about this?"

"I thought I'd tell you first, see if you had anything to add. Or subtract."

Desoto touched the heels of his hands together, then meshed his fingers. "No, you better play straight with Burr, *amigo*. He's federal; he can put a permanent kink in your cane. He might be a by-the-book pain in the ass, but he's got us all by the short hairs. And that map with the area marked off in red really might have to do with a drug deal of some kind." He pulled his hands apart slowly, as if a delicate magnetic field that he didn't want to break had developed between them, then leaned farther back in his chair and clasped them behind his head. "Does Edwina Talbot still believe so firmly that Willis Davis is alive?"

"Even more firmly," Carver said. "I think he's alive, myself. Alive and wandering around somewhere with Ernie Franks's money."

"And somebody else's name."

"Which brings me to the main reason I came here," Carver said. "It occurred to me that if Willis used or was prepared to use either of the identities he had stashed in his apartment, he might have been using a false identity when he met Edwina. He might not be Willis Davis." Very carefully he picked up the black attaché case at his feet and laid it on Desoto's desk. "Willis's," he said. "His prints, or at least a good partial, should be on it somewhere, a smooth section of leather, one of the clasps, glossy paper, the calculator that's in here. Match them with his prints, which should be all over Edwina's house, so you know you've got Willis's prints, and run a check on them through the FBI's master file. Maybe we'll discover his genuine identity."

"Such a crafty bastard you are," Desoto said. "So much more clever than the police."

"Not really," Carver said, playing it as straight as Desoto. "It all comes from not regarding Willis Davis as a suicide. I have a different angle of approach. That's an advantage. I'll fix it with Edwina so your fingerprint crew can get in her house."

"Will she cooperate in an attempt to prove her Willis told her another lie?" Desoto asked. "And such a big lie."

"I think so. She wants the truth. At least some of the time. She's come that far."

"Some weaker sex, your Edwina Talbot."

Carver planted the hard rubber tip of his cane and stood up. "Now you know what I know, and soon I'll tell Alex Burr so he'll know."

"Like a child's game, eh, Carver?"

"Only when you win," Carver said. "The losers don't see it as a game." He started toward the door.

"You take care, *amigo*," Desoto said. "What you've gotten yourself into can be dangerous."

"Marielitos are bad-asses," Carver said, "but they're not possessed and protected by the devil."

"I wasn't talking about Marielitos," Desoto said. "They might kill you, but there are slower, more exquisitely pleasurable ways to die."

Edwina again. "Sooner or later, one way or the other, everybody dies," Carver said.

He looked back as he limped out the door.

Desoto was grinning his erotic-romantic's grin.

CHAPTER 22

After leaving Desoto, Carver drove the relatively short distance to the University of Florida and managed to catch the dean of the science department still in his office. Professor Raymond Mackenzie was on sabbatical, the dean said. He didn't know the purpose of Mackenzie's trip to the Everglades, but he assumed it was to gather information for a scientific paper. It was publish or perish in academia.

The university supplied Carver with Mackenzie's address. Carver hadn't mentioned the student Mackenzie was living with; he wasn't sure what the dean's attitude was about that, or even if the university knew that one of its faculty was dallying with a co-ed. That might be perfectly acceptable, or it might be a sticky point with the dean. It all depended on the circumstances.

Mackenzie lived in an apartment development in Catanna, a small town less than an hour's highway drive from the university. Carver was told by the apartment manager which building the professor lived in. Mackenzie's name, along with a Lottie Kenward's, was typed on a white card and slipped into the slot above 2-C's mailbox. Lottie must be Mackenzie's live-in co-ed, probably a middle-aged professor's youth fantasy.

Carver punched the elevator button with the tip of his cane. On the second floor, he went a short distance down the hall and then knocked on the door to 2-C.

Almost immediately he heard movement inside the apartment. He wondered if Mackenzie himself might answer, if he'd for some crazy reason left his Jeep and camping equipment and returned home to hearth and co-ed.

The woman who opened the door was hardly the bubble-gum ingénue Carver had naïvely expected. She was tall, slender, attractive, black, and at least thirty-five. She was wearing a bright blue dress of some kind of silky material that draped gracefully from her wide shoulders.

"I'm . . . uh . . . looking for Professor Raymond Mackenzie," Carver said.

"He isn't here," the woman answered. Her voice was velvet and deep. Her large dark eyes were steady, inquisitive yet guarded. They didn't blink. "Who wants him?"

"Fred Carver. Who am I talking to?"

"Lottie Kenward. I live here. With Professor Mackenzie. He's out."

"I know that he disappeared from his campsite in the Everglades," Carver said. "I'm a private detective, Miss Kenward. It's possible that Mackenzie's disappearance has something to do with a case I'm on."

Breath trailed from Lottie in a soft sigh. She stepped back to let Carver enter.

The apartment was small, but well furnished and clean. Sliding glass doors opened out to a balcony that overlooked the swimming pool. There was a long leather sofa, glass-topped end tables, chrome-framed wall hangings. A stereo was set up unobtrusively in one corner. Everything was modern. In good taste.

"What do you know about Ray's disappearance?" Lottie asked.

Carver leaned on his cane on the soft carpet. "Nothing you don't know, I'm afraid," he said. "He seems to have suddenly gotten up and walked away from his campsite."

Lottie shook her head and sat down on the sofa. She crossed long and elegant legs. "Ray doesn't do rash things like that."

"How long have you known him?" Carver asked.

"Three years. We met when he was in Chicago for a Save the Whooping Crane seminar." She didn't smile.

"You were that interested in saving whooping cranes?" Carver asked.

She looked at him levelly. "Yes. I still am. They're worth saving. I'm interested in most of the things that interest Ray. Except for the swamp; I wouldn't go with him there. It gives me the creeps."

"But he liked the swamp."

"He loves it," Lottie said, neatly changing tenses. "Do you know that there's plant life in the Everglades that can be found nowhere else in the country? Hurricane winds blow the spores over from Cuba and the West Indies. Ray's fascinated by the variety of vegetation there."

"Did he go into the swamp often?"

"No, not really. He was spending most of his sabbatical here, with me, working on his book. He's writing a novel. A mystery. I was doing some of his typing. Then he got the phone call."

"Phone call?"

"Yes. He wouldn't tell me who from. Said he'd explain later. And we weren't getting along, not as well as we thought we would be with all this time together. He told me he was going into the field, somewhere in the Everglades near a town called Solarville. Then he left."

"He didn't tell you why?"

Lottie ran a hand through her mop of black hair and shook her head. "No, he was supposed to phone me from Solarville, but he didn't."

"Are you one of his students?" Carver asked.

"I was last year. My required science course. Four years ago I quit the business world and decided to become a teacher. Just got fed up with all the lying and all the crap and swimming against the current. They make it tough."

"Because you're black and a woman?" Carver asked.

She raised an eyebrow in surprise. "No, I've been black all my life. Female, too. I didn't really experience discrimination I had trouble coping with until I began living in Florida with a white man. Chicago's no cosmopolitan paradise, Mr. Carver, but this place has a way of castigating interracial couples. Stiff-backed, fundamental religion rules down here. Even the places you do business with identify themselves with God. Honestly, some of the people here, their idea of God is like He's president of some celestial chamber of commerce."

Carver thought about Ernie Franks and his crucifixion oath for Sun South employees.

"The way the people in this area, the neighbors especially, looked at us, treated us . . . it put a strain on our relationship that hadn't been there before. A couple of the tenants even paid us a visit one night and hinted that they were Ku Klux Klan members, suggested we move out. Ray got mad and told them he had a shotgun and if they tried anything he'd put holes in their sheets."

Carver was beginning to like Ray. He shook his head slightly. The Klan and Mickey Mouse and drugs and the Bible and sunshine and murder and palm trees. Florida had become some state. "Why do you live here?"

"Ray's work at the university. And the swamp. He's doing ongoing research on its vegetation."

"Ongoing can be a long time," Carver said.

"You're dead right about that."

"Did Mackenzie ever mention my name?"

Lottie thought for a few seconds before answering. "Not that I can recall."

"Do you have a photograph of him?"

She stood up and walked lithely into the bedroom. Carver

could see an unmade bed beyond the door. She walked around it, letting her long fingers drag along the bunched sheets at the foot of the mattress. There was something infinitely sensuous in the gesture. The women men sought and then left. What the hell was wrong with his gender? Carver wondered. What was Mackenzie doing in the swamp instead of here?

Lottie swayed back into the living room a minute later with a photograph of a thin, mustached blond man in his early fifties. He was grinning and touching the frames of his round-lensed glasses, as if he were about to peel them from his head in the manner of people who put on and remove reading glasses frequently. He was wearing a checked flannel shirt and there was a rock formation and some pine trees behind him.

"I took that shot in Colorado," Lottie said, "and had it enlarged."

Carver stared at the photograph. He was sure he'd never seen Raymond Mackenzie or his likeness before this moment.

"Did you try to find out exactly why he was going into the swamp this time?" Carver asked.

She put the photograph down, faceup on an end table. "At first I did. But he wouldn't say. If things had been better between us just then, maybe he'd have told me. But we'd just come from the bank, where he tried to get a loan for a new Jeep. He made the mistake of taking me in with him. The loan officer wanted to know more about me, about us, than whether Ray could afford the payments. Too many of the questions were personal. I excused myself and left. It was no big deal compared to the kind of bigotry that goes on around this place, but Ray was mad at me for not telling off the loan officer. Things had piled up; this happened right after the Klan conversation. Ray and I had an argument. The next day he took the old Jeep and his camper trailer and left. He didn't phone me when he got where he was going. And he never called anyone at the university, either. I kept on them over there, finally got them to get someone in Solarville to investigate. Then I learned that Ray had disappeared."

"Has he ever dropped from sight like this for any length of time before?" Carver asked.

"He's not the type just to up and disappear," Lottie said. "Not even for a few days. He's no adventurer except when it comes to saving whooping cranes or snail darters."

Carver thanked her for answering his questions, assured her the Solarville police were still looking for Mackenzie, and limped toward the door.

"You'll let me know right away if you find Ray, won't you?" Lottie asked. Desperation drew her words taut.

He swiveled his body with the cane and nodded. "The tenants who threatened you and Ray," he said, "do you think they're really Klansmen?"

"Who knows?" she said, shrugging. "They wear hoods when they're out in their white linen jammies. My impression, though, was that they were mostly talk."

Carver wished her luck, and left the apartment.

As he walked toward where he'd left the Olds parked in the shade, he noticed half a dozen tenants lounging around the swimming pool, working on their tans.

CHAPTER 23

C arver was sitting on his porch the next morning, still wet from his swim, watching the sun climb slowly higher as if it needed to gain leverage to bear down and burn the low haze off the Atlantic. It was still too misty to see the wide swells off the coast, but he could sense the waves forming out there, water rising massively as it met the backwash from the shore. And he could hear them roar in with ponderous force to become visible through the mist, showing whitecaps like teeth, hungry for the beach.

The rhythmic, rushing sound of the surf relaxed Carver. He was still breathing a bit rapidly from his swim, and his eyes were half closed as he leaned back in the webbed aluminum chair in the shade of the porch roof.

Everything was under control, sort of. At least put in abeyance for a while. He'd aired out the cottage, watered the plants, and found it easier than he'd anticipated to get back into his therapeutic swimming routine. He'd talked to Desoto and Burr the day before, called Ernie Franks and told him there was nothing substantial to report, and left Edwina preoccupied with catching up on real-estate business. She'd told him there were contracts on two of the houses she had listed, and she was sure she had a client for a third. She hardly had time for Carver. He was pleased to see this healthy streak of greed in her.

There was a soft scuffing sound to Carver's right.

He didn't move as alarm erupted coldly in his mind. The arrangement of light and shadow on the porch changed subtly. His heart skipped and then picked up about twenty beats per minute.

He knew it was better to stay quiet for now, then move fast and surprise whoever was casting the unfamiliar shadow.

With seeming idleness, he closed his fingers around his cane, tensed his body for action. The taste of fear lay heavy and acidic on his tongue.

"You're easy to sneak up on," Alex Burr said.

Carver let out his breath and felt his flow of adrenaline slow. His heart stopped banging against his ribs.

He relaxed his grip on the cane, swiveled his body, scraping an aluminum chair leg on the porch's plank floor.

Burr was standing about five feet from him, just off the edge of the porch. He was wearing a short-sleeved white shirt with a tie and had his suitcoat slung over his shoulder. Probably his idea of dressing down for the beach.

"I was just about to release my dogs on you," Carver said.

For an instant Burr believed him; his single blue eye widened slightly and rolled side to side. Panic glittered there.

Then he smiled and stepped up on the porch. "Been swimming?" he asked.

"Yeah. I go just about every morning."

"For the leg?"

Carver didn't answer. His therapy was none of Burr's business. He hadn't asked Burr about his eye.

"You've got a well-developed upper body," Burr said. "You look strong."

"It got built up dragging around my lower body."

Burr walked over and half sat, half leaned on the wooden

porch rail in front of Carver. He folded the suit coat neatly with the lining turned out and draped it over an arm. It hung like expensive material. "Desoto says you were a good cop who made cases, that you're the tenacious type that always finds the only way possible and then does it. He says it's a flaw in your character."

"He should know about character flaws."

"I don't consider tenacity a flaw."

"You wouldn't."

"And shouldn't," Burr said. "Any leads on Willis Davis?"

"None. Other than the junk stashed in his apartment. But I don't consider that a lead. It doesn't move me any nearer to finding him."

The breeze ruffled Burr's straight blond hair and momentarily revealed the black straps of his eye patch. "It means Willis Davis was no stranger to narcotics."

"Him and fifty million other people."

"That coke you found in the coffee can was rich stuff. As high a quality as I've ever seen, and not cheap."

Carver was getting tired of Burr, and he still resented being sneaked up on. "Nothing points to Willis being a coke snorter," he said, "although the can pretty much confirms he's a coffee drinker."

"I wouldn't worry about him if he were just a snorter, and I'm willing to look the other way from his caffeine habit. But maybe the stuff in his apartment was a sample. Part of what will be a bigger shipment."

"It's possible," Carver admitted. The gun, the red-penciled map, the phony I.D.—none of it sat quite level for Carver, though he wasn't sure why. Burr might very well be right about an impending drug buy with Marielito involvement. "Why didn't you tell me Silverio Lujan had a brother?" he asked.

"I didn't know it at the time," Burr admitted. "It got by us. I'm sorry." He admitted the mistake and apologized with an easy grace. Carver thought a little better of him. Or maybe

Burr was used to admitting mistakes and apologizing, had gotten good at it.

"Will brother Jorge forgive and forget?" Carver asked.

Burr shook his head no; the blue eye was bright as a stalking bird's. "You spilled Marielito blood, family blood. That's why I came here, to warn you and ask if you wanted protection. Someone to watch you, maybe move in with you until this is settled."

"It seems a long way from being settled," Carver said. "You don't even know where Jorge Lujan is, or if he knows his brother is dead."

"He knows by now," Burr assured him.

"I'll live alone," Carver said. "Not that I don't think your protection can be effective. But it has its time limit. And I can't do my job with a DEA man following me around on his scooter."

Burr didn't acknowledge the mild slur tossed at his organization. He turned and gazed out at the rolling ocean. "So many damn miles of coastline," he said. "So many ways to get the stuff in from Mexico or South America. And so many people making so much money the easy way, at other people's expense, off other people's misery." He turned back toward Carver. "You got any ideas on how to stop them?" he asked.

Carver had been put in his place for that scooter remark. He had no idea, short of moving the citizens out of Florida and the U.S. Army in. And probably that would only slow the drug smugglers. "You've got a tough job," he conceded. He held up a hand like a traffic cop warning a speeder to put on the brakes. "But please don't bore me with statistics."

"I wasn't going to. But I think you might have grabbed a thread leading to something big. With more people involved than if this were simply a hundred-thousand-dollar buy."

"Maybe the money's a down payment."

"These folks don't extend credit, Carver. It's all cash up front. That way they don't have to get mad over a deadbeat or bad check and carve up someone. They do business in a very direct way."

Carver knew just how direct. "What do you make of the map?" he asked.

Burr looked up and watched a sea gull glide over the cottage. He obviously wasn't sure how much he should confide in Carver. Finally he said, "My guess is that the red-penciled area on the map is a drop point, where somebody's going to pick up a load of smuggled narcotics."

"Can a boat get that far into the swamp?"

"Maybe. But it might not be brought in by boat. The area circled is large, maybe three square miles. Most likely a plane will drop the shipment by parachute somewhere in the swamp inside the red-penciled area, and whoever's going to pick up the drugs will go by boat to retrieve it. They install electronic signaling devices in shipments delivered that way; a man in a boat can hone in on them with a receiver tuned to the same frequency and go right to the drugs."

"Wouldn't he have to move fast, before someone else might pick up the signal? Someone like you?"

"Sure, but the smugglers have the jump on us; they know the frequency beforehand and the approximate location of the drug drop."

"Sounds risky," Carver said.

"It is risky. So's stocks and bonds and betting on horses and cards and on where bouncing little balls will land on numbered wheels. But people do all those things because the potential payoff can be worth the risk. This is big business, Carver. We might be talking about a multi-million-dollar deal shaping up in the swamp near Solarville. I'm interested in making the potential profit not worth the risk this time around."

"I'm only interested in finding Willis Davis," Carver said. "And speaking of finding people, has Raymond Mackenzie been located?"

"You know about him?"

"Chief Armont told me."

"He hasn't been found yet. I'm aware of where he disappeared from; there might well be a connection with what interests us."

"Or might not be."

Burr straightened up and tucked in his white shirt more neatly. He wasn't a large man, but he was built with compact strength, lean-waisted and with a springy kind of erectness to his posture. Carver wondered if there was military service in his background; he wondered about the eye.

"I lost the eye in Vietnam," Burr said, experienced and sensitive enough to suspect what Carver was thinking. "Stepped on a Claymore mine." He crossed his arms and looked directly at Carver. "What about the leg? How did it happen?"

"A holdup kid's bullet," Carver said. "I got careless. I should have checked the back room in a store that was being robbed. A kid with a gun was back there."

"Don't flog yourself about it," Burr advised.

"I don't," Carver said. "Everybody gets careless now and then, and usually gets away with it. My timing was off."

Screaming and squawking from the beach made both men pause and watch a couple of gulls fight over a dead something that had washed up onto the sand. They watched until one of the gulls flapped away with an object grasped in its beak. The defeated gull flew off in search of easier offerings from the sea.

"The way of life, huh?" Burr said.

"Some lives."

"The way it is in our line of work, with the people we deal with. Maybe the way it is in most lines of work."

Carver wasn't sure about that. He didn't think most assembly-line workers had to worry about being met on the road by a man with a knife. Burr walked over and stepped down off the porch. Carver envied him his two good legs.

"Don't be careless again," Burr cautioned. "You might be onto something bigger than you know. Be on the alert, think before you jump, be careful." He made it sound like a Boy Scout oath.

Carver nodded to Burr and watched him round the corner of the cabin. A few minutes later a car engine about a hundred yards away racketed to life.

As Carver listened to Burr drive up the road toward the coast highway, he understood why the DEA man had parked so far away and come up on the house quietly. He wanted to demonstrate to Carver that his advice was sound. Be careful; you're not as secure as you might think.

Carver decided to be careful. But he knew that being careful wouldn't have made any difference on the road with Silverio Lujan. People like Burr fooled themselves about how much control they could exercise over events. So much of what happened in life, good or bad, was the result of luck. Or if you weren't a gambler, you could call it fate. Carver didn't think it made much difference what it was called; people had to learn to fend it off or roll with it in order to survive.

He went inside out of the sun, sat for a while gazing at the sea beyond his hanging plants, then called Edwina and made a date for lunch.

CHAPTER 24

C arver showered, then dressed in worn jeans, gray sweat-socks, his moccasins, and a black sportshirt with a riotous pattern of colorful tropical birds splashed over it. Edwina had an afternoon appointment to show some citrus-grove property outside of Del Moray, so she and Carver were going to meet where she recommended, a restaurant called Orange We All, on Highway 17 near Sanford.

Orange We All was quintessential central Florida. It was built to resemble a huge half-orange, complete with a stem and artificial leaves on top to hide the air-conditioning unit, and had laughing Disneylike characters painted all around it halfway up.

As he parked the Olds in the crowded lot and saw a family with half a dozen kids tromp into the restaurant, Carver had misgivings about agreeing to Edwina's choice of a place to eat. He liked kids, but he didn't care for the idea of eating lunch within range of a two-year-old's highchair. His own kids, Fred Jr. and Anne, had seen spoons more as launching devices than eating utensils at that age. Carver remembered thinking that was cute, but that had been Fred Jr. and Anne.

Edwina had gotten there ahead of him and had somehow secured a quiet booth near the back of the restaurant. She had on the gray tailored business suit she'd worn when Carver had first seen her, and a large blue leather briefcase was next to her leaning against the back of the seat. The attractive, modern career woman, taking time from her busy schedule to meet someone for lunch. She looked like an ad for *The Wall Street Journal*. What would the conversation cover today? Carver wondered. Missing lovers, the sweet agony of passion, or tax-free municipals?

"Do they serve orange juice here?" he asked, sliding into the seat across the table from her.

Edwina smiled. "And good food. And they see that adults by themselves are seated away from the kids. You shouldn't judge things solely on the merits of their exteriors."

"You and Burr are throwing worldly philosophy at me today too fast to comprehend," Carver said.

She sat forward, interested. "Where did you see Burr?"

"At my place this morning. He wanted to warn me that what we're involved in might be a big drug operation, with accompanying danger. He thinks Willis might be a low-level player in a high-stakes game."

A large-busted young waitress in an orange uniform and wearing a hat with Mickey Mouse ears on it approached the table. A balloon twisted into the shape of some animal Carver couldn't identify bobbed after her with helium buoyancy on the end of a long string attached to her belt. No wonder the place had tourist trade.

Edwina ordered the Dieter's Delite. Carver asked for a hamburger, french fries, and something called an Orange Sloshy.

"I bring clients here sometimes," Edwina said. "I've closed several deals at this table."

"It's probably the Orange Sloshy that gets them," Carver said.

Edwina ignored his wisecrack. She was looking at him with an interest he hadn't seen before in her gray eyes. The intensity of that look scared Carver. It suggested that they had turned a corner. Now their fates were linked. She was a little bit afraid, too, and curious about where this was all carrying them. The three of them, Carver, Edwina . . . Willis. Or was he gradually displacing Willis, becoming what Willis had been to Edwina? Willis the perfect, gentle lover; she'd moaned his name beneath Carver. Carver didn't want to be Willis, not to that extent. Is that where this would end? How it would end?

"He's a thief," Carver said softly. She knew who he was talking about. Willis. Always Willis. "He ran out on you; he didn't have to do that."

"I don't know the circumstances. You don't, either. Maybe he had to leave. Maybe he did it for me." She didn't sound convinced. "I have to give him the benefit of the doubt," she said earnestly.

"He doesn't deserve it," Carver said.

She sighed, toyed with the menu, then placed it back in its metal clasp at the side of the booth, near the miniature orange salt and pepper shakers. "I should have guessed it would go wrong for Willis and me," she said. "There were signs, but I couldn't see them, not knowing what I know now."

"Signs involving drugs?"

"No. Nothing like that. Like the time Ernie Franks caught him going through his, Franks's, desk. That happened right after Willis started working at Sun South. He explained to Franks that he had a customer on the line and needed some information fast on one of the new units, thought he'd find it in a hurry in one of Franks's drawers. Franks believed him; he's kind of a gullible sweet bastard despite the business he's in. I wanted to believe him too. And Willis is convincing. Nobody thought much about it after a while. Then there was the time Willis disappeared."

"Disappeared?"

"Only for a few days, not long before he moved in with me. He stood up some customers, cost the company at least one deal. Franks was furious, but Willis, being Willis, was able to smooth things over."

"How? What did he tell Franks?"

"I don't know, exactly. He told me he had to go to Miami unexpectedly."

"Did he say why?"

"No. Only that it concerned some past business. You see, Willis went to Miami before he and I . . . became close."

"I thought you became lovers before he went to work at Sun South."

"We had." She gazed directly at Carver. "We became close later."

The tone of her voice said it even if the words didn't: The closeness of complete commitment was what had come later, the absorption of self. Desperate love, like in one of the old movies Desoto watched. Some women still thought that way. And men. They shouldn't. Carver had found that out. People continued to buy into that kind of thinking, that kind of love, because they had no choice. The idea made Carver uneasy.

"Maybe when Willis disappeared he saw some people he didn't want anyone to realize he knew," Carver said. "People on the wrong side of the law, in the drug game."

"*Burr* would think that," Edwina said.

The waitress brought their food. On the way back behind the counter, she paused and gave the balloon animal to a squirming preschooler at one of the tables. The kid promptly stuck it with a fork, popping it. Mom frowned. Dad thought it was funny. Family life.

Edwina was right, Carver decided. The hamburger was surprisingly good, the French fries were crisp, and the Orange Sloshy was delicious in its waxed cup.

They ate silently for a while, the way people do when they're hungry and the food is simple and up to taste.

Carver watched Edwina across the table. Her dark hair was carefully brushed and arranged and she was wearing a minimum of makeup. She didn't seem aware that Carver was studying her, but he knew the mask of Edwina could be un-readable. What was the mask hiding? What wasn't she telling him?

"When will you be finished working tonight?" he asked.

"I don't know. Late."

"Do you want to drive up to my cottage when you're free?"

She didn't hesitate; she'd thought about it before he asked, had her mind made up. "I don't think so, Carver."

"If you can't forget about Willis," he said, irritated, "can't you at least put him aside for a while?"

"Not at my discretion."

"I was thinking about indiscretion," Carver said.

Edwina pushed her cottage-cheese-and-orange-segments concoction away, no longer hungry. Or maybe that was the idea of the Dieter's Delite.

"You're acting like a moody adolescent," Carver told her. He was angry with Willis again, taking it out on Edwina.

"I know," she said. She wasn't being emotional, nowhere near tears, merely assessing herself, like someone with a fixa-tion they've learned to live with because there's no available cure. "But I need to know about Willis so I can lock my mental door on him and go on. Can't you understand that?"

"I can understand it," Carver said. "I can't accept it. You're making life too damned complicated."

Edwina stood up, then stooped slightly and picked up her blue briefcase. "I better go," she told Carver. She didn't sound angry or upset. "I probably shouldn't have taken the time to come here, anyway."

Carver didn't say anything. He took a huge bite of his ham-burger. If she wanted to leave, let her. He could be a brooding adolescent, too. Edwina stood staring down at him.

Then she surprised him. She bent down and kissed his forehead softly, lingeringly, and turned abruptly and walked from the restaurant.

He would have called after her, but his mouth was full of hamburger. By the time he'd washed it down with a sip of

Orange Sloshy, she was gone. He heard her car pull out from the parking lot.

When Carver was almost finished eating, the waitress brought the check. Edwina had let him pay for her lunch. For her, that was a gesture of intimacy. Like her unexpected kiss. Carver shook his head. Edwina's moods confused and astounded him. They were like violent weather before a seasonal change: rapid, unpredictable. Her life shifting in juxtaposition with the thing that warmed and sustained it, her earth rotating away from Willis, into what she dreaded would be her winter.

He paid the cashier, got another Orange Sloshy to go, and went out into the heat of the parking lot.

As he settled into the Olds, he spilled some of the Orange Sloshy down the front of his tropical-bird shirt, but the stain was lost in the colorful maelstrom of bright curved beaks and beating wings. The sudden coldness on his chest and stomach made Carver shiver.

He started the Olds and drove for home.

When he parked in front of his cottage, he saw Desoto waiting for him on the front porch.

The lieutenant was wearing an elegant gray suit with the coat buttoned, and he appeared even more out of place on the beach than Alex Burr had that morning. Desoto looked more like a handsome Spanish don with an eye for royal coquettes than a cop.

"Ah, Carver," he said, as Carver stepped up onto the porch. He breathed in deeply, making it a meaningful gesture. "I love the smell of the ocean. I don't get to the coast often enough." As if to punctuate his statement, a particularly large wave broke on the beach with a slapping, backwashing roar. It seemed to bring with it a breeze carrying the faintly rotted, fishy yet somehow fresh scent that Desoto missed inland in Orlando.

"What brings you to the coast this time?" Carver asked. He unlocked the door, pushed it open, and stepped aside, leaning on his cane and waiting for Desoto to go in. A porch plank squeaked under the weight concentrated at the tip of the cane.

"Willis Davis," Desoto said, moving gracefully past Carver into the cottage and looking around.

Carver followed. "I've heard enough about Willis for one day."

"He's a problem for you in more ways than one, no doubt," Desoto said. He shot his white grin at Carver. "She needs to find him, see him again maybe, to forget him."

"That's what she seems to think."

"You should be tolerant, Carver."

"Oh, I am. Jesus, I am! Want a beer?"

"Yes, in a glass."

Carver went behind the counter, got a Budweiser from the refrigerator, and found a clean water tumbler for Desoto. He watched Desoto pour the beer carefully, as if he were a chemist, so that the head of foam was precisely as he wanted it.

"Aren't you drinking?" Desoto asked, putting down the empty can.

"No, I just had two Orange Sloshies."

"Hm." Desoto took a sip of beer, smiled with the satisfaction of sated thirst, and licked his lips. "We ran the Willis Davis prints," he said. "His real name is Willis Eiler, a.k.a. William Corker a.k.a. Willis Davis. He got out of federal prison in Marion, Illinois, eight months ago after serving five years on a narcotics charge. He sold some cocaine to a federal agent. Eiler also has been convicted of swindling a wealthy widow in a real-estate scam in Missouri."

"What are his stats?"

"Thirty-nine-year-old male Caucasian, five-foot-eleven, brown hair, hazel eyes. They wired me his photo." Desoto reached into an inside pocket of his suitcoat, pulled out a black-and-white photograph, and handed it to Carver.

As he accepted the photograph, Carver realized he was breathing rapidly and his hands were unsteady. Finally he was going to see Willis Davis—or Willis Eiler.

It was a prison mug shot, full front and profile.

Eiler didn't look worth all the fuss. He was an ordinary type with even features, a certain stubbornness in his eyes, and handsome not so much for any distinctive quality but because there was *nothing* distinctive about him. No rough edges. Nothing not to like. He'd have been good at modeling suits in the Sears catalogue.

So this was Willis, Edwina's all-or-nothing bet. Maybe his Everyman quality made him a sort of blank canvas that women like Edwina longed to paint their dreams on.

"Keep it," Desoto said, when Carver held the photo out to return it.

Carver glanced again at the regular, bland face in the photograph. "A crook and a con artist from the time he met her," he said.

"Did you ever doubt it?"

"Yeah," Carver said. "She had me doubting it for a while, off and on."

"Even she can't doubt it now," Desoto said. "He was using her. He ingratiated himself with her so she'd help him get employed at Sun South, so he could set up his phony time-share racket."

"He had to be good to fool her," Carver said.

"He is good. And Edwina Talbot was ripe to be fooled. Wanted her last chance. Men like Eiler, they can sense that kind of yearning in women, *amigo*. They feed on it."

"Knowing who he really is doesn't get us any closer to him," Carver said.

"Not yet, maybe. But it might." Desoto tossed back his head and drained the rest of his beer.

"Another?" Carver asked.

"No, I have to get back to Orlando. I wanted to give you the information and photo personally. And to see the ocean. I'll come out here for a while on my vacation, Carver, and we'll do some surf fishing. You can tie a line on the end of your cane, eh?"

"Sure," Carver said. Six months ago, a few weeks ago, he might have taken offense at a remark like that, even from Desoto. The Edwina effect, he realized. Damn her, she was good for him.

After Desoto left, Carver got himself a beer from the refrigerator, then propped up the photograph on the table and sat looking at it for a long time, wishing there were some way he could crawl inside the mind of Willis Eiler.

That night Carver dreamed about sinking slowly in the dark ocean, opening his eyes underwater and seeing faces drift by—Edwina, Desoto, Willis Eiler, and there was Verna Blaney, with her scar blanched white by the sea. They might have been the faces of the dead; Carver couldn't be sure. He called out to them underwater, silently. Only Desoto replied, seemed to shout a warning that was whirled away by the current as a thousand tiny, glittering bubbles. The face of Silverio Lujan floated past slowly, troubled, eyes closed. A man with Latin features seemed to drift straight up from the bottom of the ocean, extending his arms toward Carver.

Something—a sea creature?—closed its tentacles around Carver's neck. He suddenly couldn't breathe; his lungs were working in violent spasms; he was drowning. Someone was cursing hoarsely in Spanish. A huge man with foul and beery breath had his hands clamped on Carver's throat, digging blunt, powerful thumbs into his windpipe.

Carver woke up. Suddenly. Seeking the reassurance of the real world. Finding instead vacuum and panic.

A huge man with foul and beery breath had his hands clamped on Carver's throat, digging blunt, powerful thumbs into his windpipe.

CHAPTER 25

Carver was instantly aware of the pressure on his chest. The man choking him bore down with the weight of a building.

Terror struck cold in Carver as he tried to draw breath and got only pain. His ribs seemed about to cave in; he thought he could hear the cartilage in his neck cracking under those probing thumbs that felt as if they were touching together *inside* his throat, pinching off his air. The man's rancid breath was hot on his face in the darkness as the attacker muttered a throaty stream of Spanish. Carver caught only one word: *"hermano."* Brother. He knew he was meeting Jorge Lujan, and that this was violent vengeance for that day on the road outside Solarville.

Carver squirmed convulsively and managed to get his own arms inside Lujan's thick, locked arms. He clasped his hands tightly for leverage, bent his elbows as much as possible, and pried his arms out sideways against Lujan's.

The pressure on his throat gave some, but not much. He kicked with his good leg, twisted, struggling to get leverage, focusing every measure of strength he had on separating Lujan's muscular arms, parting those digging thumbs the precious thousandth of an inch that meant life.

Lujan was straining hard now, cursing more violently with a desperation of his own. This wasn't turning out to be as easy as he'd thought. Warm spittle sprayed on Carver's face with each barking, hissing oath.

Lujan's grip gradually loosened, then suddenly broke free.

He tried to regain his hold on Carver's throat, but Carver parried his thrusting hands, knocked his arms away.

"*Bastardo!*" Lujan hissed.

Carver punched upward with his right fist, felt a jolt of pain as his hand bounced off a hard cheekbone or forehead. Then he had his palms pressed flat against Lujan's chest and was sucking in air and holding it like a weightlifter for added strength, breathing in, pushing, *pushing*.

Lujan grunted and his body rose. He was surprised by the awesome strength in Carver's arms and torso. The physical compensation and unnatural upper-body strength of the lame.

Carver forced the much larger man sideways and managed to slide free on the mattress. His right hand found the cane leaning against the wall near the bed and he gripped it and slashed out with it. It connected hard with flesh and bone; he heard an enraged shout, so abrupt and loud that it startled him.

His eyes had adjusted and he could see well enough now in the moonlight bouncing off the ocean and filtering in through the wide window. He caught the glint of a knife blade, struck at it with the cane. Connected again.

The knife skittered across the floor to the far side of the room. He heard it clatter against the far wall. Lujan spat a fresh, wet series of curses. He was breathing hard, his chest heaving. When he began to move forward, Carver lifted the cane, ready to strike again, and he stopped.

Lujan smiled. There was an easier way, the smile said. A better way. His breath still rasping from the exertion of the struggle, he stooped almost in an incongruous bow to acknowledge Carver's gameness, then moved to the other side of the room to recover the knife, withdrawing into shadow.

Carver's own breath was hissing, whistling in his throat. He watched Lujan back away to search for the knife. It might take him a while to find it in the dark. Carver had two choices: Go after Lujan now with the cane and hope he hadn't found the knife. Or get out of the cottage and try to escape.

He knew he'd been lucky with Silverio Lujan. And Jorge was much larger, more deadly, dedicated through vengeance. Living only to see Carver die.

Carver realized he was nude; he always slept that way and had forgotten he had nothing on. The sudden realization of his nakedness made him feel even more vulnerable, doomed.

He clutched the cane, fell hard, and half rolled, half scurried to the door, pulling himself along with his arms and hands. He shoved the door open and scrambled outside, then remained calm long enough to regain his feet.

With a rattle of his cane on the planks, he was off the porch. He knew Lujan would follow him as soon as he found the knife.

Carver began limping toward the churning, glistening white surf, toward the sea. There was nowhere else to go.

The tip of the cane kept sinking into the sand. He stumbled but managed to stay upright as he limped onto the deserted beach. The soft sand, with its array of minuscule shells, stabbed between his bare toes. Then it smoothed out and became cool and packed when he got near the surf; the work of the sea.

When he looked back he saw the bulky form of Jorge Lujan, shoulders hunched and head thrust forward stiffly in determination, swaggering slowly toward him. He was hefting the long-bladed knife in his right hand, knowing Carver was his. There was only the stalker, the stalked, and the wide, black Atlantic.

Carver broke for the ocean. Not out of strategy but out of fear. He was stumbling now, dragging his bad leg like a penance. The roar of the oncoming waves seemed to mock him, and the sharp scent of the sea was a whiff of death.

He fell, losing his cane, and heard Lujan laugh. For an instant panic took him. He worked his good leg beneath his body, supported himself with his hands, planted his bare foot. He screamed with an eruption of energy, felt his body respond remotely while his mind reeled: all like a dark and explosive dream.

Then, miraculously, he was on his feet. He'd gotten there with his arms and good leg. He looked around for the cane. It was nowhere in sight among the shadows. The moonlight played tricks on the wrinkled sand, keeping it hidden.

Somehow he lurched forward step after step without it. He got the impression that he was moving quite fast.

But when he glanced back at Lujan, Carver was surprised by how much nearer he was.

Lujan clamped the knife in his teeth, then bent low and picked up something. Carver squinted and strained to identify it.

His cane. Lujan had found his cane.

Grinning, still holding the knife in his mouth, Lujan lifted the cane high so Carver could see it clearly. Then he disdainfully snapped it in half over his knee. He tossed the broken pieces in opposite directions, then smiled a creepy smile and began advancing again. He was enjoying this more now, knowing Carver was hobbled by his handicap, was trapped.

Carver felt the cold surf lick at his ankles as he stood watching Lujan walk toward him, still grinning like a pirate around the knife blade.

A coldness moved into Carver's mind, a calm stillness and a fierce will. He wasn't ready to die. Someday he'd die, maybe even tonight, but Lujan wasn't going to choose the minute, the second. Lujan wasn't going to play Destiny.

He backed into the surf, watching Lujan.

Lujan seemed to sense some change in his quarry. He held

the knife in his hand now and was moving more slowly, still with a swagger, but also with a hint of caution.

When the big man was less than fifty feet away, prepared to move into killing range, Carver dropped down and did his contorted backward squirm into the rolling surf.

Lujan was surprised by the maneuver, by its awkward speed. He hesitated, then sprinted forward. He'd had enough of this Mickey Mousing around; it was time for blood.

He was almost on top of Carver when a large wave roared in. Timing it perfectly, Carver waited, then hurled his body backward into the rush of water, felt it embrace him and carry him away in its backwash.

Carver was floating. Lujan was ten feet from him now, still standing in shallow water, a faintly amused expression on his broad, peasant's face. So, this was getting complicated, he seemed to be thinking. But the night was middle-aged if not young. *Tiempo.* There was time. This was a new game, but one he could play. And win.

As Carver began swimming away from him, out to sea, Lujan methodically removed his shirt, then took off his shoes. He ran splashing into the waves like a kid on vacation, waving the knife in his right hand. Then he began swimming after Carver with a strong crawl stroke, the blade winking in the moonlight with each powerful arc of his thick right arm.

They were on even terms now, Carver knew. His bad leg was little hindrance in the water; he could maneuver with his enemy.

He kept swimming straight out from the beach, letting the bigger man tire out. There was no sound now, only the roar of the incoming waves, lifting and lowering both swimmers with the sea's ponderous eternal rhythm.

Carver began swimming more slowly, holding back slightly, hoarding his strength. He looked back and could see Lujan about a hundred feet away, still swimming strongly, closing on him. Carver thought he could see the son of a bitch grinning again.

Letting the rage, the indignation at this man actually trying to take his life well up powerfully in him, infusing him with energy, Carver took the initiative. He surface-dived, flattened out underwater, bobbed up just ahead of Lujan, and saw the startled expression on Lujan's face.

Carver stroked to the left, to confuse his pursuer, fixed Lujan's exact position in his mind, then went under again and swam toward that point.

Still beneath the surface, he waved his arms about, groping. He felt nothing. He surfaced just behind Lujan.

Lujan was whirling around in the water as Carver drew a deep breath and submerged again.

This time he found Lujan's legs easily, avoided a kick, clutched a knee, and worked his way down a bulging calf. He tried to grab Lujan's ankle, then decided a pants leg would provide a better grip.

Bunching a thick cuff in his fist, he began to stroke in upward motions with his left arm and good leg, forcing himself and the struggling Lujan deeper.

In the darkness of the depths he felt Lujan writhing above him, trying to kick free, trying to bend his body enough to strike at Carver's hand with the knife. But as long as Carver maintained their downward momentum it was impossible for Lujan to reach him with the blade. And as long as he held his grip on the pants cuff, it was impossible for Lujan to break free.

Carver's lungs were burning and he was tiring rapidly as he took them deeper and deeper, into blacker, cooler water. Something brushed his leg. A fish? A strand of drifting seaweed? Whatever it was, it floated away like a brief premonition.

Lujan began struggling more violently above him, panicking. His free bare foot was beating with increased fury at Carver's fist clenching the pants leg, but the resistance of the water robbed him of any power.

Carver forced them still deeper, feeling his ears pop from

the pressure. Inanely, the words to an old seafaring song ran through his mind: "Many brave hearts are asleep in the deep. . . ."

Then Lujan seemed to stop struggling. The leg in Carver's grasp moved limply, lifelessly.

Carver could go no deeper. He was afraid he might not have enough air in his lungs now to reach the surface. He released his grip on Lujan's pants leg and pushed himself away, flexed his aching fingers, and let himself rise, hastening his ascent by paddling with his hands and his tired good leg.

At least a minute passed, he was sure. Certainly it felt that long.

Then he broke the surface and saw a star-scattered dark sky that had never looked so vast. He sucked in a long, rasping breath, rolling onto his back. He rotated his head, looked around him.

He was alone on the moon-splashed, undulating surface of the sea.

Breathing deeply and regularly, getting his strength back as the burning sensation in his lungs lessened, he floated loosely.

He was farther from shore than he'd thought. The light of the channel marker seemed almost near enough to touch, the lights along the beach so distant, impersonal pinpoints like low stars.

It was oddly restful out there alone—relaxing. He rose and dropped with the sea rhythmically, softly, and it seemed from time to time that he actually fell asleep. He was strangely at home in the water, as if he belonged there and not on land: evolution in reverse to a point no one had anticipated—not Carver, not his therapist. His hours in the ocean had altered his being, saved his life.

The sea seemed to swell and ebb within him as he drifted in solitary peace.

Then, with a chilling jolt of fear, he imagined that Lujan might still be alive. It was possible. The man might be beneath him now, shooting up underwater with torpedo speed, the knife extended to slash into Carver's vulnerable submerged softness.

He told himself that was absurd, that Lujan was dead.

But there was no way to be positive. The high and lonely yellow moon glowed down at him in benevolent warning. The sea rose and fell and sighed and urged caution, and return to life on land. "That's where you belong," it whispered. "Where you belong. . . ."

Carver shook himself, rolled onto his stomach, and stroked toward shore.

CHAPTER 26

The corpse was found bobbing in the surf the next after-noon. A honeymooning couple from Detroit had spotted it on the beach at Okadey, a small beachside community six miles south of where Carver had gone into the ocean with Lujan pursuing him. At first the honeymooners had thought they'd spotted some sort of sea animal; the body was bleached almost white from the salt water. Then they'd seen the dark of the pants just beneath the roiling surface and realized what it was and notified the authorities. Carver wondered if their discovery had ruined their honeymoon or added spice.

Carver had phoned the local law after he'd made it back to shore the previous night. Then he'd called Desoto and Burr. Burr had turned up at the cottage within an hour. He let the locals do their jobs, staying in the background, watching. Now and then, in an almost noncommittal way, he'd offer a suggestion, probe for an answer or explanation. He knew his stuff. Very professional. Carver had to admit his opinion of Burr had been raised a notch. The DEA agent's cool yet fervent dedication might not be an endearing quality, or make for the complete man, but it was the sort of dedication that brought results. Not unlike Carver's dedication.

The Coast Guard had searched for Lujan for six hours before giving up and assuming he was dead and would be easier to find in daylight. If he could be found at all. Sometimes the sea kept its dead forever; sometimes it toyed with the dead for a while before returning what was left to land.

They were out there again just after dawn. Carver stood at his window and saw two small craft silhouetted in the early sunlight, tacking in slow circles off the shore. The Coast Guard was patient, systematic. But they had read the currents wrong, and Lujan's reappearance on land had been a surprise.

Carver drove the Olds down to Okadey that afternoon and met Desoto in the back room of the tan brick funeral parlor that served as a temporary morgue for the small community. There were yellow canvas awnings over the windows, and a bell mounted like a chimney on the low, sloping roof, doubtless to be tolled as part of the services. Carver imagined that cost extra. MAHON'S MORTUARY, the black-lettered sign peeking from among the hibiscus in front of the place had read.

Lujan wasn't refrigerated, but the back room was cool, down in the fifties, probably, and he'd keep until the body was identified and taken to Orlando. There he'd be autopsied, methodically dissected and discussed by the big-city experts.

Somber introductions were made. Mahon himself, a short, animated man in a muted plaid sport jacket, who would have looked more at home selling aluminum siding, drew a sheet away from the body.

Carver flinched inwardly, as he always did when viewing a dead body; then he sent that part of his mind away, as he always managed to do. The emotional vulnerability had lasted only a few seconds before professional detachment took over. Mental armor. Sanity retained.

"It's got to be him," Carver said. The sea and its inhabitants had worked on the face, making what was left of it unrecognizable, but the pants looked the same, and the general size was the same. There were slashes near the left pants cuff, where Carver had gripped it and had barely avoided Lujan's knife blade. And how many bodies dressed this way were bobbing around in the ocean off the resort beaches of central Florida?

Desoto nodded to the unconcerned Mahon, and the pale yellow sheet was drawn up again over Lujan's ruined face.

"A closed-casket ceremony would be my recommendation," Mahon said in a cigarette-throat wheeze.

Neither Carver nor Desoto offered a comment on that professional assessment. It was Mahon's backyard they were playing in, and he was welcome to it, headstones and all.

"I'm surprised to see you here," Carver said, as he and Desoto walked outside into the sun, Carver with his replacement cane.

The day was hot and humid, but after the chill of death in the back room, the heat felt fine to Carver. The mosquito that sampled his right forearm, the dank smell of the sea, the pelican that skimmed the blue water offshore, all represented life.

"We've opened the case wider," Desoto said, "so the game has changed somewhat. It's thought officially, and in some quarters unofficially, that Willis Eiler might have been murdered."

"Not a Missing Persons case?"

"No, not with dead Marielitos turning up wherever you go looking for him. Death by violence is contagious."

"He's still alive," Carver said.

"I think so, too." Desoto reached into the pocket of his tailored suit, withdrew a folded white handkerchief, and used it to wipe his hands thoroughly, as if he'd touched the body inside the mortuary and encountered some kind of contamination. "But I'm not positive about what I think; that's what's interested me about this case from the beginning: the possibilities."

Carver nodded, understanding. Traffic on the coast highway whizzed past them, eddying the air and spreading wind

190

patterns over the grass. They were standing only a hundred feet or so west of the pavement. An odd location for a mortuary; too near the living.

"How do you see it now?" Desoto asked.

Carver leaned on his cane, thought for a moment. How *did* he see it? Really. He said, "Drugs, probably. The hundred thousand was seed money to buy a shipment of something that could be cut and resold at four or five times the price."

"Not big money for a drug scam, Carver. My friends on the narcotics squad talk in terms of millions, not thousands. They do so with a certain arrogance."

"Burr thinks Willis might have partners, that the deal is bigger."

"Sam Cahill?"

"And others. Maybe two swamp turkeys called the Malone brothers."

"What about Raymond Mackenzie?" Desoto said. "He's still missing."

"I can't see him involved in a drug-running scheme," Carver said. "But it's possible; with so much money at stake, he might forsake the whooping crane and the snail darter. And his campsite was within the area red-penciled on the map I found in Eiler's apartment."

"You figure Burr is right?" Desoto asked. "About this being a major deal?"

"He might be. But even if he isn't, there'd be enough money to provide plenty of incentive for Willis and Cahill. People have been murdered for less."

"People have been murdered for bottlecaps," Desoto said. "That's irrelevant. You think Willis and Cahill hired the Marielitos to try to kill you?"

"It's possible. Even likely."

"What bothers me," Desoto said, "is that the Marielitos wouldn't be satisfied to be hired help; they'd cut themselves in on the deal. Or maybe they were in it from the beginning and it really is as big as Burr thinks."

"The cut will be even bigger now," Carver said, thinking about the Lujan brothers, wondering if there might be a third brother, or a homicidal cousin. Blood feuds tended to be longer-lived than their participants. "You're right," he said, "some of the pieces don't quite fit."

"Either that," Desoto said thoughtfully, "or as we get older and more experienced we notice the irregularities around the edges."

That could be, Carver thought.

"Have you told Edwina Talbot about what happened last night?" Desoto asked.

"Yes, I phoned her this morning."

"And she was upset?"

"I couldn't tell." He wished Desoto would mind his own business.

"Ah, a lovers' quarrel?"

"I don't know," Carver said. "Our last parting was ambiguous."

"Love is ambiguous, *amigo*."

"You don't know love," Carver said, "you only know sex."

Desoto exposed a toothy grin to the sunlight, made a wavering gesture with a palm-down hand. "A gray area." He looked beyond Carver, beyond the highway, out at the shimmering ocean. Carver followed his gaze. The pelican was making another determined pass at lunch, inches off the sun-shot water.

"I didn't feel like driving out here today," Desoto said. "I promised to take my nephews fishing, then to Disney World. They want to see EPCOT there, the society of the future."

"Your nephews Huey, Dewey, and Louie?" Carver asked.

"You're in the wrong cartoon, my friend."

"Yeah, that's the feeling I've had lately." Carver remembered his own trip to Disney World a few years ago with Anne and Fred Jr. He'd been more impressed than the kids by the Haunted Mansion, Tomorrow World, Space Mountain, the monorail system. Disney World was more than simply a magnificent theme park; it was a startling example of lockstep efficiency and the reach of technology. It left on its adult visitors subtle impressions not anticipated.

Desoto sighed. "My day off. I was looking forward to deep-sea fishing and Mickey Mouse. I guess instead I'll go home and watch television."

"You watch too much television," Carver said.

"I know, *amigo*, I'm a vast wasteland." Desoto grinned and wiped a finger across his teeth, as if he suspected spinach might be stuck to an incisor. A good-looking guy protecting that smile. "What about Willis Eiler?" he asked. "Have you told Edwina that her Willis is another Willis?"

"Not yet," Carver said. "I will today. Soon."

"I don't envy you, telling her that."

"It's not an enviable job," Carver said, "but it's a necessary one."

"You'll find the right time to tell her," Desoto assured him. He lifted a hand in parting, sparking sunlight from a gold cufflink. "Maybe then love or sex or whatever will lose some of its ambiguity." He turned and walked toward where an unmarked car with a driver was waiting.

Maybe, Carver thought.

They sat in the shade of the fringed umbrella, at the white metal table on Edwina's veranda, where Willis Eiler had sat as Willis Davis and had his breakfast the morning of his disappearance. The departure point where, in one manner or another, he had left his lover in one of the ways not covered by Paul Simon's fifty.

Carver had told Edwina of Willis's real identity, his background, the inescapable conclusion. Her expression remained impassive as she listened. The reaction to his words must have been violent, but she'd kept it inside her. There was no indication of the cold shock of the undeniable, the burgeoning emotional storm. That scared Carver. It was as if she'd chosen not to face the truth but to recede further back into delusion. He had to stop her, draw her out.

"He used you," Carver told her. "That's what it was about from the beginning. He wanted you to help him get employed at Sun South so he could work his phony time-share racket. He'd probably done it before, knew it was his quickest route to a lot of money."

Edwina stared across the table at him; a wavering reflection of the sea behind him played subtly in her gray eyes. What was going on behind that reflection? For an instant he wondered if she had known Willis's identity all along.

"I don't sense pity in you," she said.

"I'm frustrated," Carver admitted. "Scared, and a little angry."

"At me?"

"At you. At Willis. At the situation. He used you. You're still letting him. He's causing you to suffer, even from a distance. Even if he's dead."

She shook her head slowly. "He isn't dead."

"No," Carver said, "he isn't. That was only something else he wanted you to believe."

"You seemed to relish telling me this." There was a kind of agonized disbelief in her voice, a note of betrayal.

"I hated telling you," Carver said. "But I relish the fact that at last the truth is out about Willis. I regard that as the necessary first step in you finally freeing yourself from him."

She caressed the warm metal of the tabletop with her fingertips, as if it were a live thing that might respond to her touch. "There's a cruelty in you; I knew that from the beginning. Maybe I was attracted to it. Me looking for trouble in men again. I'm like that, I suppose."

"Maybe I am cruel," Carver told her, "if doing what has to be done is your idea of cruel. Maybe it takes someone like me to push you out of the prison of your obsession and into the light."

"Light?" she said, with a vagueness that disturbed him. She seemed to be slipping away, into a dimension of pain where she'd be alone and he couldn't follow. "Is it light you're moving me toward? Or is it darkness? Emptiness? Where there's nothing to hold on to. Other times, other places, people we know, eventually they all leave you, gone away into nothing, remembered, fading, taking part of you with them."

"You have to learn to let them go," Carver said, "grab the future." He was terrified by the way she was talking. "You use the years you have left."

She cocked her head to the side and stared at him. "Are you the future? You and your drugstore philosophy?"

"Maybe. But that's irrelevant. The future is on the way, the past is receding. Willis is over, but that doesn't mean the end of your life."

She smiled dubiously. "A new beginning?"

"A continuation," Carver said. "New beginnings are mostly bullshit. We're only allowed so many of those and we tend to use them up in a hurry. I'm talking about a continuation of you as you. The you that was getting by before you met Willis."

"You seem to have this all worked out for me."

"I worked it out for myself, and not so long ago."

She stood up and walked to the low wall around the veranda, looking out to the sea. Then she stepped over the wall and walked to the edge of the drop, the point where Willis had left his folded jacket and his shoes and allegedly leaped to his death.

Carver wanted to jump up, shout her name, run to her and snatch her back away from the edge. But he didn't. He knew that kind of rescue would be only temporary, and he was sure she wouldn't follow Willis's imagined plunge to the sea. She knew he hadn't leaped. She knew now what he was. She had to know!

But she was leaning outward, her hair flung like a pennant in the breeze. The wind off the sea might grab her, claim her.

Carver stood up, bumping his head on the damned umbrella.

She turned, as if sensing his movement.

Then she walked back onto the veranda.

They both remained standing.

Keep it out in the open, he thought. Keep it out where she has to face it. She was strong enough now; he could see that in the depth of her eyes, the raised, smooth sweep of her jaw. She was one of this war's survivors. He said, "Ask yourself how you feel about Willis. How you really feel."

She crossed her arms, hugged herself as if she were chilled in the ocean breeze. "I don't feel love anymore. But there's something—a kind of passionate need I can't identify."

Carver walked over to her and stood beside her but didn't touch her. Without speaking, she moved as if drawn toward the house.

He walked beside her with the cane, and she slowed her pace to match his.

Inside the house, she slid the glass doors to the veranda closed. The roar of the surf became distant, a constant, seductive whisper. Carver circled her waist with his free arm, kissed her.

In the bedroom the sea was louder. The window was open and the drapes swayed lazily. Carver lay on the bed and watched Edwina undress. She was no longer even slightly shy with him; there was, in fact, a meticulous, unhurried grace to her movements that suggested she enjoyed undressing before him.

She walked over and stood nude next to where he lay, so he could reach her. Her sun-darkened flesh had goose bumps on it and she was breathing rapidly, quaking so that he could see the vibrant trembling in her breasts. He reached out and with the backs of his knuckles caressed the paler, smooth flesh of her inner thigh. She jerked a breath inward, lightly closed her eyes.

The telephone jangled. Neither of them moved.

It rang again. Twice. Three times. Four.

Persistent.

Women and phones. Edwina touched Carver's face gently, then stepped aside and lifted the receiver.

She said "yes" three times, hoarsely, then she turned and held out the receiver for Carver. "It's for you. Desoto."

Carver twisted his body, took the receiver, and reached out to drop it back in its cradle.

Edwina gripped his wrist, stopping him from hanging up. "He'll call back," she said. "Better to talk to him now." She ran a hand across her stomach, leaving faint scratches from her fingernails. "Maybe it's not important; get rid of him."

Carver was staring at the pink tracks on the smooth flesh of her stomach; his heart was racing, his blood roaring like the sea in his veins. He pressed the receiver to his ear and identified himself. *Not important, get rid of him.*

"*Amigo,*" Desoto said, with exaggerated geniality. "Feel like looking at more dead bodies?"

Carver made the conversation with Desoto as brief as possible, then clung enthusiastically to life before leaving to look again at death.

CHAPTER 27

"Do you know them?" Desoto asked. "They knew you."
Carver stood beside Desoto and a gum-chewing attendant in the morgue in Orlando. This time it wasn't so tough. Maybe that was because the spaciousness and business atmosphere of the place made the bodies on the carts, a man and a woman, seem somehow unreal, like wax creations set out for display. Or maybe it was because these were people he hadn't killed.

"I'm not sure," Carver said. "They look familiar."

For an unsettling instant, the two pale, nude cadavers reminded him of himself and Edwina just a few hours ago; he wondered if that accounted for the disturbing sense of familiarity. Every cop knew love had too much to do with death.

The man and woman were both slender, and looked as if they were in their mid-forties when they died. There were cleaned-up contusions on both their foreheads. The woman's frail body was slightly misshapen, bent, just beneath her pointed breasts. One of the man's legs obviously had been broken, and his nose was mashed.

Carver breathed in some of the mint-disinfectant scent of

the morgue and swallowed. Now this scene was quickly becoming too real for him. Too much death for one day. "How did they die?" he asked.

"Instantly. A one-car accident on Highway 75. They went off the road, down an embankment, and hit a concrete bridge abutment at high speed. There was some heavy vegetation down there and the wreckage wasn't found until this morning. Time of death is placed as late last night, about when you and Jorge Lujan were trying to teach each other to swim."

Carver looked away from the bodies, at Desoto. "Is that all that ties this accident with me, the time of death?"

Desoto arched a hand and delicately smoothed his dark hair, almost as if he had a mirror before him. In the presence of the dead, the vain and commonplace gesture was strikingly incongruous. "That, and the woman had your name written on a piece of paper in her attaché case. Along with a receipt from the Tumble Inn Motel in Solarville, dated one of the nights you stayed there."

Recognition rushed at Carver now. "Was the car a black Lincoln?"

Desoto nodded.

Carver looked again at the bodies, tried to reach beyond the impersonality of death and imagine them in life, without their injuries. The man in a three-piece suit, the woman not nude and crushed, but sleek and fully dressed and with a diamond, gimmick wristwatch. People with grand desires and petty grievances and places to go. The executive types he'd seen in the motel restaurant his first night in Solarville. The wealthy tourists.

"I don't know their names," he told Desoto, "but I remember them from the motel. They seemed to have money. I pegged them for a rich couple roaming around doing Florida. You know the type: travel as a hobby."

"They weren't married," Desoto said. "Maybe they were sleeping together; people do. He was David Panacho, with a wife and kids in Gainesville, and she was Mildred Kern, single, from Orlando. They were employees of Disney World; the Lincoln was a company car."

"An exec and his secretary on vacation," Carver suggested.

"They were both executives. We're checking now to find out more about them."

"An accident," Carver said. "I don't see how this fits in with me, with Willis Eiler. Or don't you think it was an accident?"

Desoto shrugged inside his elegant suitcoat. "Who knows for sure about this kind of crash? One car involved, nobody around to see it happen. Someone could have driven them to the edge of the embankment, then sent the car over. Or possibly it was a suicide pact, or suicide and murder. Death by misadventure, *amigo*. There were no skid marks."

"Or whoever was driving could have fallen asleep at the wheel and the car went off the road."

"That's the hypothesis," Desoto said. "Whatever's simplest is most likely. But why would the Kern woman have your name written on a scrap of paper? Nothing else, just your name?"

Carver didn't answer. He didn't know. Maybe it all meant nothing. It could be that Desoto was making too much of this. Possibly he'd seen the old movie *Out of the Past* the night before, the ending where Robert Mitchum and Jane Greer careened to their deaths in a '46 Chevy.

But he knew Desoto had something else in mind. "You think they were in on the drug deal?" Carver asked.

"It's not impossible. Burr's almost convinced of it. He's looking into their lives right now. Panacho's wife told him her husband had phoned and had hinted he'd unexpectedly discovered something important. He wouldn't say what it was about. She said he sounded scared, but that might only be the hindsight of grief. Burr's on his way to talk to the Disney people: Fearless Fosdick in the Magic Kingdom."

Desoto nodded to the gum-chomping attendant, who ushered them into the warmer area of the morgue. Carver followed the lieutenant out of the building, onto the hot sidewalk. *Déjà vu*. Carver had had enough of looking at corpses and then going out to stand in the heat. He felt nause-ated, chilled despite the sun.

"You okay, *amigo?*" Desoto asked, staring at him.

Carver nodded. "Yeah, relatively."

"Not an easy world sometimes."

"Not easy ever, it seems for some people."

"Maybe it's meant to be that way. A test for us."

"That is a lot of crap perpetuated by the folks who like to wear hair shirts."

"Oh, probably. You told Edwina Talbot about her Willis, eh?"

"This morning. Just before I drove here."

Desoto's features sharpened in concern. "How did the news set with her?"

"I'm not sure yet. It was rough on her at first. She tried not to accept it."

"But you wouldn't let her lie to herself. Not anymore. Not you."

Carver squinted against the lowering sun and stared at De-soto. Sometimes the handsome lieutenant's perceptiveness surprised him. "That's how it was," he said, "and I think she has stopped lying to herself, stopped idolizing Willis. But I'm not sure."

"You're going back to her now?"

"Yes," Carver said. "Then we're driving to Solarville."

"Under it all," Desoto said, "she's strong. I found that out during her visits about Willis. Someday you'll be surprised by how strong she is."

"I hope so," Carver told him, and left him standing there in the slanted, burning sunlight.

Carver limped across the street and got in the Olds. As he started the engine and pulled away from the curb, he saw Desoto still standing on the sidewalk, thinking. Adding, sub-tracting, not getting answers, wandering through the obscure and trying to bring it into focus, make sense of it, not having any luck.

Carver knew how he felt. Every turn seemed to lead to more

turns; every frustration seemed to beget more of the same. The search for Willis Davis had about it a dreamlike quality of quiet madness. Carver felt at times as if he were trying to feel his way through the miasma of nightmares. Then there were times when he seemed to see clearly, but objects on his mind's horizon simply receded further out of reach as he advanced, eluding him. He wondered how it would be to forget all of this and get a job selling insurance. Or maybe even real estate.

But he only wondered for a moment; he'd never make a salesman. "What other kind of work do you know?" Desoto had asked. Carver knew the answer to that one and had to live with it.

After wending his way out of Orlando and onto the highway, he drove fast back to Del Moray.

CHAPTER 28

E dwina looked put together, in control. She'd brushed her dark hair, put on a blue cotton blouse and a crisp tan skirt. She was wearing blue socks, and the kind of jogging shoes they sew a lightning streak on so they can jack the price up to forty dollars. The outfit made her appear young, interested and interesting. There was an awareness in her calm gray eyes that offset the sadness.

She was holding a drink in her right hand, a whiskey sour in a stemmed glass. As she let him into the house, Carver looked closely at her. She didn't appear at all sloshed.

"Want one?" she asked.

He said that he did and sat down in the cool living room. Beyond the sheer curtains over the wide window, the still-bright evening continued to simmer. The only intrusion from outside was the whisper of the sea. Everything was neat and in place, clean, as if she'd dusted and straightened the room, the house, while he was gone. A life in order, at least on the surface.

He wondered how she was now, how what had happened played on her mind while he was away. Sometimes there was a delayed reaction to the kind of information he'd thrown at her. Carver felt miserable about what he'd done. Doing the tough but essential tasks in this world exacted a price. Someone once said that sooner or later every man had to shoot his own dog. Carver felt as if he'd been shooting his own dog all his life.

Edwina returned with another whiskey sour, handed it to him, then sat down across from him in a low chair. She said, "Who's dead?"

"Two people," Carver said. "Man and a woman. A car accident on Highway 75."

"How does that concern you?"

"I saw them when I was in Solarville. They were staying at the Tumble Inn."

"Do they have anything to do with Willis?"

"I'm not sure. My name was written on a slip of paper in the woman's briefcase. They were both Disney executives. Her name was Mildred Kern; the man was David Panacho." He watched Edwina's face as he spoke; she gave no sign that she recognized the names.

"Maybe the Kern woman saw you in Solarville," Edwina suggested, "found out you were a private detective, and wrote down your name with the intention of hiring you someday. Were the two lovers?"

"Possibly. They appeared as if they might be, but I can't be sure. And Solarville is the kind of out-of-the-way place two employees of the same company would go for a romantic tryst if they didn't want corporate gossip to affect their careers."

"It could be that one or both of them are married," Edwina said. "You might eventually have been contacted by the woman and asked to follow a spouse, to learn about another affair in order to temper a divorce settlement."

"Or follow a child or a business associate or a mother or father or find something that was stolen . . . maybe a black bird. I've thought about the possibilities. It's a futile exercise.

204

The woman is dead, so we'll probably never know what she was doing with my name written down, what she intended."

Edwina sipped her drink deliberately, then slowly lowered her glass. He watched her, concerned, wondering. She looked as if she felt fine, as if crush had led to bounce, but you never could tell about people. And he needed to be sure about her. He parted his lips to speak.

"I'm all right," she said, before he could ask.

He smiled and tapped the cane on the blue carpet. It made no sound.

"Really," she said, smiling back. "I have wounds, but they're healing. This is the other world with different, sweeter songs, isn't it?"

"It can be if that's what you want."

"I do want it that way," she said.

He believed her, but he wasn't so sure she could bring it off. Not by herself, anyway. He hoped Desoto was right about her surprising him with her strength.

Outside, some sort of bird wheeled close to the window and screamed, as if it wanted in. Like madness circling. Edwina winced at the sound. Carver decided he wanted her with him. He wanted to help her, to protect her, even if she did think she'd made the necessary painful adjustment and had managed some kind of peace with herself. He wished he could be sure about her.

"We're going back to Solarville," he said.

"When?"

"Unless you can't make it, when we're done with these drinks. We'll drive by my place so I can get a few things, and we can be in Solarville within a few hours."

"I can make it," she said.

She finished her drink and placed the glass on a table by her chair. There was a steady calmness about her now, a sureness of movement and a directness in her eyes. Carver didn't know if that was good or bad. The ongoing disillusionment she'd suffered since Willis's disappearance had to have taken a serious toll. He knew it was important to keep her oriented, stable.

She apparently felt the same need for orientation. "You think Willis is in Solarville," she said. "Why?"

Carver finished his own drink, then he sat back, toying with the damp, cool glass. "Willis pulled out of Sun South early," he said. "Franks found out about the time-share scheme only because the bank contacted him, and that happened only because Willis drew virtually all the money out of the secret account. Willis had the opportunity to steal even more money from Sun South customers without any real danger of discovery. Which means he probably left when he did because he had enough money to suit his purpose."

"Which is what?" Edwina asked. The bird made another pass and screamed again, louder, as if it desperately wanted something. Carver wished it would hunt up a worm.

"To make even more money," he continued. "It has to be a drug deal. And it probably had to be financed by a certain date, which also helps to explain why Willis abruptly pulled out when he had slightly more than the nice round figure of a hundred thousand dollars. The red-penciled area on the map hidden in his apartment is swampland just south of Solarville. And it's in Solarville that Willis's old friend and fellow dreamer Sam Cahill is living beyond his means and selling backwater real estate. I think Willis and Cahill are partners who needed the hundred thousand to make a drug buy, possibly to take place when the Malone brothers receive a shipment. It could be that the drugs will be smuggled in by plane and dropped into the red-penciled area of the swamp, then picked up and sold to Willis and Cahill." Carver stopped handling the glass and set it aside. "Which means that Willis Eiler must be somewhere around Solarville, waiting with Cahill for the deal to be consummated."

Edwina sat back and seemed to think about what Carver had told her, finding it easier to digest than it would have been the day before, when she hadn't known that Willis Davis hadn't really existed, that he was an act, a production, Willis Eiler.

She said, slowly, "There's something I have to tell you. Something it's past time to tell."

"There's no need for any kind of confession," Carver said. But he suspected there was a need, in Edwina.

"Because it isn't required, I want to tell you. I was married for five years to a husband who beat me. Badly. Systematically. It took a broken collarbone and blood transfusions finally to convince me I had to leave Larry." She laughed softly, deep in her throat, and shook her head. "Sounds dumb. The battered-wife syndrome. Classic, huh?"

"Classic," Carver agreed, watching her with a neutral expression.

"The trouble was, when I left Larry I found that what he'd done to me went with me. At first I didn't know what to do. I was terrified being alone. I'd hole up in my apartment; the walls seemed to scream at me. I learned how lonely someone could be. After a while I tried the singles bars. I started going out with men, too many men, looking for a lover who didn't exist, looking for him in a lot of lovers."

There was no apology in her voice when she said this. Carver liked that.

"Finally I realized what was happening, how hopeless it was. I quit craving love, sex, men, almost everything. I was repulsed by what I'd become; I thought hard about suicide. A year of analysis helped to pull me out of my depression. And my work helped. I went into real estate as much for therapy as to make a living; that's why I got so good at it so fast. Still I had problems, with men, sex. I didn't want to get involved; I was afraid." She bowed her head slightly, not looking at Carver.

"Then I met Willis," she said, "just the way I told you, at a time when I thought I might be ready again for one more try at a relationship, my last. And he turned out to be the lover I'd only dreamed existed, the one I'd searched for after playing punching bag for Larry, before my illness. He knew exactly what I needed. He was gentle and compassionate."

"It was his business to know what you needed," Carver said softly.

She looked directly up at him. "I know that now; I can face it. When I told you about going up to Willis's room with him at the sales convention, that was true. But we didn't make love. I told him about me. Everything. About how the violence and shame had made sex impossible for me with other men. And he understood, held me to him all that night. He was the only man who ever stayed with me without sex. He didn't demand, didn't rush things. He had more patience with me than my therapist had shown me during analysis." She drew a deep breath, then said, "The only time Willis and I made love was the night before he disappeared. That's how I know it was a good-bye, Carver. It was the only time."

Carver sat silently. He wondered if Willis would have been so understanding and gentle if he hadn't had an ulterior motive. All that time with a beautiful woman, without sexual union. . . . He didn't voice that thought to Edwina, who had lived so long with brutality and then found the gentleness she'd sought. Her gentle man.

Carver understood now why Willis had meant so much to her. And he understood why she'd been vague, why she'd kept this part of her life secret: She'd taken a chance on Willis and lost. She had to know Carver before she could trust him with her past.

She smiled, a soft smile he was seeing for the first time. "Despite your cynicism and hard exterior, there's a gentle compassion in you, too."

"Is that why you called Willis's name that night at the motel, when you were with me in my bed?" Immediately he realized the selfish cruelty of his question and regretted it.

Her smile dimmed and she seemed surprised. She had no answer. Her face was transformed to the familiar mask again, but it wouldn't hold. Her lower lip began to tremble; the mouth of a ten-year-old beneath those calm and knowing eyes.

Carver took her hand and drew her to him, gently.

When they emerged from the house into the heat, Edwina locked the front door behind her and got in the Olds with Carver. She had a leather overnight bag slung by a strap across her shoulder. She worked it free and turned to place it on the backseat.

"I didn't pack a lot of clothes," she said. "How long will we be in Solarville?"

Carver shrugged and started the engine. "Maybe not long. It depends on how things go. On how right I am."

He backed the car away from the small but plush house that had been home to Edwina and Willis, in that simpler world before the truth, then drove north along the coast to his cottage.

While Edwina waited, he packed a few things in the new suitcase the Tumble Inn had provided after the fire. This time the zipper stuck and he had to wrestle with it, snagging a fingernail before he finally had it zipped all the way around.

Then he phoned Ernie Franks at home and explained where he was going and why.

It all sounded good to Franks; the odds on Willis Eiler being found, and at least some of the Sun South money being recovered, had suddenly improved. His elation and hope throbbed in his voice. Franks and Edwina; maybe there was something in sales that eventually engendered desperate faith.

"Let me know," Franks said, before hanging up. "When whatever it is that's going to happen is over, you let me know about it, okay?"

Carver assured Franks that he would. That was the idea behind their arrangement. That was why Franks had offered him a percentage of the money, wasn't it?

As Carver and Edwina drove south, then cut west on 70 toward south-central Florida, Carver watched the lengthening shadows along the flat highway and began to feel the same heightened optimism that Ernie Franks had voiced. Not because of the money, or the possibility of a cracked drug operation, but because it seemed that at last Willis Eiler could be put to rest alive or dead.

That might be the final stage in the exorcism of a demon.

CHAPTER 29

D aninger seemed surprised to see them again at his motel. He smiled, bowed, smiled, genuflected, smiled, smiled, and gave Carver and Edwina adjoining rooms near the deep end of the Tumble Inn's swimming pool. The possibility of litigation still ran strong.

Carver slept late the next morning, but he was still awake before Edwina. He left her sleeping and drove into Solarville to check in with Chief Armont. At the rear of the headquarters lot, Mackenzie's Jeep was parked, its wheels and fenders caked with mud.

The chief said he was glad to see Carver but didn't put on nearly as good an act as Daninger. But then, he didn't have the motivation. He asked Carver what he was doing back in town.

When Carver told him, Armont didn't seem to like it. He knew there was plenty of drug trafficking going on in and around Solarville. He also knew that some of the people involved had the influence to cost him his job. He didn't like the fine line he had to walk; he did what he could without committing professional suicide, kept his town as straight as possible and only looked the other way when he had to. Carver sympathized with him, but at the same time wondered exactly how much Armont did or didn't know. A man could keep his eyes clenched shut only so long.

"I didn't figure you were the sort a few murder attempts would keep away," he told Carver. "I knew you'd be back. You're the dog-with-a-rag type: won't let loose because you can't." He sounded as if he were that type himself, only circumstances kept him from acting on instinct and sinking his canine teeth into the rag. His flat, cop's eyes narrowed. For an instant it was apparent that he envied, and admired, Carver. "You've got leeway. You'll always find a way to get the job done."

"I'll always try, anyway," Carver said. "You know how it is."

Armont nodded. He did know. That was his burden.

"Have you checked on Sam Cahill?" Carver asked.

"His house has been staked out. No Sam Cahill anywhere around here lately, if you ask me."

And no Willis Eiler, Carver thought. It was possible that the hand Willis and Cahill were playing had folded of its own accord and they'd moved on to new hunting grounds. They were both men who had disappeared with daylight before.

After leaving police headquarters, Carver drove the short distance down the hot and dusty street to The Flame. He parked on South Loop, directly across from the restaurant, and was starting to get out of the car when he noticed there were few other cars parked nearby and there was no sign of life inside the restaurant's tinted windows.

It was Sunday; he'd forgotten. Apparently The Flame was extinguished for the Sabbath. That meant that to talk to Verna Blaney and try to get an inkling if she knew where Cahill had gone, he'd have to drive out to her cabin.

He got directions easily enough from jug-eared Wilt at the Shell station, then drove to the south end of town and then farther south on a series of narrow, elevated dirt roads that ran through thick swamp, between tall cypress and mangrove trees, their limbs laden with Spanish moss and dangling creeper vines. An otter glared at the car from the side of the

212

road, then disappeared back into the swamp. Carver realized he was inside the red-penciled area on the map he'd found in Willis Eiler's apartment in Orlando.

Verna Blaney's place was in disrepair, but it was more than simply a cabin. It was isolated well off the road, at the end of a long gravel driveway. Low and ramshackle, it had a flat-roofed front porch with three wooden steps leading up to it, and curtains pulled closed at all the windows. The grayish clapboard house sported black shutters and a tall brick chimney. There was a screened-in porch built onto the west side, but the screens were rusty and torn, hanging in flaps as if objects had been hurled through them. Behind and to the left of the house was a crude wooden dock, and near it, resting on dry ground, was one of the flat-bottomed airboats some of the Everglades residents used to navigate the swamp.

These boats drew hardly any water, and were often powered by a military-surplus aircraft engine or a converted automobile motor, with a propeller above the stern set to blow backward and power the boat over narrow stretches of flat land as well as shallow swamp water. The large propeller whirled inside a wire cage to prevent anyone from accidentally reaching or walking into its blades. Doing that would be like stumbling into a giant blender.

At full throttle an airboat roared like a plane and gave passengers the sensation that they were flying at high speed an inch off the ground or water. Sometimes they were. Carver remembered that Verna's father had made his living taking tourists for airboat rides before his death last year. The airboat by the dock was dusty, had thick, leafy moonvine intertwined with the propeller cage, and obviously hadn't been moved for a long time.

Not far from the house sat a rusty Ford pickup truck that might have been drivable, but didn't look as if it had been moved for quite a while, either; but Carver remembered seeing it parked near The Flame.

He walked across the bare plot of ground in front of the house. The earth was dry and packed hard, without the slight-

213

est vegetation, as if weed and grass killer had been sprayed on it to hold back the swamp. Racketing with the screams of cicadas, the swamp bent green and malevolent around three sides of the low house, which seemed to be hunkered down, threatened and cowering.

"I ain't never shot nobody before," Verna Blaney said. "It'd be a new and interesting experience."

She was standing on the porch with a double-barreled shotgun cradled in her arms, tucked beneath her high and ample breasts, which were straining the seams of a yellow cotton dress.

Carver stopped walking and stood very still about fifty feet from the porch steps. Verna was barefoot and had a puffy, sleepy look about her eyes, as if she'd been taking an early afternoon nap and he'd awakened her. Or maybe she'd still been asleep from the night before. Late to bed, late to rise . . . was that the real Verna?

"What do you want?" she asked. And she asked it as if Carver didn't have much time to frame an answer.

"I want to talk."

"I don't want to listen. Get out. Fast. Now!"

Carver leaned on his cane, didn't move as if to leave. "You're being unreasonable, Verna."

"I don't think so. You ain't the first man to come out here way to hell and gone to see me. And it ain't because they enjoy the drive, or my company. They don't have to look at the scar, they figure, or listen much to what I got to say. It's the body they think is just fine. And a woman like that, with that mark on the side of her face, why she'd be just aching all over for male companionship."

Carver was getting the idea. Verna Blaney thought she knew men through and through, the single-track, rutting beasts that peopled her dreams. He thought about her living all these years there alone with her father. He wondered about Ned Blaney. What kind of father had he been to give her that impression of men? What had he done to her? Or maybe there was something to what she said, considering some of the male

Solarville natives Carver had seen. Might the Malone brothers have been two of Verna's crude and carnally intent visitors?

"I only want to ask you a few questions about Sam Cahill," Carver said.

Verna was running a hand down the shotgun's twin barrels now, curving her fingers around them lightly, almost sensually. Carver couldn't help it; his eyes flicked downward and up, taking in her ripeness. Something exotic that had grown in the swamp, primitive and dangerous.

She'd expected his involuntary reaction; it seemed to confirm something. She glared icicles at him. "Put a bag over her head," she spat. "You ever hear that expression, mister? Put a bag over her head and she'd be a good fuck?"

"I've heard it," Carver said.

"So've I. Most all my life." She turned her head defiantly for a moment so Carver had to look at her scar. "Damned propeller from a swamp boat my pa was tinkering with did this, when I was only twelve. They said I was lucky to be alive, still have my head." She was holding the shotgun at the ready now, aimed at a spot on the ground not far in front of Carver. "I ain't so sure of that."

"The scar isn't as bad as you think," Carver said. "And plastic surgery—"

"Good-bye," Verna Blaney said in a flat voice.

"At least you've got two good legs," Carver said.

Oh-oh, the wrong thing to say, considering what Verna was sure he was thinking.

"And don't bother coming back," she said sternly. She took a step toward him and aimed the shotgun.

Carver felt the flesh bunch up on the back of his neck. He used the cane more nimbly than he thought he could and backed up several steps, staring at the black eternity inside the gun barrels. This was a tortured woman he'd caught at a bad time, one who saw before her a member of the sex she feared and distrusted. And she'd obviously had experience in handling a gun. A body sunk in the swamp's quicksand might never be found.

The shotgun's long barrels didn't waver.

It was too nice a day for death. Carver continued his retreat.

When he was on the gravel driveway, near his car, he finally turned his back on Verna Blaney. He opened the door and tossed his cane on the seat.

"Mister!" Verna called, as he was about to lower himself into the Olds.

He turned, standing balanced by supporting himself on the open door, one hand on the warm chrome windshield frame.

"I don't know anything about Sam Cahill," she said. "Haven't seen him in a long spell. Don't want to. Don't want to see you again, neither." She raised the shotgun and fired a blast into the treetops. Birds screeched and flapped into the sky, like a scene from an old Tarzan movie; something Carver didn't recognize gave an animal scream deep in the swamp.

He climbed the rest of the way into the Olds and drove away from there in a hurry. Verna Blaney still had the shotgun's other loaded barrel to use against her fear and pain, and Carver's flesh and blood.

He'd known women like her; she wanted male companionship more than she would admit to herself, and she hated men for that persistent desire, and for shunning her because of her scar. For what one or more men had done to her. Making her different. She was twisted and agonized in her loneliness.

And maybe able to kill.

When Carver got back to the Tumble Inn, he found Edwina sunning herself by the pool. She and two skinny, preteen boys in the deep end were the only ones there. One of the lads appeared to have an erection.

"Where have you been?" she asked, lowering her oversized sunglasses and peering coolly up at Carver above the frames.

"I wanted to talk to Verna Blaney."

"And did you?"

"Not in any way productive. She ran me off her property. Threatened to shoot me. I would say she hates men."

"Or would like to think so," Edwina said. Savvy. Catty.

"I thought she might have some idea where Sam Cahill is, but if she does, she isn't willing to share it." Carver felt a bead of perspiration play over his temple, run down his cheek to tickle the side of his neck. Like an insect. He wanted to get in out of the heat. "Had lunch?" he asked.

"I was waiting for you."

"Get dressed and we'll drive into town," Carver said. "Have us a bite. Maybe talk to Chief Armont again."

Edwina hitched up the top of her suit and stood up from the chaise longue. The two boys splashing around at the other end of the pool took time out from any pretense and gaped at her in unabashed admiration. Carver thought they were developing good taste young.

Armont laughed when Carver told him about his encounter with Verna Blaney. "She usually reacts with disfavor toward men who drive out there uninvited to sweet-talk her, but I'll admit she's been a little extreme this time."

"I wasn't there to sweet-talk her."

"Sure, but she don't usually give her surprise callers a chance to say what they want, just runs them off. Generally she only uses shouts and threats, though, not a shotgun. You want to press an assault-with-a-deadly-weapon charge?"

"No," Carver said. "Has Verna ever been really serious about a man?"

"She's had her beaus," the chief said, "but not for long. She doesn't have any illusions about what men want from her. That scar disfigured her inside as well as out. Her daddy's fault; he should have had the damn thing stitched up right after it happened. But he didn't, cantankerous old asshole, and now it would cost a fortune to have a plastic surgeon fix that scar, and even then there'd be no guarantee. At least that's what old Ned Blaney used to say whenever anybody brought up the subject."

"What kind of man was her father?"

"Nobody really knows," Armont said, pecking out a rhythm with a pen point on his desk. "Kept to himself, ran his airboat rides for tourists who were driving by on the main highway and got steered to his place by the signs he had up and down the road. I think he was fond of Verna, and a good father in his way, but crude. Too crude to realize how deep a scar like that might run in a pretty young girl."

Carver thanked the chief and turned to Edwina.

"You two looking for a place to eat lunch," Armont said, "The Flame should be open now."

"I drove by there this morning and it was closed," Carver said.

"They only serve lunch and supper on Sundays," Armont explained. "Folks like to sleep in late or go to church Sundays in Solarville, depending on what they been up to the night before." If there was irony in his voice, Carver couldn't catch it.

He and Edwina left Chief Armont and had salads and coffee at The Flame. There weren't many customers, but people were wandering in at a steady pace. Soon the place would be crowded. Emma and the horsey waitress were on duty, but not Verna Blaney.

When Carver asked Emma about Verna, she said that Verna wouldn't be in that day or any other, except possibly as a customer. She'd quit the day before yesterday, and rumor had it that she'd sold her house and ground and was moving away. She'd had enough of Solarville, she'd said. Couldn't blame the woman, the waitress confided in a lowered voice. Emma cautioned Carver that what she'd just told him was only rumor.

Twenty minutes later, at the cash register, the tall waitress with the equine features told Carver and Edwina the same story and assured them that it was fact. The truth was slippery at The Flame, just like everywhere else.

"What next, O Sleuth?" Edwina asked, on the sunny sidewalk outside the restaurant.

Carver leaned on his cane with both hands and glanced up and down the street. There was little traffic, no pedestrians other than the two of them. "We go back to the motel and swim," he said.

"I've already been swimming," she told him.

"Then we'll find something else to do. I can think of a few things. But we're at a standstill right now because it's Sunday and city hall won't be open until tomorrow."

Edwina looked curiously at him. "What's city hall got to do with why we're here?"

"We'll go there tomorrow," Carver said, "and use your real-estate expertise to find out whether the Blaney property's been sold."

"If it was sold recently, it might not be recorded yet."

"That's where your expertise comes in," Carver said. "If it isn't recorded, do you think you can talk to the right people in the right way, find out whether there's been a transaction?"

"I think so. There can't be that many title companies in town, and I'm in the business."

That was the way Carver had it figured.

He drove them back to the Tumble Inn. But they didn't swim. Instead they made love that afternoon in Edwina's room, ate supper in the motel restaurant, and made love in the evening in Carver's room. Each time they were together, lost in the exploration phase of their affair, it was better. Exhilarating. Bad memories were fading. They were both beginning to think highly of the Tumble Inn.

Carver was asleep when the jangling phone by the bed dragged him from deep, indecipherable dreams to the surface of wakefulness. He resisted, so the dreams couldn't have been bad ones. As he pulled the ringing, vibrating instrument to him, he dropped it onto the floor. It bounced with a jingling protest.

He cursed, retrieved the receiver, and pressed it to his ear. He found the wrist near the end of his left arm and squinted at his watch: 10:35. A glance at the window told him it was dark outside. The 10:35 was P.M.

"Carver?" a voice buzzed in his ear.

"I think so."

"This is Alex Burr. I'm here in Solarville. We've got some action tonight. Wear some old clothes and meet us on South Loop, where it curves near the swamp just outside of town."

Carver wondered who the "us" were. The DEA? He supposed so. "When?" he asked.

Burr seemed surprised by the question. "Now. As soon as you can." He hung up.

Carver listened to the static of the broken connection for a few seconds, then terminated his end of the conversation.

He decided not to wake Edwina. He slipped into an old pair of jeans that he'd brought in his new suitcase, put on his wrinkled shirt with the sleeves rolled up above the elbows, and pulled on a fresh pair of socks and his moccasins. Then he got out of there, walking as lightly as he could with the cane.

"Now," the man had said. Federal man. DEA. Best to listen. Now.

Carver carefully locked the motel-room door behind him, breathed in the warm swamp air with its fetid, primal scent, and woke up all the way.

The swamp loomed close and black around him, loud with the croaking cacophony of a thousand bullfrogs and the shrill, frantic buzzing of night insects. The moon was full and suspended low over the treetops, like an extraterrestrial mother ship overseeing all the wild madness below.

Working his tongue around the insides of his cheeks to remove the dry, sour taste from his mouth, Carver got in the Olds. He started the engine without gunning it, then pulled the car slowly and as quietly as possible from the parking lot. Then he drove fast toward South Loop.

He was eager now to find out what all the rush was about, and to learn what kind of action Alex Burr had planned for that night.

CHAPTER 30

As Carver slowed the Olds and steered it gently into the curve on South Loop, a uniformed cop stepped out of the brush and into the glare of the headlights. He held up a rigid arm and hand almost in a Nazi salute, as if he were halting three lanes of traffic.

Carver pressed his foot on the brake pedal hard enough to make the Olds's long hood dip. The cop waved him over toward where he was standing, waiting for him like a Berlin Wall guard.

"You Carver?" he asked, when Carver had stopped the car and stuck his head out the window. The cop was young and already thick around the middle. Another ten years of sitting in patrol cars or at a desk and he'd be downright fat; already his face was the jowly one of a middle-aged man, but his eyes were young, consciously expressionless peering out from the curved-moon shadow of his cap's visor. He was putting on the tough front, hardening to his trade.

Carver showed him some identification. Official paper. That did it. The pudgy cop smiled a one-of-us smile and said, "Follow that road, sir. They're waiting just over that rise. And

I've been instructed to tell you to turn off your headlights."

Carver didn't see any road, but he killed his lights and aimed the Olds's long snoot at the blackness of the swamp. Then, by moonlight, he did see that there was a narrow, mostly overgrown road leading to the rise the cop had pointed out. It wasn't a dry road. Long bent grass glistened wetly between the shadows cast by the trees. Carver could see recently made tire ruts in front of him, and now and then the car would lurch and he could hear the sucking sound of swamp water beneath the wheels, telling him he was driving where no car should go.

As the Olds's hood topped the crest of the rise and then dropped, Carver saw four cars parked close to each other near what looked like a broken section of fence. Two of the cars bore Solarville Police markings. There was a knot of men standing by the cars. Carver recognized Alex Burr, the cop Rogers, who had retrieved his cane from the smoked motel room, and the aggressively paunchy form of Chief Armont.

When he parked the Olds by one of the police cars and got out, he could see the dark, humped shapes of two airboats. What had appeared to be broken fence was part of a decrepit dock; the two boats were moored to it. Though Carver could hear water lapping, the airboats weren't bobbing. They were sitting in the kind of shallow water they were made to skim.

Burr said hello to Carver and introduced him to two other men who were DEA agents. Armont nodded to Carver. He was wearing dark slacks and a short-sleeved blue shirt. His two men were in uniform. The DEA agents, including Burr, wore dark pants and black windbreakers with *DEA* lettered on their backs in foot-tall orange letters. The better to know friend from enemy if the action got heated. And heated action seemed to be anticipated: two of the agents were carrying semi-automatic shotguns as well as the handguns Carver was sure were concealed beneath the windbreakers.

Everyone except Burr seemed calm. He was in control, of himself and the operation, but it was easy to see that his adrenaline was pumping. There was a stiffness to his features and his single eye moved rapidly. When he spoke, tension like taut, vibrating wire grated in his voice. "Come on," he said to Carver in his DEA way. "I'll explain as we go."

Carver didn't ask where they were going. He limped to the nearest airboat, almost stumbling as his cane sank into the soft ground.

"Need some help?" Burr asked, trying to hurry him.

Carver declined, and almost dropped his cane as he scrambled into the boat and sat next to Burr. The boats were aluminum, about twenty feet long, with the familiar wide propellers in high cages mounted on the stern, well out of the water. They had everything to make them aircraft except wings. Armont, along with one of the DEA agents and the two uniformed cops, got in the other airboat. That boat was older and sat higher in the water. Carver peered at the two boat trailers half concealed in the reeds but couldn't make out the license plates. He guessed the newer boat he and Burr were in was a DEA boat, the other belonged or was on loan to the Solarville police. A DEA agent sat behind the low windscreen in front of Carver. Up in the bow, a boyish blond agent with a pug nose, whom Burr had introduced as Marty something or other, was hunched over what looked like a small radio and was wearing bulky earphones that lent him a curiously mouselike appearance. Marty made a circular motion with his right arm, then pointed toward the swamp.

Lines were unlooped from the moorings, and the two airboats came alive with sputtering roars and hunkered lower in the water. Carver could feel the powerful vibration shake the boat, run up his back from the base of his spine. The seats they were sitting in were hard, with straight backrests, bolted to the standard bench-type seats built into the boat.

"Better strap yourself in," Burr said.

That seemed like sound advice. Carver felt around, found a

safety belt, and fastened it, yanking it hard a few times to make sure the buckle had caught. He stuck his stiff leg out in front of him to get as comfortable as possible.

The throbbing rumble of the engines rose, and the boat Carver was in led the way into the dark swamp. Carver was aware of thick saw grass and reeds bending and parting in front of and under the boat. Now and then there was a rough bounce and hard vibration beneath the hull as they briefly skimmed over land rather than water. They were only going about fifteen miles per hour. The propeller that drove them forward made a muted beating sound like a helicopter rotor, barely audible beneath the roar of the converted aircraft engine that powered it.

Marty raised his arm again in a silent signal and held it steady.

The engines of both boats died, and they were drifting in a shadowed clearing, surrounded by the black trunks of partly submerged trees. Moonlight silhouetted the branches and the elegantly drooping Spanish moss and vines. Some of the vines dangled all the way down into the water. Carver couldn't see much on either side; the reeds they were near were taller than the boat.

The boats bobbed silently in softly lapping water. No one in either of them talked for a few minutes, until Burr leaned close and said to Carver, "The Malone brothers are out there somewhere in their airboat."

"How do you know?" Carver asked.

"We hid a bumper beeper on their boat. Kept a man on the signal, and when they went into the swamp, we knew about it."

A bumper beeper was nothing more than a tiny radio transmitter that emitted a steady pulsing signal. They were magnetic and could be affixed to the bumper, or any other metal part of a car, and a listener tuned to the beeper's frequency could follow the car, track it from a distance, unobserved. No reason it couldn't work with a boat.

"The Malone boat is sitting motionless now," Burr said. "Just like us. We're about a quarter of a mile from them. They're waiting for something, and we're waiting right along with them."

"You think they're waiting for a drug drop?" Carver asked.

"They're not out here fishing," Burr said. "When they meet another boat or go to pick up anything dropped from a plane, we're going to be there right afterward and see what we can find on them, who they're dealing with."

Carver wondered if Willis Eiler or Sam Cahill might be out in the swamp with the Malone brothers. "Are they alone?"

Burr slapped a mosquito. "No way to know. All we've got is a radio signal that gives us direction and distance."

Carver was getting uncomfortable. He shifted position and was warned to move around as little as possible. Aluminum boats made noise when they were bumped, and sound carried far on the water. The frogs in the area were getting used to the boats' presence now and started croaking again, providing a counterpoint to the hum of insects.

The swamp had accepted them, if grudgingly. Persistent mosquitoes reminded Carver of how grudgingly.

After about ten minutes, Burr stood up and leaned forward. He touched his forefinger to his lips in a gesture for complete silence, then he pointed skyward.

Carver could hear it now: the distant drone of a small plane. The noise seemed to be to the south, moving nearer. He tried to find the plane's running lights but couldn't. Either it was flying without lights or the canopy of moss-and-vine-draped trees completely blocked the view.

When the drone of the plane was nearer, it suddenly became much louder, as if the craft had dropped to a lower altitude.

Then it became fainter again, began to fade. The plane was climbing and flying away from them now.

Marty of the huge headphones said with urgency in his voice, "They're moving!" The Malone brothers were on the prowl. Marty pointed out the direction to the agent at the controls.

The motors of both boats roared to life again, and they were off at high speed in the direction the agent had pointed. The police boat was behind and about a hundred yards to the left, keeping pace with them like a dark shadow of their boat.

The agent manning the controls was good and appeared to know the territory. The roaring boat vibrated, veered to miss trees by fractions of inches, shot through fields of reeds and tall saw grass that bent and snapped and whipped at Carver's exposed right arm. The wind forced him to squint as they skimmed the water and sometimes the land as they sped through the moonlit swamp. He glanced behind them; the boat with Armont in it was still back there, a dark specter flitting among the partly submerged tree trunks and foliage. Neither boat was running with lights, which struck Carver as strange considering all the noise they were making.

Burr seemed to know what he was thinking. He leaned close and yelled, "The Malones can't hear us over the sound of their own engine when they're moving! And we only move when they do!"

Carver braced his body with his stiff leg and nodded. It seemed pointless to try to scream an answer over the din.

Marty raised a forefinger and made a rapid circling motion with his hand, then he looked back and grinned like a schoolkid on a snipe hunt. He was having a grand time.

So was Burr. He was grinning, too. This was what his life was about. "We're getting the signal now from the homing device on the packages dropped by the plane!" he shouted.

Now they didn't really need the signal from the bumper beeper to keep from losing contact. They and the Malones were tuned to the same guiding signal emanating from the transmitter packaged with whatever had been parachuted into the swamp. The beeper on the Malone boat was being used only to track it in relation to the DEA and police boats. The signal from the swamp was drawing all three boats like a magnet; only the timing of the operation was in doubt.

The boat changed direction slightly, continued at high speed through the swamp. Whenever it skipped over dry land the thumping and jolting on the hull seemed about to tear it apart. Carver bounced constantly and would have left the seat if he hadn't been belted in. He didn't see how Marty, up in the bow, where the motion was more violent, could stay in the boat even with a seat belt. The DEA agent swayed and rolled with the thrashing of the bow, as if he could read the dark terrain and anticipate the boat's reactions.

He raised a hand. The boat slowed, the bow dropped, and water began to slap at the sides of the metal hull. They began to drift. The other boat also had slowed. It moved in closer, and both idling engines were cut off.

Now the silence of the swamp closed in.

But not quite.

Carver could hear the rising, falling drone of the Malones' airboat in front of them. Except for its warbling, it was similar to the sound of the plane that had dropped the drugs.

The drone changed pitch drastically, remained steady for a while, then died.

"They've picked it up!" Marty said.

Burr shouted something Carver didn't understand, waved his arms, and both engines kicked over, then snarled to full throttle. The bow of the boat rose again and they were speeding toward a rendezvous with the unsuspecting Malone brothers and their smuggled drug shipment.

Both boats had spotlights switched on now, playing brilliant white beams over the swamp in front of them, sending reflected light dancing like wild spirits among the trees. Secrecy and silence were impossible now, and unnecessary so close to the end of the hunt. Their quarry would know they were being pursued. The airboat with Armont in it even had a siren, which howled an eerie singsong yodel as the two boats screamed across water and lowland and closed in on the Malones. The police boat pulled wide left, circling like a night predator among the trees.

And Carver could see the Malone boat ahead, in a clear pool of moonlit black water beneath huge, overhanging moss-draped limbs.

There appeared to be four men in the boat. One of them—it looked like a Malone—stood up and turned to the others. The Armont boat was almost on the other side of them now, threading its way through the trees and hanging vines. Both boats would be on them in less than a minute.

The four figures in the Malone boat milled around frantically. Carver saw the stern drop, then rise again as they tried to start the engine. Apparently whoever was at the controls was too panicky to get the boat going.

Then the Malone boat did start. Its bow rose unbelievably high, and it shot off among the vertical shadows of tree trunks, toward the deeper, denser swamp.

Carver was shoved back in the seat as his boat gave chase. Wind blossomed his shirt, and small vines and branches whipped at his arms and face. He leaned toward the middle of the boat to avoid them. A large flying insect bounced hard off his forehead; for an instant he heard it buzz past his ear as it tumbled behind into the whirring propeller.

The airboat suddenly skidded sideways over dry land, dropped jarringly back in the water, roared ahead several hundred yards, then stopped with the huge propeller barely ticking over inside its cage.

Carver was still leaning forward, his seat belt digging into his stomach. He peered ahead over the lowered bow.

The Malone boat sat dead in the water. Rather, it sat on land. The Malones had tried to breach a bar of grassy ground that was wider than they'd thought. Their boat had become lodged; the engine had died.

Armont's boat came into sight, slowed, and drifted in closer to the Malone boat. Two of the men in the boat stood up. Carver heard the pop of gunfire.

Burr yelled and their own boat leaped forward. Marty had the big earphones off and was standing precariously in the bow, blasting away with a handgun. Like Mickey Mouse transformed into Dead-Eye Dick. Burr had a gun out too, and had tripped his safety-belt buckle and was out of his seat, scrambling toward the bow. Carver hit his own buckle, was jarred loose from where he was sitting, and rolled as low as he could between the seats. His cane was bouncing and clattering in the bottom of the boat. He wished he'd brought a gun.

The boat skewed sideways, stopped, bobbed violently. Carver's right arm was wet from the spray of water topping the hull. More shots. And the resonating roar of the shotguns with their heavy loads.

Then shouting. Some of it in Spanish.

"Okay! Okay, you bastards!" a voice yelled. "We give up, dammit! We fuckin' give up!"

The boat was drifting sideways. Carver poked his head up. Armont and his cops, and the DEA agents, were all in the knee-deep water, leaning forward and pushing and splashing toward the Malone boat. Two of the drug runners in the boat were standing, their hands raised. Another was slouched in a seat. The fourth lay facedown in the moon-illumined grass beside the grounded boat, with outflung arms, and what looked like a wide-brimmed straw hat upside down next to his head.

Carver cursed his bad leg. He wanted to get out of the boat, wade over, and help out, see what the hell had happened. Instead he sat and waited. He didn't feel like having to be rescued when he and his cane got stuck in the mud.

"You okay?" Burr yelled over at him, while the agents swarmed around their suspects, frisking them, reading them their rights, tending to the man in the seat, who apparently was wounded. They were ignoring the man on the ground. Carver knew what that meant.

"Okay!" he yelled.

Goddamned cane!

The three padded and plastic-wrapped packages in the Malone boat contained raw heroin and were equipped with homing-signal miniature transmitters. Neither of the men with the Malones was Sam Cahill or Willis Eiler. They were Latins, probably Marielitos. One of them was dead. Gary Malone was shot in the shoulder, and was sullenly waiting for an ambulance back on the side road off South Loop.

Carver and Burr had tried to get the Malones to tell them where Willis and Cahill were, but nobody with anything more to lose was talking until they'd met with their attorneys. They'd been caught in this phase of the game before and knew the moves.

By midnight Gary Malone was being operated on for removal of the bullet. The body of the dead Latino had been taken away for autopsy. And Sean Malone and the surviving Latino were in jail in Solarville, awaiting transfer to federal custody and arraignment on controlled-substance charges.

"You guys do acceptable work," Carver told Burr.

Burr nodded, then brushed deftly at a mosquito near his eye patch. The black patch had remained firmly fixed through the night's action. "Sometimes it's a fun job," he said.

Carver remembered the expression on Burr's face back in the swamp and knew that he meant it, dead Marielito and all.

When Carver got back to his room at the Tumble Inn, he saw the mound on the mattress, and the spray of dark hair on the pillow, that was Edwina curled beneath the thin white sheet in the coolness of the air-conditioning. She was still in the fetal position. Apparently she hadn't awakened while he was away. As far as he could determine, she hadn't even moved.

He undressed and lay down beside her, listening to his breathing slow until it was in gentle rhythm with Edwina's rising and falling breathing. He reached out a hand and lightly touched the warm curve of her hip beneath the sheet. She caught her breath, stirred, but didn't wake.

Her breathing leveled out again, in perfect time once more

with his. The sound was soothing, oddly mesmerizing; it seemed somehow to deepen the silence in the room.

The phone call from Burr, the wild chase through the swamp, the gun battle and arrests: It was all taking on the unreality of a dream.

That was okay with Carver. It hadn't been a dream. In the morning it would again acquire the firmness of hard fact. A fun job well done. The Malones would inevitably talk and implicate Willis and Cahill. Reality would wait patiently for sunrise.

In the cool, protective darkness, Carver closed his eyes and slept.

CHAPTER 31

C arver woke slowly, not quite sure why he was relinquish-
ing sleep. He could hear the steady, watery hum of the
air-conditioner, and the rolling, crunching sound of gravel
beneath the tires of a car outside on the motel parking lot. He
wrestled himself over onto his back, used his good leg to kick
free of the twisted sheets, and opened his eyes.

The venetian blinds had been tilted to admit the morning;
the room was bright with slanted bars of sunlight, golden
swirls of dust particles. Edwina was sitting in the chair by the
bed, fully dressed in jeans, a white blouse, and her lightning-
streak jogging shoes.

She said, "I've been out. I heard about last night."

Carver raised his arm and squinted at his watch. Eleven
forty-five. He'd been even more exhausted than he'd realized
when he went to bed. His mind and body hadn't come down
yet from the chase through the swamp. And when finally he
did relax, it had been completely and he'd slept deeply and
long.

"Have they gotten anyone to talk?" he asked.

"About what?"

"About Willis. And Sam Cahill. The prevailing logic is that they were in on this drug-smuggling deal, the secondary buyers."

"After last night they'd be on the run, wouldn't they?"

"If they heard about what happened. But they might not have tried yet to contact the Malones for the drug shipment."

"It wouldn't take the Malones to alert Willis and Cahill," she said. "Everyone in Solarville heard about what happened."

Carver sat up, maneuvered his body on the mattress until his back was against the cool headboard. He raised his good knee, leaned forward, and rested his forearms on it. He could hear his watch hammering away time. His mind was beginning to catch up with this business of being awake.

He rolled out of bed good-leg-first. Balancing himself by leaning against the mattress, he snatched his cane from where it was propped against the nightstand. Then he limped into the bathroom and took a quick shower.

When he returned, toweled dry, he began to get dressed. Edwina watched as he worked his stiff leg into his pants. She helped him stand while he slipped into a shirt. Then he sat on the mattress and put on his socks and shoes. She didn't attempt to help him with that.

"City hall should be open by now," he said, using his hand to smooth back the damp hair above his ears. "We're going to check into their records and see if the Blaney property's been sold." He made his way toward the door.

They went out into the heat and got in the car. Daninger, lecturing a maid pushing a cart loaded down with folded linen near the office, glanced over and saw them. He began walking toward them, probably intending to talk about the previous night. Carver didn't want that; he started the car and drove from the lot, pretending he hadn't seen Daninger.

Outside the miniature grandeur of the domed city hall, it occurred to Carver that he hadn't had breakfast and he was hungry. He asked Edwina to drive to the McDonald's down the street and bring back a couple of English muffins and coffee, while he began checking records inside.

He found his way down a short hall to the recorder-of-deeds office, and talked to a clerk who appeared to be about sixteen but had the serene manner of a forty-year-old. He gave her the necessary information, and she went away, then returned five minutes later with what looked like a huge ledger book. She went with him to a table in the corner, looked up a page in the oversized book, and punched up the locater number on a computer. On the green-tinted computer screen immediately appeared the status of the Blaney property.

It was all so quick and easy that it threw Carver for a few seconds. The young clerk had walked back to her desk, and he sat for a moment absorbing the information on the monitor. He thought again of the area encompassed by the red pencil marking on Eiler's map.

What was on the screen made no sense, fit no pattern.

Or did it? He sat still for a while, letting the doors spring open one by one in his mind, each leading to a room larger and brighter than the last.

Then he got up, thanked the clerk, and limped out.

In the marble-floored hall, he used a pay phone to call Ernie Franks at Sun South. Then he called Desoto and Armont. The chief wasn't in his office, so Carver left a message.

When he got outside, Edwina was starting up the city hall steps, carrying two white McDonald's bags. She stopped, then went back to the bottom of the steps to wait for Carver in the sun.

"They don't serve breakfast after ten o'clock," she said, "but I talked them into a couple of cinnamon danish."

"Fine," Carver said. He could smell the warm cinnamon.

"Did you find what you wanted so soon?"

"I did. They're more up-to-date in there than you'd imagine," Carver answered. He began walking toward the parked Olds.

"Where are you going?" Edwina asked, surprised.

"To Verna Blaney's place. I'll drop you at the motel. No time to explain."

"No," she said calmly. "You won't drop me off. I'm coming along."

Carver thought about that. He didn't see why she shouldn't go, and there were solid reasons why she should. There was little time to try to talk her into staying behind even if he decided to give in to his impulse to protect her, leave her safe and confined. That was the sort of thinking that had led to trouble for him before.

He tapped the pavement with his cane and said, "Come on, then. We can eat breakfast on the way."

Carver knew where he'd been misled. Since Eiler had been in prison for drug dealing, and since Florida, and Solarville in particular, was an active area of drug trafficking, he'd suspected that whatever scam Eiler was executing involved drugs. The packet of cocaine and the red-penciled map found in the apartment seemed to confirm that drug dealing was the game. Carver knew now that the coffee can containing them had been planted in Eiler's apartment *after* the police had conducted their search; that was why Desoto's men hadn't discovered it when they went through the place. They probably had looked behind the kitchen plumbing access panel and found nothing, because at the time there was nothing there.

After the two unsuccessful attempts on Carver's life in Solarville, the fire at the motel and then the knife attack, Eiler had decided on diversion rather than a third attempt. A second obvious attempt to murder Carver then, successful or not, would almost certainly have drawn attention to Eiler as doubts about his own death, or fake suicide, had grown. Jorge Lujan and his cohorts, such as brother Silverio, were working for Eiler and Cahill, and had planted the coffee can in the apartment after the police search so that Carver, or whoever else conducted a deeper search, would assume that Eiler was involved in a drug deal.

But the two Disney Productions executives, David Panacho

and Mildred Kern, had somehow stumbled onto what Willis was really doing, and had to be killed. And they had become curious about Carver nosing around in Solarville and had found out his name, possibly what he was doing in town. If they had to die, it now made sense to Willis and Cahill to wipe Carver off the slate, also. And the Marielitos involved in the deal were probably pressing for revenge for Silverio Lujan's death. They'd already murdered the naturalist Mackenzie, to buy time or his silence.

So Jorge Lujan, or possibly one or more confederates, had killed the Disney executives and faked their accident on the highway. That same night, Jorge tried to murder Carver and wound up dead himself.

Within a few minutes, Carver and Edwina were on the road outside of town. The sun seemed unnaturally large and hot, as if it had slipped a million-mile notch nearer to earth. The stark contrast between light and shadow was vivid enough to cause mental jolts as the car sped through alternating patches of brightness and darkness, as if some of the shadows might be solid enough to cause impact.

Carver pushed the Olds hard on the highway, then along the narrow dirt road that led to Verna's sanctuary deep in the swamp.

CHAPTER 32

S he must have heard them drive up; she was waiting for them on the front porch. Verna was barefoot, as she'd been on Carver's first visit, only this time she hadn't yet dressed and was wearing a faded blue robe. Her dark hair was mussed, and her eyes were intent and red-rimmed, as if from lack of sleep. She was carrying the shotgun this time, too, cradling it gently beneath her breasts, almost as if it were an infant.

"Just there's about right," she said, shifting the long shot-gun so that her finger was on the trigger and the twin barrels swung like bleak fate toward Carver and Edwina.

Carver reached over and touched Edwina's arm. They simultaneously stopped, then stood motionless on the bare earth in front of the porch. The huge sun pulsated above, its heat weighting them down.

Carver probed the ground with the tip of his cane, found it as hard as it had been the day before, and set the cane and leaned on it.

"We have to talk," he said.

"I do doubt that."

Carver was sweating miserably. The humidity had risen.

Despite the relentless sun, black clouds loomed high and heavy in the west; a storm gusting in off the gulf. Distant thunder rolled across the shadowed swamp, like the rumbling of dinosaurs roaming where they had lived forever.

"I'm no more interested in what you have to say today than I was the first time you came poking around out here," Verna said.

"You'll be interested if you take the time to listen," Carver said. "Is Willis inside?"

"Willis?" Her voice took on a hollow quality; she was no good at deception. She tightened her grip on the shotgun. Carver watched her right forefinger caress the trigger guard with an odd kind of affection.

"Willis Eiler," he said. "He's your husband, Mrs. Eiler."

Beside him, Edwina took an involuntary step back and to the side, as if Carver's words had struck her with solid force. Then she moved forward again, beside Carver.

Verna stood quietly, considering. Carver and Edwina stood just as quietly and waited. Insects buzzed and chirped frantically around them in the swamp, sensing the coming storm. The birds that had been singing were silent, as if they'd already taken shelter.

"How'd you find out we was man and wife?" Verna asked.

"Checked the real-estate records at city hall. I wanted to know if you'd really sold your property. There hadn't been a sale, but the property had been retitled in the names of Willis Eiler and his wife Verna."

"Why was you interested in my property changing hands?"

"I thought your leaving town might be pertinent to a narcotics case, but I was wrong. About almost everything. I was being led. Now I understand. The object of the game was never drugs, it was real estate. Land. Willis stole money to purchase your property through his partner, Sam Cahill. When you wouldn't sell to Cahill, Willis courted and married you to get the land." It probably had been simple for Willis, Carver thought, looking at Verna. Lonely, more easily understood than she imagined, she was easy prey for a handsome, experienced con man with a hundred-thousand-dollar bank-roll.

None of this made much sense to Verna. "Is Willis why you're here?" she asked softly.

"Partly," Carver said. "But I'm also here because there's something you should know, Willis or no Willis. The Disney corporation is interested in using this area to create a theme park they'd call Everglades Kingdom, an expansion of Disney World into southern Florida. They're keeping their intentions as quiet as possible to prevent land prices from soaring. Willis Eiler found out about the project when he was going through his boss's desk in Del Moray, where he was selling time shares that didn't exist, and came across some Florida Real-Estate Commission correspondence. Disney plans to drain some of the land here, build up roads, create a scenic waterway and a monorail system serving luxury hotels and tourist attractions."

Verna seemed vaguely disbelieving of what Carver was telling her. "Tourist attractions, monorails, luxury hotels . . . here?"

"We're standing right in the middle of the proposed area," Carver told her. "Your property. Land Disney will pay a fortune to acquire because they must have it."

Verna's jaw set firmly and something cold moved into her eyes. Her hair was brushed down and forward to conceal her disfigurement, but Carver saw the lower half of the scar flush bright crimson. A breeze danced through the leaves, parted the folds of her robe for a moment to reveal one of her fine, bare legs halfway up her thigh.

She knew how to get to the point: "You saying Willis married me for my swampland and this tumbledown place?"

"He knows what it's really worth," Carver said. Let her put the pieces in place, figure it out for herself. It didn't take Sherlock Holmes, just someone with the proper slant. Even Watson might have managed it.

"We was keeping our romance and marriage a secret until we'd moved away, because Willis said we could expect trouble from his ex-wife." Verna motioned smoothly toward Edwina with the shotgun barrels. "This her?"

"No," Carver said. In the corner of his vision he saw Edwina straighten and stand tensely. "This is a woman he was living with, another woman he took advantage of to get what he wanted. He served prison time for cheating a widow out of her property in Missouri. You're the latest in a succession of women in Willis's life, Verna. He uses women then throws them away. He's using you."

"He was gonna sell the place and get outa here," Verna said, "away from Solarville. Sam Cahill was going to handle the deal for us."

"I told you Cahill is Willis's partner. He did try to buy this place from you, didn't he?"

Verna nodded. "Tried every way he could. I wouldn't sell at any price, though. I couldn't. I'd have had no place to go then. All alone."

"And when Cahill couldn't convince you to sell to him, Willis came here to charm you into marriage and get the property that way. Isn't that the way it was, Verna?"

There was a faint noise from inside the cabin, like someone walking with a heavy tread.

Carver knew who it was; it would have been unwise to stir from cover so soon after the night before, with so many law enforcement officers still in the area.

The door opened and Willis stepped out onto the porch.

He let the screen door slam shut behind him; the sound was like a rifle shot that resonated briefly and then was absorbed by the calm swamp.

Carver stared at the man, the myth brought down to life-size. Willis was like his photograph, handsome in an ordinary, even-featured way that served him well in his illicit work. He was wearing faded Levi's, a white dress shirt with the sleeves rolled up, and, incongruously, dusty black wingtip shoes. The dandy adapting to his new and temporary environment; evolution in the swamp. Willis didn't look directly at Edwina.

Carver was aware of tension flowing from her like an electric force.

"Any of this true?" Verna asked.

"Some of it," Willis said. "Not the part that means I don't love you."

Carver watched Verna as her mind grappled with yet another disillusionment. Life was like that: illusion, delusion, deception, self-deception, worlds and castles constructed of our personal perceptions, masquerading as reality until something interfered. Verna's magic kingdom had been built here before Disney's, and now Carver was tugging at the cornerstone of her castle.

Willis reached out for the shotgun, then withdrew his hand as two more cars flashed into view through the palmetto trees and parked at the end of the gravel drive.

Chief Armont and a uniformed cop got out of one of the cars. Another uniformed cop, the going-to-fat young one who'd stopped Carver on the road the night before, climbed out of the other. He looked more puzzled than official today.

Verna raised the shotgun, aimed it directly at Carver. "You folks stay right there by your cars," she said. "Somebody dies otherwise."

Armont stood still. He floated a hand upward to signal his men to do the same.

Verna nodded toward Edwina. "This your former wife, Willis?"

"Of course not. She's a woman who used to work where I worked. She thought she was in love with me." He barked a sharp, incredulous laugh, as if he were amazed at the audacity of those two people who had turned up there where they didn't belong. "I never loved her. I never lived with her."

"He speaking the truth?" Verna asked Edwina.

Edwina said nothing. The front of her blouse was trembling, rising and falling rapidly.

"He's murdered to try to get this land," Carver said to Verna. "He's even murdered *on* this land—a naturalist called

Mackenzie who was cataloging wildlife for the Disney corporation."

Willis shook his head, almost in amusement. "Another lie."

Carver blinked perspiration from his eyes. Even the breeze was warm and fetid, the swamp breathing.

Willis began shifting his weight from leg to leg. He was getting nervous; his mind must have been darting around like a wasp in a jar, searching for openings, angles that might lead to escape. Carver wondered if Willis, there in the cabin, had heard or seen any of what had gone on in the swamp the night before. The lights might have been visible through the trees, and the wail of the siren must have carried for miles. But then it wouldn't have mattered much to him; none of it actually involved him. They'd only thought it had. Just as he'd planned.

Chief Armont's voice boomed out. "I think you oughta put the gun down, Verna, and we can talk."

She ignored him.

"Verna!"

She moved the shotgun barrel almost imperceptibly to take in Armont and his men. The message got across. She was capable and willing. Armont knew her; he kept quiet, waiting for it all to play out. The sky darkened, and the insects in the swamp became silent. A few drops of rain fell.

"The law want you, Willis?" Verna asked, not looking away from Carver and Edwina.

"The law wants me," Willis said. "But not for what Carver says. What he says is a lie."

"This isn't your former wife? You ain't just using me?"

"No, no! For Christ's sake, no, Verna!"

A good actor, Carver thought. A great actor.

"He's the one who's lying," Carver said to Verna. "He doesn't love you." He knew he didn't sound nearly as convincing as Willis.

"He's a gimpy private eye who peeks through keyholes," Willis said, pointing at Carver, managing disdain in the gesture.

242

"And her?" Verna asked, moving the shotgun's twin barrels in the direction of Edwina.

"She'd say whatever he told her."

The low thunder was rolling closer now. Carver watched the raindrops spot the bare ground in light patterns determined by breezes high above. They made a faint pattering sound on the leaves and hard earth.

Verna raised the shotgun a few inches and held it with fresh purpose. She'd made up her mind: Willis. His luck ran on.

"Go on back along the path behind the house," she said to Willis, not looking at him. "You'll come to a big live oak with lots of old hatchet marks in the trunk, cuts I made when I was a girl. Make a right turn there, just the other side of the tree, and go through the swamp. In about a hundred feet you'll be on an overgrown dirt road that poachers used to travel. You wait right there and I'll pick you up in the truck." She moved her head toward the rusty vintage Ford pickup. "I want to talk some to Chief Armont."

Willis looked at the truck. "I couldn't get it started yesterday. Will it run?"

"It'll run. And I'll see they don't follow us."

Willis obviously didn't fancy the idea. But he did like the notion of getting away from there as quickly as possible. He leaned close to Verna, whispered something in her ear, then jumped down off the porch and jogged around behind the cabin. He had a loose-jointed, athletic way of running. Boyish.

Verna said nothing, swept the long shotgun slowly from side to side to make it clear she might fire at anyone who moved. The rain, still light, picked up a bit. Lightning played among the clouds in the west, getting closer.

"Time to talk some sense now, Verna . . ." Armont began, urging her to speak to him.

But she didn't have anything to say, and a quick, chopping motion with the shotgun's twin barrels told Armont he didn't have anything to say, either. Verna waggled the barrels from side to side. No one was to speak.

243

When several minutes had passed, Willis began to shout.

At first Carver couldn't understand what he was screaming. Then, when he did understand, he lifted his cane from the ground, reset it, and took a step forward.

Verna tightened her grip on the shotgun. Carver stopped and stood still again. Armont and his men were poised tensely, but they hadn't moved.

The screams became louder, higher-pitched, like a woman's screams.

Verna stared at Edwina, who stared back. Their stoic expressions revealed nothing, but Carver knew something was happening between them; he could actually feel its subtle vibrancy. It was like an understanding beyond words, between sisters. Maybe it could have passed between them only there, in the deep swamp.

Willis began screaming Verna's name. Then Edwina's.

The two last, maimed women in his life stood motionless and unfeeling, statues in the rain.

Carver shivered. He held tight to the crook of his cane with both hands and bore his weight down on it to steady himself.

Willis screamed Edwina's name last.

Three times.

Pleading.

In tearing, banshee wails of horror.

Then suddenly he was quiet. Sunk beneath the quicksand where Verna had directed him. The abrupt silence rolled from the swamp and settled heavily over the clearing.

Verna slowly lowered the shotgun and bowed her head.

Carver heard footsteps behind him, then Armont and his men passed him at a fast walk, moving in on Verna.

Armont gently removed the gun from her hands, then held her arm tenderly, like a concerned lover, and led her into the house.

The rainfall became heavy, steady.

CHAPTER 33

The storm was still attacking the swamp, Mother Nature miffed, hurling down lightning bolts and sending sheets of rain sweeping across the flat road, when Carver, with Edwina beside him, drove from Solarville and turned onto the main highway.

Armont had taken charge and sorted things out with a finesse that surprised Carver. The chief was tough and a pro, but he was tuned to human sensitivities. A good man in a bad job.

By late that afternoon, just before Carver and Edwina left Solarville, word had come that Sam Cahill had been stopped by state troopers on Interstate 75 in his red Corvette. When told that Willis Eiler was dead, he demanded legal counsel and became closemouthed. Most of Ernie Franks's money was in a suitcase in the car's trunk.

There was a bad exchange rate on that money; it had cost far more than it bought.

The rain had slacked off to a mist that the sun was working to burn away, when Carver glanced sideways at Edwina and turned the Olds north on Route 1, toward home, his place on the edge of the sea. He was sure that they were finally and in every way free of Willis, that the obsession had ended.

But Carver didn't go to his place. Instead they drove to Del Moray. To her place.

Their place.

In the middle of the night she called him Willis.